THE BIRDS OF PREY

THE BIRDS OF PREY

JOHN RALSTON SAUL

McGRAW-HILL BOOK COMPANY
New York • St. Louis • San Francisco
Düsseldorf • Mexico

2 3 4 5 6 7 8 9 0 B P B P 7 8 3 2 1 0 9 8

First published 1977 by
Macmillan London Limited,
London and Basingstoke.

Library of Congress Cataloging in Publication Data

Saul, John Ralston.
The birds of prey.
1. Birds of prey.   I. Title.
QL696.F3S28   1978   598.9′1   78-8415
ISBN 0-07-054860-9

to
Charles de Gaulle
from a disciple

Sans peur
et
Sans regret

Plots true or false are necessary things,
To raise up commonwealths and ruin kings.

DRYDEN

The Large Birds o' Prey
They will carry us away,
An' you'll never see your soldiers any more!

KIPLING

Prologue

St Denis, La Réunion (AFP), 10
March 1968. General Ailleret's Indian
Ocean tour ended in tragedy at 11.00
p.m. last night. Following an official
dinner and reception at the Prefecture,
he left for Gillot Airport with his wife
and daughter. He was joined by four
members of his staff and a crew of
thirteen.

It was a dark night — raining. The
DC6 was weighted down by a heavy
load of fuel: special reserve tanks were
filled to allow a direct flight to Djibouti.

At 11.15 the four-prop machine
rolled down the runway. In the control
tower they noticed that the plane had
some difficulty getting into the air. The
runway is parallel to the sea. On its
right, hills, and behind them the vol-
cano, 'le Piton des Neiges'. Straight
ahead, slightly further away, more hills.
On the left, water. Take-off is along
the beach, and the moment the machine is in the air it must turn sharply
to the left. But the Chief of Staff's
plane appeared to turn to the right.
The control tower warned the pilot
that he was heading into a dangerous
zone.

It was too late. Seconds later the
plane struck an electric cable, plung-
ing the island into darkness. Then a
row of trees. Then the rising ground.
The 18,000 litres of fuel exploded on
impact. All but one of the passengers
were killed immediately. A stewardess,
who had been at the rear of the plane,
was cut out of her seat by a young
peasant from a village only a few yards
away. She is in a critical condition.

The accident occurred eighty seconds after take-off.

The reader looked up from the bound volume of newspapers,
put his head back. His eyes drifted over the vast nineteenth-
century dome decorated with naked figures reclining in the
name of literature or struggling for history or working for
any of the other virtues that had been admired in Louis-
Napoleon's Paris. He closed his eyes and tried to re-create the
scene in La Réunion through the sparse words of the slightly
discoloured newspaper more than four years old.

The plane in a thousand pieces scattered over fields of
sugar-cane. A filthy drizzle dampening the fire. The peasants
thrown from their beds by the explosion, creeping out of
their homes, walking slowly, warily towards the flames,
stumbling in the darkness relieved only by yellow flames over
bits of the wreckage. Hundreds of half-burnt photographs
floating down, witnessing the General's official tour of the
Indian Ocean, even photographs of his triumphant arrival in
La Réunion that same morning at the same airport. His arm
waving from the charcoaled corner of a proof caught in a
branch, his sharp uncomfortable eyes hidden by sun-glasses
on another shred of paper where the childish cheeks had
burnt away. Bodies. Parts of bodies lying calmly in unnatural

poses, as if they had always been there, separated from the rest of their former selves. The peasants drawing back in horror before this contact, then hearing the feeble cries of a survivor, finding her, bloodied, lacerated, clothes ripped away, bones crushed, still strapped to her seat, thrown clear and sitting upright like a lunatic cinema spectator waiting alone surrounded by ten-foot-high sugar-cane which blocked her view of the spectacle — a young man pulling out a simple farm-knife and liberating her from the sad remains of this miraculous bird with one slice, as he might slaughter a chicken.

The Prefect of the island and the other officials arriving from the dinner which Ailleret himself had left only an hour before, still in their dress uniforms, wandering nervously about the filth trying to protect themselves from the drizzle, vainly organizing rescue operations where there was no one to rescue.

The reader opened his eyes to escape his macabre imagination, looked to his left. There was an old woman in an elaborate dusty hat poring over a collection of eighteenth-century fashion-plates. On his right, a young American student, apparently unclean, leafing idly through pages of defunct socialist monthlies. Outside the massive, windowless hall of the Bibliothèque Nationale it was 8 May 1972. A fresh spring morning.

He turned back to his desk.

Chapter One

6 May 1972

The grey stones of the Gois stretched out flat and sinister across the horizon. The smell of the sea crept up dark from beneath them as if they concealed a monumental graveyard of everything the Atlantic takes and strangles and reduces to primary matter.

A black line cut across this vision. The line was constructed of heavier flat stones, chiselled square to lie close together, heavy enough not to be carried away when the tide swept over the natural causeway twice each day. This was the rough road which joined the island to the Continent four miles distant. For anyone setting out from Noirmoutier, down into the long, low, sloping bowl of the uncovered Atlantic without knowing that the western coast of France lay at the other end, it would have seemed a sure descent to some desolate river of death.

François de Maupans did not have this fear. He stepped out before his wife and his four guests, down from the island and briskly along the road. His heavy frame followed obediently in his steps, his boots falling flat and sure on to the stone, still slippery from its last drowning.

He always insisted on showing the Gois to those who were there for the first time. So contemptuous of man and unbroken by him, it seemed newly discovered by whoever ventured on to its rock.

He twisted his head about, already sweating, and shouted back to the others, more hesitant on the wet surface.

'Before they built that obscene bridge at the other end of the island, everyone had to come here on this road, across the

Gois. And if you started too late the tide caught you. Your car was swept away and you, with a little luck, spent the night on one of those.' He pointed toward the row of stone towers clinging to the road at two-hundred-yard intervals. They appeared as gallows in the grey light.

The group strode on, gathering speed until they met the returning water a mile out. They stopped and watched it creeping up before them, covering the road. Then turned about and walked back slowly, the tide following on their heels.

'It was here I had my most startling revelation.' Maupans spoke with satisfaction. 'No man is born banal. It is something he becomes.'

A few moments later one of the guests stopped, letting the others walk on ahead. He turned his back on them and faced the water swirling faster and black in the evening light. He looked down at his feet and watched the liquid crawling over the crevices of the stone, filling the hollows in his gridded soles, rising up over his boots.

He was a tall man, finely cut, his shoulders broad but too clearly drawn to be heavy. One could sense his back, calm beneath a thick sweater, resigned in the sea which engulfed him. He appeared a silent man.

The sea began to pull at his ankles, gently, so gently at first. He looked down at it inquisitively, looking for the message in this coaxing, his eyes green, perhaps by reflection. He appeared to examine his legs as he watched them disappear. Impassively. His friends were lost in the distance on the black line. He turned about slowly and found their silhouettes. The light caught his face. It was a young man's face. A man in his mid thirties. The sea had run a hundred yards beyond him. He looked down again at the water rising over his calves to the top of his boots and then suddenly began to stride forward without lifting his feet, pushing the sea aside until it fell behind.

The other five waited for him on the rise at the end of the road. He joined them in silence. They looked back out over the rocks now covered by the sea and the gallows towers floating void of victims.

The guest took Maupans by the arm and drew him on towards their car as if they were alone – a gesture of natural self-confidence.

'You were right', he said, 'about men becoming banal.' Maupans glanced at him. 'You were right. But do you know the cause? I'll tell you. A man becomes banal if he has never been afraid.'

'But Charles' – Maupans laughed – 'I know too many boring heroes.'

The guest cut him off.

'Boring is the opposite of banal.'

'Is that why you waited down there for the water to sweep you away?'

'Good God, François, I always get out before I'm afraid.'

It was a statement of fact. He then dropped Maupans' arm and turned to one of the women, whispered something which began with her name: Agnès. She was gracefully hard and moulded automatically to his side. They walked ahead down the narrow road until the car, with Maupans at the wheel, came up behind and stopped for them to climb in.

François de Maupans, in his father's eyes, was slightly degenerate. He did not quite blend in. He dressed too well. He ate too well. He knew too many people his father couldn't place. He enjoyed running his company, his estate. He enjoyed life.

His wife, when they first married, had been a model of perfection in his father's eyes. Once you knew her name you knew where she lived, had gone to school, who her friends were, her children's names, what she thought if she thought; above all that because she thought the same as you.

Under her husband's influence she had abandoned the
formula of her class and tried to imitate him. What for him
was natural for her was a strain; often a misdirected strain.

Noirmoutier was an escape for her. She brought only one
maid to the Spartan house. Her guests were served simply,
and she encouraged them to drink so that she might drink
more herself, as a good hostess. Drink was a simple pleasure
she had discovered to enhance her moments of relaxation.

Maupans didn't mind. His wife's figure was unchanged and
his pleasure in her undiminished.

It was ten o'clock. They sat around a large table outside,
under a dark sky pricked with specks of light. The scent of
hyacinths rose out of the jungle-like garden on all sides, and
they were hemmed in by the silhouettes of the stunted,
twisted, prickly oaks which dominated that part of the
island. The oysters had been taken away. The baked sea-bass
had just arrived.

Maupans had placed Agnès de Pisan, the woman Charles
Stone had suggested he invite, on his left. She was, as he
had expected, charming. Beside her was Stone, in easy
reach, where he wanted him. Then Hélène, then one of
Hélène's cousins whose name he could never remember. Ah,
he thought, the all-destroying grace of conventionality. And
beside him was a woman called Mélanie Barre. She was
pretty, because Maupans had eliminated all his wife's friends
who were not.

Hélène appeared nervous. Nervous because Stone was
beside her. At least, that was the surface of her problem. Its
real origins were far deeper. Noirmoutier was her house – hers
in the sense that Maupans let her run it as she wished. It was
her world, her escape, her return to the more certain and
clear-cut world of her childhood. She peopled it with her

friends. People who neither did nor said surprising things. People who acted as she knew and expected they should — family friends, people who fitted in.

Stone was one of her husband's friends. He was amusing, attractive, civilized — for that she didn't fault him. However, he was an unknown factor, not quite categorizable, an outsider like all her husband's friends and therefore not quite reliable — or was the word 'relaxing'? And Agnès de Pisan was exactly the same.

Normally Maupans didn't mind being separated from his Parisian circus for a few days. He either ignored his guests and concentrated on the surrounding country or he acted as the resident outsider, shocking and amusing everyone as best he could.

From time to time his wife allowed him to bring one of his people along, usually when the party was staying for more than a weekend; otherwise he became restless. As with this evening, she rapidly regretted her weakness.

Charles Stone was exactly what Maupans called a .friend. They had met fourteen months before in New York. They had met a second time three months later in New Delhi. Maupans had been on business. Stone was simply there. He gave no reason for his existence. He didn't seem to have one.

He confessed to Maupans that he knew Paris well, came often, knew all sorts of people Maupans knew, all different people who didn't know each other.

Maupans once asked him what he did in life. He replied that he wrote. Nobody really believed that. He seemed far too occupied with the pleasures of life; no, not the pleasures — it was more with the details of life, the perfection of its form. He left no impression of stopping periodically to contemplate anything and therefore perhaps to write. The impression he did leave was one of self-confidence; not in the aggressive manner of someone justifying himself, but in the

calm, disinterested way of someone who was blissfully
unaware of the word 'doubt'.

Why would he write? In any case, what did he write?

Not very much apparently. Stone showed Maupans an
eighty-page published essay on jungle warfare in Malaysia.
There was no real reason for the subject except that it had
interested him. That was what he had said. And he had gone
as an observer during the Malaysia troubles. He had managed to
have himself attached to a parachute company in the jungle on
the understanding that he would write something which might
help the world understand the worthwhile task the British
Army was carrying out to protect them from revolutionaries.

The paper which resulted was written under a pseudonym
and was far more a study of what happens to the human
mind under extreme stress than a political justification for
one side or the other. Over the next few months Maupans
came across two newspaper articles signed by that name on
opposing subjects from different places.

He was more and more attracted to Stone. At first he had
believed him English, then American or mid-Atlantic. He
once managed a fleeting glance at Stone's passport. It was
Irish.

He asked him a month later if he were Irish. Stone looked
at him blankly and firmly. No, he wasn't.

He had just returned from Morocco and was telling them
what he had seen.

'It must be rare: such a perfectly egotistical dictatorship.
The King exploits the country for his own benefit as if it
were a small estate. He lives in complete luxury and absolute
fear. He shuts himself up in his palaces surrounded by guards.
The people hate him. Rather than take one of his own
airplanes, he commandeers regular flights without warning so
that no one can tamper with the machine. What a dreadful
waste. All that power and he's nothing more than a silly little
playboy.'

'Then you lied!'

Stone looked across the table. Maupans put his arm around the woman on his right.

'My dear Mélanie, that's a bit strong. I'm not used to hearing such vehemence from you. Has Hélène been giving us all too much to drink again?'

'Probably,' she said. She half smiled, half sulked. 'But he did lie. He agreed with you earlier that no one was born banal. He said fear saved you from it. What about his king, a silly little playboy terrified all the time.'

'You're right.' Stone shrugged obligingly as he spoke. 'I lied for him, not for myself.'

She waved him off. She was annoyed with herself for speaking up, but having started wouldn't stop.

'More than that. You are completely wrong. Men are born banal – lots of them. Look, I married one. He was the most banal man I ever met. That's why I married him. He was ordinary every day. He never stepped out of his limits.'

'You're an uncharitable widow, Mélanie.' Maupans laughed. 'I'm not sure I'd have liked to be your husband.'

'I wouldn't have had you. I wanted what I got. And, just to show you how wrong you were, I shall tell you a secret. My husband was banal in everything except his death, when by your definition he should have been afraid – instead of which he was drunk.'

Stone's eyes were fixed on her. The others sat in embarrassed silence.

'And why do you say that?' he asked.

'Charles!' Maupans cried. 'We know the story. I don't want it again over dinner.'

'My husband was in the Air Force. He was one of the officers flying the Chief of the General Staff back to Paris. That was four years ago. March 1968. The plane fell out of the sky and everyone was killed.'

'I can see that an insult for you is a compliment. So far he seems quite banal.'

'Except that there was no reason for the accident. Absolutely none. No explanation was ever given. They brought the bodies back from the God-forsaken island in the Indian Ocean where it happened and let us bury them without knowing why. And then they hinted unofficially that the crew had been drunk. And that, you see, was a lie.'

'You may not know, Charles' — Maupans cut her off by laying his hand on her arm and reached across the table in a weary manner to explain something a foreigner couldn't possibly understand — 'that every time some important Frenchman is killed in an accident somebody else claims it was an assassination. We are violent in our imagination, even if we aren't in our acts.'

She had withdrawn into her place again. The light came from behind, leaving her inclined head in shadow. She spoke in a whisper which brought Maupans to silence.

'I wanted to believe it was an accident. That was all I wanted. I wanted to keep my memory of him as ordinary as he was. But I couldn't, you see, because they lied. Poor Thomas, he was so banal he didn't even drink. He never drank.'

Stone moved his eyes. They were clear, questioning. Maupans looked up at him, relieved by the silence.

'Well, that calls for a celebration,' he cried. 'Another bottle. The least we can do is drink to his memory again. And you are wrong, Mélanie. It isn't a God-forsaken island. You are prejudiced. It's normally called the Île des Poètes.'

The next morning Maupans and Stone took two horses out on to the island's flat prairie. It was early. The sky was almost Italian, for no known reason. Very blue, low, stretched-out clouds pulling by, a pristine clear atmosphere streaked by the rising sun. Maupans told him it was often like that. They rode quickly over the soft ground in the direction of the Gois. When they arrived low tide had just begun and the causeway was bare, shining in the sun. The black rocks had become reflections of the light. The seaweed was a bed of jewels. They drew up and stared out at it.

'A strange woman, your Mélanie. What was that all about?'

Maupans did not reply at first. He was leaning forward in his saddle toward the Gois, sniffing to draw in some of the rising smells.

'A rather lovely woman, I've always thought. Her name is Barre. That won't mean anything to you. As she pointed out last night, Thomas Barre was hardly a startling personality. You might know her father's name, Rogent.' Stone nodded slowly. 'A Resistance hero. Captured. Tortured. He's still alive. Just alive. I don't know how he manages it. They cut out half his guts. And her mother was another Resistance hero. Also captured. Also tortured. She didn't survive. I understand the Germans returned her body to be buried in pieces, as an example.

'That was why she married Barre. All Mélanie wanted in life was calm and stability. He reeked of it. And they gave her back his body to be buried, in pieces. Funny kind of destiny.'

'Was it an accident?'

Maupans shrugged and moved his horse forward.

'Let's ride back by the beach while the tide is low.'

That afternoon Stone suggested to Mélanie a walk along the beach, around the island if necessary, long enough to realize he didn't lie all the time.

Stone was a tall man – just tall enough to assert himself without effort and yet short enough to melt away if he wished. He was perfectly integrated. That was a peculiar characteristic, but very real. He appeared at home with himself. His strength was deceivingly hidden because his lines were smooth and clean as if he were slight. His character appeared in the same way, deceptively hiding in its own good balance. And yet .he was not slight, and his character, on closer examination, was more restrained than balanced.

And so his stride became more carefully fitted to the ground, perfectly calm, restrained, scarcely appearing to disturb the world about him.

He wore baggy light cotton trousers which floated in the slight breeze and no shirt. His hair, just slightly too long, blew in gentle disorder, like a baroque decoration on an immaculate form.

Stone had a way of feeling what people wanted to hear and see. Even better — what it was they wanted to see in him. And he had the remarkable talent of becoming exactly that. Not from weakness of character. No. As a boy he had done it first out of delicacy. People were so unhappy talking to someone different. He tried to blend in so that they might relax. Later his delicacy was blunted, but he saw that people were nervous, defensive before outsiders. And so he kept his habit. There was nothing more sure to open a woman's heart — or a man's — than to know she was preaching to the converted.

Without thinking, without meaning to, as he scuffed his feet along the beach, he became Mélanie's shadow. He avoided anything depressing. He talked about the sand, quoted all the English poetry on sand that he could remember. Bits of Eliot —

I grow old . . . I grow old . . .
I shall wear the bottoms of my trousers rolled

— and 'The Walrus and the Carpenter' and even, reaching back into the past, Ozymandias' lone and level sands stretching far away.

She was delighted. She had a wide, strong mouth which came suddenly into prominence when she smiled, and a funny way of laughing straight ahead without any armour when she did laugh. That was not something he had expected — yet another person coming out from under her cover, laughing, and retreating again a few moments later. In those few moments she was a light and airy being, matching him with pieces of French poetry. Some Hugo, some Baudelaire and then, almost to herself, Saint-John Perse:

Les armes au matin sont belles et la mer. A nos chevaux
livrée la terre sans amandes
nous vaut ce ciel incorruptible. Et le soleil n'est point
nommé, mais sa puissance est parmi nous
et la mer au matin comme une présomption de l'esprit.

After a few more lines her voice faded away and she stopped and looked out at the calm sea, meek and obliging. They laughed. She seemed to have forgotten about the night before when Stone brought the conversation around to her own world, and on that empty open space of sand she didn't seem to mind. .

She told him about her life. Her life as a child. She had never known her mother — only through her father's eyes. He had spared no details, either of her heroism or of her suffering. Her father lived, camped, in Paris in a flat on rue de Constantine, refusing to make it comfortable. He imagined life as one unending flight of flexibility, instability and upheavals. He would plan nothing practical for tomorrow. What was the point? Tomorrow might bring. . . . And, anyway, he had abandoned the practical things of life long ago.

When she found her Thomas Barre it had been a marvellous dream. A man who cared nothing for ideas or vague dreams or flexibility. A man who was well planted in the ground, who lived for the little things, who moved slowly in order not to miss them.

'Then why was he in the Air Force?'

'Most pilots are like him. The old adventurous breed are gone because they were too dangerous. Pilots are all careful, thorough, efficient men today. There is no room for risks. And Thomas' — she stopped for a moment on the sand and gave him an embarrassed smile — 'was more careful than the rest. That was why he flew for GLAM.'

Stone looked questioningly.

'The Ministerial Air Liaison Group; with customary Anglo-Saxon obstinacy the name is reversed in English. Air Force planes whose job is to carry about important people. Two weeks before the accident Thomas flew de Gaulle down to Toulon in the same airplane for a memorial service. The *Minerve*, a submarine, had disappeared.'

'And two weeks later he was in the Indian Ocean.'

'That's right.'

She left him and walked down to the water, kicking the sand into the waves. Stone watched her from behind. She carried herself like a child, slightly ephemeral, light, isolated. It was a conscious effort at self-protection. She had a child's grace and calm; but, like a child's, it was an assumed calm. Her short hair was disordered in the breeze, but seemed comfortably disordered as if always that way. In fact, it suited her. He walked down to the water's edge, put his hand lightly on her shoulder. She turned automatically, like a machine, and began again.

'They flew Ailleret out for an official visit to Madagascar and on the way back stopped at La Réunion.'

'But what happened?'

'I told you. It was 9 March. They took off in the night and crashed into the mountains. An investigating team was sent out on the plane which had brought the bodies back, but they never published what they found in their investigation. Everyone was given a hero's funeral at the Invalides, thanks to Ailleret being on board, and we heard unofficially through our friends that there had been a human error; that our husbands had been drunk. Touching contrast. One heroic moment of de Gaulle, head bowed before the coffins, followed by eternal slander and doubt.'

'No one would kill eighteen innocent people to get rid of one man. There are too many other ways.'

'Look, I didn't say a word! I didn't say a thing.' She took hold of his left arm. 'I don't want to hear your doubts or your questions. You provoked me last night.'

'You provoked yourself,' he broke in.

She waved him off.

'All I said was that my husband didn't drink. And I have a hard time imagining old Bradiet or any of the others whooping it up before a long, overnight flight. That's all. I knew them. They were like my husband — careful people. Now let's talk about something else.'

'I went down to the sea,' he began,
To see what I could see,
Down by the sea side
Down by the sea.

I went down to the sea,
To hear what I might hear,
Down by the sea weed
Down by the sea.

I heard my future floating,
Light through the blue waves,
To through the water
Fro through the sea.

I saw my future sinking,
Down through the dark brine
Down through the water
Down by the sea.

She laughed at his melancholy face.
'Are you the only one allowed to be sad?' he asked.
'Yes. Didn't they tell you?'

Chapter Two

Stone's eyes snapped open, hazy in the half-light. It was five o'clock the next morning, Monday. The pupils focused with difficulty on to a mass against which his face had been resting. It had the texture of peach skin. He recognized the back of Mademoiselle de Pisan's shoulder and rolled away from it out of the bed.

Reaching about for his dressing-gown he found it and groped down the corridor to his own room.

His apologies had been made the night before, saying that something had happened in Paris and he was forced to go back. This appeared an acceptable excuse, having been preceded by a telephone call which lasted for twenty minutes despite the bad line to Paris. The call was made in a closed room to a journalist, Bernard Kaplan, who was an old friend and doyen of the American correspondents in Paris. Even on the crackling line Kaplan was sardonic and eloquent. He had known Ailleret slightly, at receptions, exercises to which the press were invited and so on. He knew just enough about the man to encourage Stone with his idea.

Stone left alone, creeping out of the house into the half-light of retreating darkness. At that hour he would be able to go as fast as he liked and reach Paris within six hours. The first two hundred kilometres were winding country roads — one and a half lanes wide at best. After that they straightened out, and at Orléans the Autoroute began.

He thought of nothing except the road, driving down the centre with calculated fatalism. The car was rarely below 70 m.p.h. on the bad stretches and was pushed quickly up to 110 each time the road was clear. He didn't like going fast.

Nor dislike it. Speed left him indifferent – indifferent with the exception of a movement of skin over his rather sharp cheek-bones in the last moment before he rounded each corner. He was protected from any sensation inside the car and that suited him perfectly. It wasn't a subject on which he used his imagination.

If he went fast it was because he had a fast car. It suited him to keep an Alpine in Paris. Elsewhere he was just as happy to roll along slowly.

If any thought went through his mind, it was Maupans' remark on banality. He was anything except banal; that was what most people thought. And yet he felt a terrible dust building up around his soul, and the dust was banality. Lack of fulfilment. He was too careful. He had protected himself too well from all risks and so was dying of his own superiority. A distorted joke. Perhaps that was the real reason for the twitch over his cheeks.

Each time he interested himself in something, he wondered if this time he might not frighten himself, free himself, lose control even a tiny bit. He wondered if he might not feel the sensation of movement.

Shortly after seven the Loire appeared before him, an experienced lady flowing slowly with the two banks like legs lying serenely wide apart. On the south side there was a small road, always clear of traffic, which led two hours later to the throughway across Orléans and then to the Autoroute, where it was possible to push the speed to 120 m.p.h.

At eleven o'clock he was in the centre of Paris, walking under the porch of the Bibliothèque Nationale, the national library. The library held collections of all the major newspapers since the turn of the century.

Thus, thirty minutes later he read for a second time the account of the accident. The paper was dated Monday, 10 March 1968. The accident had been on Saturday night and the report had been sent on Sunday. He read slowly in order to miss nothing, then turned to the next page. In the midst of the testimonies from various ministers and generals was the first official communiqué. He skipped over it to the last paragraph. 'Shortly after take-off the plane turned slightly to the right. The hypothesis of a technical failure which might have caused this alteration of direction is not excluded.'

He turned the pages of the large bound volume on to the next day. There was nothing except confirmation that an investigating team had flown out. He turned on again. Nothing. Again. Still nothing. Again. There was an article on the funeral at the Invalides, with a photograph of de Gaulle, the nineteen coffins behind him, bent over from his great height, talking to the families of the dead. Stone examined it. De Gaulle had one hand on somebody's shoulder and the other arm hung at his side, long and stiff with the fingers at the end clenched tightly. He thought he could make out Mélanie in the background. It was probably his imagination. The great stone courtyard appeared grey in the photograph.

He skipped through the columns. They described the funeral in detail but there was nothing about the accident itself. For the next half-hour he turned through the sheets, from day to day, eventually stopping at 14 July without finding anything more.

He asked for the volumes of the other national newspapers: *Le Monde* and *Le Figaro*. It took most of the afternoon to search through them in the same way. There was no doubt. The accident and its causes were not mentioned after the first two days. The whole subject melted into nothingness after the funeral. Perhaps that was normal. Who cares about the dead?

And yet. And yet there was absolutely nothing. He thought for a moment, looking up into the air. It was so difficult to imagine someone killing nineteen people — especially sitting where he was, in the dusty atmosphere of this library. He avoided the old woman on his right and the student on his left and gazed into the dome a hundred feet above.

There was something missing. Everything was missing.

He set a notebook on the desk before him and wrote at the top of the first page the date, '8 May 1972', and beneath it: 'The death of General Ailleret.'

He then listed all that Mélanie had told him the day before. On the next page he set down a complete summary of the newspaper accounts.

It was four o'clock. He stumbled to his feet. In his crumpled jeans and old sweater he looked as peculiar as the rest of them. Five hours in that damp air were more than enough. He drove across the river to the Brasserie Lipp where he knew he could get something to eat despite the time. The owner greeted him, managing almost to ignore his unshaven, dusty state. He devoured a mountain of choucroute, drank two large beers, drove home and went to bed.

Charles Stone lived at 79 rue de Grenelle – an eighteenth-century house divided into flats with his on the second floor. A Louis XV staircase led to his door. The wrought-iron balustrade never failed to comfort his soul. There was something about the early stages of degeneracy which attracted him.

The rooms themselves had the air of rooms only half-lived in. Which they were. Either too ordered or too disordered. The walls were covered in pictures; drawings of the late eighteenth or early nineteenth century and contemporary paintings. His collection rarely pleased those who saw it.

The French were brought up to appreciate oils for their market values (a solid market value meant an old painting) and drawings not at all. And those who appreciated contemporary art didn't appreciate his. They all thought Stone had peculiar taste. The word 'bad' would have been too strong for what they didn't understand.

The drawings were nudes. That was one of his simple pleasures. The paintings were mostly grotesque or tortured. They were his more complicated, more personal pleasures.

An angel in the arms of a tart stared coldly across the drawing-room over a curious mixture of Directory and modern furniture, out on to the building's private garden in the courtyard below. A double door led to a Sheraton dining-room — Sheraton because its lines were clean and efficient — and that into a small library, beyond which was his bedroom. His bedroom was modern because modern was perfectly comfortable.

Stone lay face down, naked, asleep in the middle of the bed. His left hand lay on the nape of his neck, its fingers twisted around his brown hair which became almost fair at the edges. The fingers were long and finely drawn without being delicate. On his left was a cognac glass which he had emptied as a last prayer to all that was good in life. On his right, on the floor, lay a blouse. It belonged to Agnès de Pisan, the girl he had taken to Noirmoutier. She probably wouldn't come back after being abandoned to the care of Hélène de Maupans.

It was a pity, he thought as he drifted into sleep. But that was the sort of risk he allowed himself so easily to take. Yet another proof of his banality.

Chapter Three

Philippe Courman was a friendly sort of fellow — extremely friendly in a distant, engaging way. Few of his friends would have said he had enemies. Even his enemies would have denied it. They preferred silence to his friendship or his enmity. With silence and time one might forget.

No, Courman was a popular fellow. You had only to look at his confident slow smile as he walked out of the Cercle Militaire, the largest club in Paris, limping slightly from the club foot at the end of his left leg. That deficiency brought even more popularity for a brave man, and he was a brave man. His lapel testified to that fact with a small collection of ribbons carefully sewn in place. The Croix de Guerre. The Rosette on ribbon of a Commandeur of the Légion d'Honneur which set him well above the mere Chevaliers and Officers who bought their honours so easily.

Next to those two lay his real distinction. The discreet ribbon of a Compagnon de la Libération. That small band of heroes; the first thousand disciples of freedom who had become hunted criminals when they abandoned their secure lives in 1940 to risk everything with de Gaulle. And how many of those medals had been given to widows of dead martyrs? How many other holders had died from the long-term effects of wounds or tortures or, now increasingly, of natural causes? Twenty-seven years after the event Philippe Courman was one of the few hundred survivors of that thousand. Each year he became a larger percentage of the nation's living heritage.

He was exactly the kind of man Stone wanted to meet as he

climbed to the monumental entrance of the club. He was slightly late for a meeting and rushed past Courman, who was chatting with a few friends half-way down the steps.

That meeting had been organized by François de Maupans. Maupans had returned late Monday evening with Agnès de Pisan, using her restlessness as an excuse to hide his own. He had rung Stone early the next morning and delivered a detailed account of the lady's monologue on the long drive home.

Stone took advantage of a short pause to break in with a request for advice. Later that morning he was ushered into Maupans' office, looking as people expected him to look — imposing and discreet. He wore a pale-grey suit, a blue shirt with a pale-brown stripe and a heavy chocolate-brown silk tie.

Maupans greeted him at the door and drew him on to a massive deep sofa in one corner.

'Now, what is the problem?'

' "Problem" isn't the right word. Interest. I am interested by Thomas Barre's death. Mélanie is obviously serious, and I am sure there is something worth discovering. But I don't know anything about Ailleret or the French Army. I need an opening of some sort to set me off in the right direction.'

'You know as much as I do. I have spent my life avoiding the French Army. They have a tendency to overwhelm anyone who comes near. Put another way, they are simply a reflection of France. Or we are a reflection of them. There are two schools of thought in France. Those who believe only the Army matters and those who believe it doesn't matter at all. I belong to the second group. Not that the second group believe their own line. It is simply a hypothetical point of view. You might call it wishful thinking.'

'You mean they do matter?'

'Too much. Too much. Every time we listen to them they destroy us with their eternal infighting. And, if we try to ignore them, they prepare our doom behind our backs. My group presents itself as the liberal left. To be truthful we are the national ostriches; we prefer not to know. The Army has always been the sickness in the Republic.'

'Where should I start?'

Maupans clambered awkwardly to his feet, as if climbing out of a bathtub, and began pacing about the room.

'Why do you want to know?'

'Any reason. Any reason at all. The truth. And, if you don't believe in truth, call it the flip-side of what we do know. I'm curious. I want to know who would kill eighteen innocent people in order to execute one he thought was guilty.'

'Ah, you have the wrong attitude. They are not criminals. They may be politicians or officers or whatever, who work in their own vicious ways, but they are playing a very private game. Do you really want to open that box and pull out all the pieces and the board? You might succeed in doing that, but they will catch you on the rules. You see, that is the really private part of the game. The rules are not written, because no one would dare write them, and even the initiated have trouble making the right moves.'

'A scintillating analogy, my friend, but apparently we have different definitions of what is criminal.'

'All right. All right. I'll give you a name. General Pierre de Portas. Here is his telephone number. He is youngish, has just quit to become general manager of a chemical firm. He is a cousin and I believe he˙thinks the way most officers think. Let him talk. Don't put your foot in it before you understand how their minds work. I promise you, those plain-looking officers conceal more secrets and secret traps than you can imagine.'

'A chat is all I want. I won't rape your cousin or his mind.'

'That's right. And keep me up to date.'

'Of course, François. You shall hear the whole of the

comedy.'

The men with whom Courman chatted on the steps were of
his age. They stood close together in order not to have to
shout over the evening traffic in Place St Augustin below
them. They were chatting not about past adventures but
about present business. They were all members of that great
Gaullist power machine, born of a thousand resisters, which
now represented sixty per cent of the population and had
succeeded in electing the nation's second Gaullist president
and had created the largest political party seen in France
since the hey-day of the Radicals under the Third Republic.

He said good night to them in a slow ponderous manner,
using the minimum of words and emphasizing each to make
it work for five.

His friends watched him climb carefully down the steps
and cross the pavement. His suit was a shade of brown. It was
always one shade of brown or another to match his beard
trimmed short like an old-fashioned naval officer – grown to
hide the grimace caused by each step with his game foot.

A black government Citroën waited for him with its
chauffeur and then disappeared smoothly in the direction of
the Concorde.

Courman played his role perfectly. He was a man of the
present, always a man of the present. Few men were capable
of remembering his past.

His first exploit had been in 1941. He was a young private
secretary to the Vichy Prefect in Blois, Vichy being the
government which Hitler allowed Marshal Pétain to run after
the defeat of France in June 1940, mainly to minimize the
quantity of German troops wasted on occupation duties.
After all, if the French were willing to oppress themselves on
his behalf, why should he, Hitler, protest? For a year and
three months Courman had worked hard to bring into effect
Pétain's pure ideals of Family, Work and Nation which were

disguised under the surprising themes of racism, exploitation and Nazism. Toward November 1941, he began to wonder if he were not on the wrong track.

By listening carefully he managed to discover a probable member of the regional Resistance, one of de Gaulle's rebels. He approached this man and offered to supply information. He was perfectly placed to tell them all they wanted to know about the Government's local plans.

The resister denied that he was other than an obedient, loyal citizen and reported the conversation to his chief, whose code name was Merle. They began to watch Courman, who continued his overtures for another month. Finally Merle decided to risk a contact. He arranged a meeting with Courman for the evening of 23 December at 10.30 in a farm-house ten miles north of Blois.

At 11.30 the code word went out to all members of the group ordering them to break and scatter — as far as possible.

Before being killed in 1944 Merle recounted his meeting to the man who had been Courman's first contact, when they met by chance during the offensive in Alsace.

Courman had been nervous, jumpy. But he brought as promised some fairly interesting documents. He and Merle then arranged a further meeting where he would produce something more important.

They were about to part when Courman blurted out: 'These documents will cost you only 10,000 francs. The next lot will be more expensive.'

Merle looked at him in disbelief.

'You mean you are selling them?'

'What the hell do you expect me to do?'

Merle tried to reach for his pistol, but the young, gangly, then unbearded man already had his out.

'If you don't want to play, I won't either. I give you two hours to get out of the region.' Courman disappeared, leaving Merle to think rapidly and act.

Merle guessed that the young man was only after money but nevertheless capable of anything. He decided to disband his group. It was eighteen months' work lost – plus the life of one member who was caught by the Milice, the French Gestapo, when he broke his cover to run for another department.

Having failed in his first attempt, Courman returned to surer ground. He had himself transferred to Dijon. There he used his position to confiscate local manufactured goods and food, which he then sold either to the puppet government or to the occupying Germans via the government at inflated prices.

By June 1944 he was a very rich young man. He was no longer gangly. His war effort had given him a certain presence – the beginnings of that friendly confidence which attracted so many to him in succeeding years. He had also built up a small unofficial organization of helpers who were either, as he put it, 'screwdrivers or bottle-openers'. The former were an assortment of toughs and the latter various useful contacts.

The unfortunate events of 1944, such as the successful Allied invasion, the advance upon Paris and so on, encouraged local Resistance groups to take events into their own hands. Courman was one of those events. In the middle of the night of 12 September he was awakened by three armed men, charged with treason and collaboration, and taken to 72 rue d'Auxonne – the Dijon jail.

There, because of his imposing manner, he was given a private cell and allowed to inform his family. He informed his chief associate, who watched and waited for two days until the local Resistance group was caught up in the overall war and went off to more important tasks. Courman was left in the hands of the regular jail officers.

His associate then arrived with ten friends. They declared themselves members of the central Resistance organization.

They discreetly shot the officer who had registered the charge 'treason and collaboration' and changed it to the Vichy charge of collaboration with the other enemy – the Resistance. They then liberated Courman, transformed by a few untidily scrawled words into a hero.

From that moment on he created a remarkable war record for himself, managing even to be named a Compagnon de la Libération. It had cost him one bribe – large and beautiful in its solitary success.

Ten thousand Resistance Medals had been given. Some three thousand of those were bought indirectly or wangled. But that award was not good enough for Courman. He had already learnt to aim high. There were only a thousand Compagnons de la Libération created, and no more than ten were suspect. Courman's was the most suspect and the least contested. He was already a great manipulator – an artist.

The first few years after the war he spent consolidating his organization and merging it with various marginal Resistance groups who were leaderless and might give him yet more levers and openings in the real web of power which controlled France.

He used his organization to work for the Government, the Ministry of the Interior, the opposition parties – in fact, anyone who would pay and could offer him a new chance to expand.

In 1958 his was one of the groups which took to the Paris streets under the general leadership of Alexander Sanguinetti, calling for de Gaulle's return. Not that he wanted it. He simply smelt what was coming.

In 1960 he began throwing his weight behind the rebellious Algerian generals but drew back at the last moment when he sensed their defeat. Then he swung round and became one of the key organizations in defeating from within the rebel terrorist organization, known as the Secret Army or the OAS – again he acted under the leadership of Sanguinetti. This about-turn unfortunately but inevitably meant Courman was forced to eliminate three of his own men who were overly compromised in terrorism.

His reward followed, as did his confidence in the regime's stability. He abandoned his fence-sitting and relaxed in the comfort of a large office in the general headquarters of the government party, the Gaullist Union of Democratic Republicans, known as the UDR. There his responsibilities were wide but vaguely defined. He was consulted on all questions of internal control and order at the grass roots. And he faithfully oiled his screwdrivers and bottle-openers, quick to rust in these days of peace.

Courman was on his way to an execution. Nothing messy. He didn't go in for that sort of thing anymore. There were so many more refined methods of dealing with people. Experience had taught him that.

His car drew up before the entrance of the National Assembly — the Palais Bourbon, a royal residence which had been transformed into the nation's parliament in the 1870s. Courman climbed out and limped into the almost oval courtyard, turned left and in through the doors. He wasn't questioned by the guards. They knew him well and greeted him as he went by.

On the second floor half-way down a corridor he stopped outside an office. He could hear voices on the other side — above all, that of his victim, high-pitched and pleading. Two other voices, calming and insistent, completed the muffled choir.

Courman pulled three sheets of paper from his pocket. They were photocopies.

'I most certainly shall not resign,' the high-pitched voice protested. 'This is hearsay!'

'Albert, you don't realize. It's only a matter of time.'

'You can't expect the Party to carry the burden when you

are publicly shown to be guilty.'

One of the photocopies was a tax declaration. Courman had not had to work for that. It had been given to him by a political opponent in the Ministry of Finance. This particular job was a commission from outside the UDR against one of Courman's own Deputies. He liked to take outside jobs from time to time just to keep his general contacts functioning.

Albert Duschêne was an old Gaullist and a virulent enemy of a senior official in the Ministry of Finance. That was not an unusual state of affairs. The Minister of Finance was not a Gaullist. He came from − in fact, led − one of the smaller parties who were loyal members of the government coalition. That loyalty extended to a shared fear of the Communist Party, but not much further.

The second piece of paper was a letter from Duschêne, Parisian Member of Parliament, to a well-known architect. In the letter he accepted a large consulting fee in return for 'aiding' the architect over a difficult building permit.

Courman had bought that letter at great cost from a former private secretary to the architect. Of course he was reimbursed for these working expenses by the man who had commissioned him. And that man in turn was reimbursed from the Ministry's secret funds.

The third piece of paper was a bank statement. It was addressed to Duschêne by a bank in Zürich. The sum on the statement was the same as the fee offered by the architect.

Courman was very proud of that paper. It had been by far the most difficult to lay his hands on. He had tried to buy someone in the bank, but the Swiss are either remarkably incorruptible or much too expensive.

In the end he simply bought Duschêne's postman. For a paltry sum one of his own lieutenants was given a quick preview glance at the Deputy's personal mail every morning for one month.

Even the simplest of men could see that the sum on the

bank statement didn't appear on the income-tax declaration.

It was a clear case of tax evasion and influence-peddling. Not that other Deputies and leading bureaucrats didn't do the same – Courman's contact in the Finance Ministry first among them. Doing wrong was of no importance. Getting caught was another matter.

Courman pushed down the door-handle and swung open the door. Albert was sitting behind his desk, worn out and embattled. His eyes were glazed like a caged animal's. He wore the same shirt he had worn the day before. Despite the heat and the oppressive atmosphere in his office he had not taken off his jacket, and sweat had seeped through the shirt, been soaked up by the suit and was beginning to show. His defences were slackening; it was the moment for the execution.

He had been under pressure from his fellow-Deputies for the last week, badgering him, questioning him. It was Courman indirectly or directly who had warned them that Duschêne was in trouble.

Poor Albert's first reaction had been to turn for help to his old friend and party organizer Philippe Courman. He would drive the wolves away. That was what Courman promised. And yet there he was, the saviour and the wolf wrapped in one, advancing through the door with a crestfallen air.

'Philippe! At last!' Duschéne jumped up from his desk with more than relief and tried to embrace Courman. 'What have you found? Who is behind these slanders?

Courman said nothing. He simply handed the three photocopies to his old friend and walked to a window. The other two men looked up expectantly while Duschêne stared at the papers puzzled. He read them twice, three times.

'But what is this, Philippe?' He held them up innocently.

'That, my poor Albert, is the end of the road for you. I have worked like the devil to get to the bottom of the rumours and those are what I discovered. Apparently they will be in the newspapers before the end of this week.'

'But, Phillippe, it isn't true. It's a frame-up. Can't you see?'

Courman looked at him as if he were too embarrassed to speak. Eventually he managed to mumble, 'I'm afraid that they are horribly eloquent. I can see no escape.'

One of the other Deputies snatched the papers from his hand and began to read them. He took on a horrified air.

'Albert, we must have your resignation tonight. We must have it before they publish. For your own sake.'

Duschêne was wandering round his office, mumbling to himself. He was in shock. He couldn't understand. He hadn't slept well for a week, not since they had begun badgering him. He was too old for this sort of pressure. He was no longer capable of reasoning things out.

Courman took no part in what followed. He sat by the window, pained by the spectacle of this old friend who had betrayed the national trust. The others applied the pressure. In the Party's interests he had to resign.

It was another half-hour before Duschêne gave in. He no longer protested. He was too tired. One of his colleagues drew up a short letter to the Speaker of the National Assembly. It mentioned health problems. Poor Albert signed almost without registering what it was.

There was nothing more to be done, so Courman threw himself into his role as a friend. He comforted and promised to stand by him. He even offered to take him home. But, no, Duschêne told them to go away and leave him alone.

'Albert, you must get some rest if you are going to defend yourself. There is no point in sitting here moping.'

'Get out. For God's sake, go away!'

They closed the door softly behind them.

It was not until the next morning that they heard the news. Albert had gone home and shot himself in his study. The bullet had gone through his skull, re-emerged and destroyed a bust by Houdon.

As all of Albert's friends pointed out, suicide was an unfortunate admission of guilt.

Strangely enough, they were wrong. It was a combination of exhaustion, frustration and despair which drove him. Duschêne had been pushed to the breaking-point and broken. He saw no solution – only a pistol stuck into his mouth, the cold steel sticking to his lips and the trigger pulled without considering the bullet which would float gently out, rip a hole in his upper jaw, searing his tongue black with powder burns as it went by, pass on through the amorphous jelly of his brain and split out through his splintered skull and fading black hair only to fly across the room and shatter Houdon's delicate, laughing terra-cotta lady.

'An unnecessary gesture.' That was what Courman said. 'And messy.'

It was he who held the widow's arm at the funeral three days later. He was a very old friend of the family. Old enough to suspect that Duschêne had really been innocent. He wondered if there hadn't been a frame-up. That wouldn't have stopped him taking on the commission – it was simply professional curiosity. He suspected that the bank statement was false.

He had a fine nose for falsehood and had fallen on the truth. The account in Zürich had been opened by someone in Duschêne's name. In fact, Albert had never accepted the architect's consulting fee. He had been tempted, had written to accept and then had withdrawn. If he had accepted, he would have declared it. But there was nothing to declare.

Albert's widow cried at the funeral. She also cursed her husband in the depths of her soul. He had betrayed her and his friends and his party. He had betrayed everyone.

Chapter Four

Charles Stone sat comfortably in an ornate reproduction armchair in a small, overly decorated salon of the Cercle Militaire. In front of him sat General de Portas, who did not resemble a general. If anything, he looked like a company director.

'Which I have just become,' he was saying. 'François told me you know nothing about the French Army, so I should tell you that we have become more technicians than soldiers. Most of us are snapped up on retiring by the private sector. Where else can they find men who know how to administer thousands of workers, understand technical problems and have good contacts? You know, the military market is a very important industrial factor.'

Their conversation wasn't turning in quite the direction Stone had expected. The man before him was of medium height, thin. He had short grey hair and a tight, slightly nervous face.

'Exactly what aspect of the Army interests you, Monsieur Stone?'

'The last ten years' – he paused before continuing – 'and the role of General Ailleret.'

'Ailleret?' Portas broke his upright pose, slightly surprised. 'Whatever for?'

'A study I'm doing. He played an interesting role. After all, he was the Chief of Staff from 1962 to 1968. He couldn't help but be interesting.'

The General had lost his neutral technician's gaze and was leaning forward – calmly, but with a certain eagerness.

'This is no place to talk.' He gestured at the officers

wandering by. 'I live not far away, just off Boulevard
Malesherbes. Come and have dinner. No, no. My wife won't
mind. She is quite used to unexpected guests.'

The General took him by the arm and led him out of the
club at a fast pace. Once on the Boulevard his strides grew
longer and even faster, each one measured as if it were
individually considered. At first he said nothing. Stone fell in
with him and followed in silence. They turned left off the
Boulevard Malesherbes on to the rue de Lisbonne. Encouraged by the intimacy of this smaller street the General looked
hard at Stone in the middle of a long stride and said, 'Ailleret
was a bastard,' then dropped back into silence.

They were greeted by a tired, plain woman, not very well
dressed. She ushered them into a large middle-class drawing-
room.

The furniture was light, unmatched – mostly collected in
foreign posts. It scarcely filled the room, which was designed
for the rich, opulent styles of Louis-Napoleon.

She apologized for the lack of comfort – 'We've been in
Government-furnished houses for the last twenty years.
There wasn't much that belonged to us, I'm afraid' – then
left them alone.

'My wife doesn't really understand. Before she complained
about having no private life. Now she has too much.' He
poured Stone a double whisky in a coloured glass tumbler,
then perched on the edge of an uncomfortable sofa. 'You
could count his friends on one hand!' Stone looked at him,
blank. 'Ailleret! Ailleret. Everyone hated him. These last
thirty years have been years of hate.' He waved his right arm
as if even the inanimate objects about them had taken to
hating. 'It would take all evening just to list all the traitors
among us in the Government and all the disasters they got us
into. But no one, no one was worse than Ailleret, not even de
Gaulle.'

'I didn't realize. . . .'

'That man never fired a shot in anger in his whole career. That's not easy. There was the war, then Indo-China, then Suez, then Algeria, and I don't know how many other little things. Never once did he see action.'

'How did he become Chief of Staff?'

'How? That wasn't difficult. Over our bodies; that means over and against the rest of the Army. Twelve years ago there was lots of room for an ambitious opportunist.'

'But he was an old Gaullist.'

'Not even that. He was half in, half out of the Resistance, and managed to get himself deported. You know, most of us had a very hard war. The Resistance took all the credit. But we did all the work. They were a couple of thousand troublemakers playing hide-and-go-seek with no responsibility. Do you know how I spent the war? Trying to hold together part of a regiment in the unoccupied zone. Do you know about that? I guess they don't tell you about that in your schools. After you English had abandoned us in the crucial moment of the fighting in 1940, and we had been sabotaged by our own communists at home, Maréchal Pétain made the best peace he could with the Germans and set about trying to rebuild France in preparation for the day when we would throw the Germans out and set up a good Christian regime with good Christian values. In the meantime the Germans only gave us the south-western half of France. They occupied the rest. So what was there left but to build as best we could with the little we had. If we hadn't held the fort the communists would have taken over in 1945 the moment the Germans were defeated. Anyway, we didn't have much; almost no weapons, and our movements were restricted so there was nothing to do. You can imagine what that does to morale. There wasn't much to eat. And most of my friends were trying to do the same, either in other parts of the unoccupied zone or on the other side of the Mediter-

ranean in our north African colonies. Thanks to us, when the
Allies landed in north Africa and later in France, there was a
French army ready to fight with them. All we needed were
the arms. Who do you think fought in Italy and in the
German campaign? It wasn't the Resistance. They had neither
the numbers nor the training.

'But Ailleret wasn't one of them and he wasn't one of us.
He was already an opportunist trying to get ahead. He
became a technician.' The word was pronounced differently,
insultingly, to imply something different from the last time
he had used it. 'In 1960 he was a brigadier commanding a
study section to encourage new weapon developments. They
were the laughing-stock of the Army. I remember once they
put on a demonstration of smoke-bomb tactics and almost
suffocated the audience. Then de Gaulle began to have
trouble finding men to do his dirty work in Algeria.

'I didn't join the OAS, but a lot of my friends did and I
sympathized with them. Nobody liked the way de Gaulle
treated us. Lying. Trickery. Shifting everyone from post to
post.

'Ailleret would have done anything asked of him in return
for promotion.' Portas had become quite excited. He seemed
intent on making his guest understand the injustice of their
position and was perched even more precariously on the edge
of the sofa. The first finger on his right hand lunged out
nervously to punctuate almost every sentence. The distance
between the two men meant that this pointed finger stopped
each time some twelve inches from Stone's face. As for
Stone, he hadn't managed to open his mouth. He had
switched on a miniature tape recorder in his pocket and sat
back trying to follow the ever more rapid monologue. 'So de
Gaulle sent him to Algeria. Promoted him and gave him the
command of a region – the North-East Constantinois. He
blew that. He was a lousy commander. Ask old Crepin; he
was his boss out there, and Crepin isn't one of us – he's one

of the original Gaullists. They had to pick up the pieces behind Ailleret. And yet when our generals rebelled against the policy of giving Algeria away to the communist Arabs, and staged the *Putsch* in April 1961 to bring down the government in Paris, Ailleret rushed off a telegram of love and affection to de Gaulle. Not many of us did that! Even if we didn't join the *Putsch* actively, we were in no rush to suck up to that sly old bastard.

'So, for the lack of other suitable traitors to support their policies, they promoted him again. And then again. In July 1960 he was an unimportant brigadier. One year later, one year, he was Commander-in-Chief, Algeria. And in July 1962 he was a full general and Chief of Staff. You might call that a minor case of rapid promotion.' He lounged back in triumph on the sofa.

'But why? Surely there were other men?'

'Who? De Gaulle had no friends. No one he could really rely on. Do you know that Larminat, one of the oldest of the old pure Gaullists, committed suicide rather than preside over the tribunal which judged Salan, the leader of the OAS, along with the other rebel generals and Secret Army leaders.

'Not Ailleret. He testified against them with all the viciousness he could muster. Go on. Read the trial records. You'll see. And do you know why? He was on the verge of being named Chief of Staff. That testimony clinched it. From then on de Gaulle knew Ailleret could never betray him; he was too hated by the rest of the Army! It was a devil's pact.

'Ailleret promised total loyalty and the purge of all anti-Gaullist officers. Ha! As if that were possible. And de Gaulle promised to keep him where he was and support him as Chief of Staff.'

'And?'

'And Ailleret kept his bargain. Do you know how many thousands of officers were unceremoniously shifted out in the next six years? Carefully chosen sacrificial lambs.

'They almost got me once but I managed to be indispensable to my immediate boss for a few months and by then the execution squad had passed on, if I may use that phrase' – he relaxed momentarily, smiled ironically for the second time – 'to describe the throwing of men unprepared and unthanked on to an uninterested employment market.

'As for de Gaulle, he had to keep his bargain. He had no choice. There was no one else. No one.' He shrugged again and almost whispered, 'No one at all. But that didn't stop him from having contempt for the man.'

The door swung open. It was Madame de Portas. 'Come and have dinner.' Stone had forgotten about his tape and quickly slipped his hand into his jacket-pocket to switch it off.

She led them into the dining-room; the furniture was no less sparse. There was a cold atmosphere which would have killed the pleasure of any good food for Stone. He needn't have worried. The meal was correct. In French terms that meant there were the correct number of courses. A plain pâté on a lettuce-leaf, some chicken with potatoes, the remaining outside leaves of the lettuce (he imagined the rest doing for tomorrow), a chalky Camembert and a slice of apple-tart. It was served by a maid who resembled Madame de Portas in every way.

The General, however, did not notice. It was his daily fare. He had long ago drawn a line between what he was served at home and what he was served outside. As if adjusting to the tone of the meal, he had partially returned to his colder, distant manner.

'Of course, times change and the officer corps with them. Ten years ago none of us knew anything about business. Now we know more than enough. There is still a hard transition, but we know how to look after our own.' He turned to his wife with a smile. 'My dear, do you know what interests Monsieur Stone? Ailleret.'

She looked away from her husband towards Stone, a potato half-way to her mouth. 'Ailleret?' She swallowed the potato quickly. 'What an odd idea.'

Stone shrugged.

'I've been explaining to him,' her husband added.

She ignored that last comment, having already slipped away into a reverie. The name apparently had some unexpected effect on her. 'The last time I saw Ailleret,' she eventually continued, 'he visited us when Pierre was commanding a division in Germany. He arrived by parachute.'

'He was a terrible show-off.'

'I have never met such a difficult, pompous man. They tell me he often arrived by parachute.' Her glance shot up to the ceiling and drifted slowly down as if she could still see him descending.

'If he had used his love for parachutes even once in action, our attitude would have been different.'

'The second-last time I saw him was in Paris, at a reception. He arrived in battle-smock. Quite extraordinary.' She sank back into her reverie.

'He often came to the office that way, ready for battle. He always said it was because he had an exercise on that afternoon. Can you imagine? Going to the office in the centre of Paris in battle-smock. Oh, and he always carried a pistol. In or out of uniform, he always had a pistol in his pocket and dark glasses to hide his eyes. We called him the cowboy general. It was all cinema to cover up his disgraceful office-bound career. And his lack of power.'

'Surely if he carried out a purge he had power?'

'Only to do that. De Gaulle wouldn't risk giving him any other role. There had been too much trouble with all-powerful generals. No. He gave a mouthful to everyone so that they were at each other's throats instead of his own.

'His office was on the same floor as the Army Chief of Staff, yet they scarcely saw each other.' Portas began laughing. 'And then there was Cabanier,' he managed to say. His wife joined in with her hollow metallic laugh. 'Cabanier was Chief of the Navy before Ailleret arrived and stayed on until 1967. He was a Gaullist, typically extremist. During the five years he worked for Ailleret he refused to shake his hand or speak to him. Can you imagine?'

His wife rang the bell and stamped her foot. 'Just like de Gaulle, he always overdid it.'

Stone couldn't help laughing with them, wondering if it were true.

'And he hated the Americans even more than de Gaulle hated them. You understand, our personal dislike of Ailleret was unimportant, but he endangered French security as well. I remember the big NATO Fall Exercise in 1965. I was at NATO military headquarters – what they call SHAPE. Ailleret ordered the French officers not to take part. Crepin was the senior French officer and he had not forgotten the problems Ailleret had caused in Algeria; above all, his great betrayal of the Army. Crepin refused to obey without a written order from de Gaulle. So Ailleret backed down because he knew he would never be given that order. Typical. And don't forget he wrote that article, "Tous Azimuts", announcing a new defence strategy against everyone including the Americans.'

Stone had seen references to it in the obituaries.

'De Gaulle must have ordered him to. . . .'

'You think so,' Portas broke in. 'I tell you, Ailleret hated the Americans. He was five giant steps ahead of de Gaulle on that subject.'

'He once told me', Madame de Portas threw in, 'that he always carried a pistol because he didn't trust "those dirty Americans". I had to stop myself from laughing. Mind you, he got it in the end.'

'Yes. And what caused that?' Stone asked.

'His own stupidity,' the General replied with satisfaction.

'There he was on La Réunion at a good party in the middle of a filthy night. The crew didn't want to leave. They were enjoying themselves. But he forced them. And the plane was overloaded with fuel. He was too proud to set down on British colonies, or even former British colonies. So they needed enough fuel to fly direct to Djibouti. Crazy.'

'As simple as that?'

'Most stupid things are. A slightly tiddly pilot and an unwieldy plane.'

'How true,' Stone agreed as the last piece of soggy pastry hidden under a thin slice of apple slipped slowly down his throat.

After a mediocre white liqueur which General and Madame de Portas had brought back from their service in Germany, Stone left them. On arriving home, he added to his tape the parts of the conversation it had missed, labelled it 'Number 1' and placed it beside his notes of the day before in a portable steel box with a combination-lock.

He lay on his bed, face up, thinking about who might possibly have done it, if Ailleret had indeed been killed:

1. retired members of the OAS
2. groups within the Army, the Navy, or the Air Force
3. the Americans
4. any individual bitter officers
5. de Gaulle or individuals within the Government; he made a note to check on Ailleret being more anti-American than his boss
6. how many other people not yet thought of?

He drank a glass of good cognac to clean the taste from his mouth and went to sleep to dream of hatred.

Chapter Five

The sun shone diagonally across the immense, flagged court-yard. It was the next morning and the air was still cool, left over from the night. He was waiting unshaven before the closed entrance of the National Library, impatiently dancing from foot to foot on the stone steps. At nine o'clock the guardian unlocked the door and Stone pushed by. The guardian watched him striding down the hall in an old sweater and jeans, and swore to himself about uncivilized foreigners.

Stone spent the next three days there. He saw nobody. Thought of nothing else. He knew that somewhere in those old newspapers and magazines he would find a hole if there was a hole. Each day he pushed by the guardian at nine o'clock and was the last to squeeze out at six. He suppressed lunch as an unnecessary waste of time and limited his food to large steaks – one each morning for breakfast and a second for dinner. After which he immediately slept to give his increasingly cobwebbed mind the time to sweep itself out for the next morning.

He began carefully with two books. The third volume of de Gaulle's collected speeches and a bound collection of the official armed forces' monthly for 1967. It was called the *National Defence Revue*.

In the December issue was Ailleret's article 'Tous Azimuts'.* There he called for a neutral France and an army

* 'Tous Azimuts' or 'All Directions', Charles Ailleret's most notorious article, was inspired by the 360° of a compass. The meaning: France should have an armed force capable of acting against anybody or anything coming from anywhere. Against Russia or America or China or Africa or anyone else.

turned even against the Allies. In the de Gaulle volume was a speech made in 1959. There, the obituaries said, Ailleret had found his inspiration and his justification for 'Tous Azimuts'. What better way to decide whether Ailleret was five giant steps ahead of his master, whether he was really obsessed by a hatred of the Americans, as Portas had claimed, than to compare their written words.

The morning was consumed by drawing out the ideas and weighing them. It was horribly tedious work, but it confirmed one thing. Where de Gaulle called for an independent France, Ailleret called for withdrawal from the complete Western political and defence network and spoke of allies who might become enemies. That was much further than de Gaulle had ever gone.

Stone closed his eyes for ten minutes, then turned to a massive pile of waiting volumes: the complete collection of the *Defence Revue* for the 1960s. He began leafing through the indexes. There was nothing. Nothing, except a February 1968 account of de Gaulle's first comments on 'Tous Azimuts'. That was two months after the article.

He read it through three times but could make no sense of it. De Gaulle seemed to agree, then disagree. His arguments contradicted each other. Was he being sarcastic or was he uncomfortable? Was he trying to avoid a commitment or was he laughing at Ailleret, at anyone who believed France was rich enough to stand completely alone and defend herself against the world?

He turned the pages and was about to give up when his eyes fell on a black-bordered page. It was the issue of April 1968. Within the black mourning-band he read:

At the moment of going to press, we have learnt of General Ailleret's death in an airplane accident.

In our next issue we shall retrace the career of our Chief of the General Staff.

Stone flipped quickly to the May issue. Nothing. 'No. It isn't possible,' he whispered loud. He turned carefully through the issue. There was nothing. The name Ailleret wasn't mentioned once. He went through the next five issues. Nothing.

There was no doubt. From the moment of his death, it was as if he had never existed.

Stone began to smile. He began to believe that he was not wasting his time.

It was six o'clock. He went home and filed his notes neatly in the steel box.

Thursday and Friday he devoted to searching through bound volumes of newspapers. They didn't offer him the opening or flaw which he sought; perhaps because he didn't yet know his subject well enough to spot it.

Gradually Stone was able to piece together the period. He discovered the ageing unknown Brigadier Ailleret grasping the limelight for the first time in 1960 as camp commandant of the first French nuclear explosion. There he gave the impression of having conceived and built the bomb himself. The papers called him its father — 'le Père de la Bombe Nucléaire' — without knowing why. Journalists liked to polarize. And Ailleret had a genius for publicity.

Then de Gaulle found himself increasingly isolated over Algeria. The whole military élite was against him. They wanted to keep the colony and, no matter what impressive posts de Gaulle gave them, they weren't grateful and wouldn't help him.

Ailleret was one of the first to leap through the door to promotion. The price? Obedience. Then came the generals' *Putsch* in 1961 and Ailleret, again first through the door, his loyalty held out before him, reached the top. There he acted tough as Commander-in-Chief, Algeria — the man who liquidated the French interest in north Africa keeping the Army in line. There he was again, after the capture of General Raoul Salan, chief of the terrorist OAS. This leader (respected even by the officers who had been afraid to rebel) was berated and insulted by Ailleret at his trial in a jittery Paris in a Palais de Justice guarded by armed troops. And finally there he was in January 1963, Chief of the General Staff, at the top of the ladder.

And yet it was true. He had almost no powers. Stone turned momentarily to the *National Defence Revue* for his specific attributions of power. He was Chief, but in name only.

And so Ailleret began his advance again. Stone found vague articles on the thousands of officers retired early — de Gaulle's enemies, Ailleret's as well — with hypocritically patriotic cries by Pierre Messmer, the Minister of Defence, for industry to employ these 'heroes' discharged from the nation's service.

Ailleret gradually becoming more active, speaking up here and there on policy matters. Rumours of clashes with the chiefs of the three services and with Messmer.

The beginning of the NATO crisis as de Gaulle announced that France would pull out. Yet another opportunity for Ailleret to take the President's side against the soldiers who wanted to stay in. And then the first departures of his main rivals. The three subordinate chiefs were older than him, well entrenched, old friends of de Gaulle. Their successors didn't have the same sure touch on their respective commands. Opposed to de Gaulle, who wanted to keep his distance from the Americans, they were gradually isolated, and Ailleret benefited, becoming increasingly indispensable. De Gaulle had no doubt hoped that four years of a heavy hand would bring the soldiers into line. But in 1966 they were even more firmly against him than at the height of the Algeria rebellion. Almost all of them, except Ailleret.

Then came 'Tous Azimuts' in late 1967 and a flurry of

articles questioning the strategy. Was it overly ambitious? What did it really mean? Who had instructed Ailleret to write it, if anyone? Who would pay the enormous weapons costs which it implied? Everybody was asking questions. Nobody appeared to be answering them. And then came his death in March 1968. And two days before his death the announcement that he would be kept on for another year in spite of having reached the mandatory retirement age. A remarkable success story, except for the end.

And none of what he had heard or read proved that Ailleret was the monster he had been painted. After all, Stone reflected, what else could his enemies call him except a grasping opportunist, just as they discredited the Gaullists by calling them fanatical extremists? Ailleret was perhaps ambitious and ruthless, but how else could one survive and succeed in such a vicious setting? And how was one to know whether Ailleret really believed in the causes he supported to get to the top? Anyone could assume that he didn't. Any outsider could assume all he wanted of one man's private conscience.

Stone sat back on Friday evening and read his notes through again. Where was the flaw? Reasons weren't lacking: hatred, jealousy, revenge, rivalry. . . . But where was the flaw?

In a moment of inspiration he telephoned Mélanie. Perhaps if he saw her she might jog something. . . . Facts. There was no answer. He didn't want to ring anyone else. He didn't want to break the spell. There were too many factors and facts and ideas floating about in his mind. He wanted to keep them in a closed circuit.

In the end he drove to Cabourg on the Normandy coast, and spent the weekend alone, walking along the endless beach, beautiful in its mournful sadness. The sea empty and rough in early May.

On Monday morning he thought of a new approach. He went to the offices of the newspaper *Le Monde* and walked into their library. His stubble was now five days' old and his clothes had the same maturity, like a cheese. No one could have denied that they had become a bit smelly. He was almost too untidy and too touchy to be admitted. That was what the librarian thought, but Stone imposed himself.

Ten minutes later a thick file entitled 'French Army Articles' was placed before him. Beside it was a thinner file marked 'General Charles Ailleret'. He picked up the latter and glanced nervously through.

Suddenly his eyes fell half-way through a sentence: '. . . that even in peace-time the Chief of Staff should have the same powers as in times of war.' He skipped further down: 'Commander in Chief of the three armed services. In the vast majority of cases, the Chief of Staff should be the only. . . .'

His eyes moved back to the top. The article was dated 18 March; eight days after the plane-crash. It spoke of a speech by Ailleret a few weeks before, in which he had called for increased powers over the other three chiefs.

Stone turned to the next article, dated ten days later. It said that Ailleret's successor would ask for the same powers that Ailleret had wanted.

He turned again. 28 April. General Fourquet, his successor, had been granted the powers Ailleret had wanted. No. He read it again. The powers that Ailleret had won just before being killed.

But they had changed their story.

He turned back to the weeks before the accident. There was absolutely no mention of a speech calling for new war-time powers. Why hadn't it been announced? And why was it partially announced after his death? And why did they change their story from having called for the powers to having won them? Was the reporter simply repeating what someone told him?

He sat back in his chair, pushed his legs out in a V under the table, let his arms go limp and closed his eyes. Then without warning he banged the table with his fist. 'That's it!' The librarian jumped at the cry. He was about to rush forward to silence the troublemaker when Stone leapt to his feet and strode over to him.

'Make me copies of these three articles.'

The other was about to protest, but Stone had recovered his presence. He gave an encouraging, gentle push and followed him out to the photocopying machine.

That evening Stone celebrated his discovery in a favourite restaurant with Agnès de Pisan, who had consented to forgive him temporarily, at least for that night. They continued the celebration afterwards in her flat. He hadn't really found anything. But he thought he had found the absence of something. A gap. What is sometimes called a hole.

Chapter Six

Charles Stone liked to gamble. He didn't like taking risks or enduring suspense. What he did enjoy was forcing other gamblers to do just that. That was one of his vicarious pleasures.

In the back of his mind he knew exactly what to do. He had only to choose a partner before dealing his cards. The man he chose was called Robert Campini. He was a Deputy, a senior member of the National Assembly Defence Committee, had lost a hand during the war, been involved in half the conspiracies of the Fourth and Fifth Republics and had been a key figure in wiping out the Metropolitan section of the OAS. He, if anyone, knew or could find out about the speech, if it had ever been given.

They had met briefly a few months before at a political dinner. Stone had been invited as the breath of fresh air, the token foreigner. He had amused Campini with his stories of the Malaysian jungle and was told to ring up the next time he was in Paris. It wasn't the very next time, but Stone took him at his word and they arranged a meeting two days later.

Campini was waiting with a generous smile in a large office of the National Assembly. It was a show office one floor above the more modest room where Albert Duschêne had lost his last round, and in the other wing. It was a mere façade for greeting outsiders. No one actually worked there. The fellow was as tough as Stone remembered, and as boisterous. He was full of his own exploits. How he had told the President this, the Prime Minister that, and was busy keeping the country moving in the right direction.

Stone sat mutely before this wall of words, making

agreeable sounds from time to time, until the monologue slackened and gaps gradually opened between the sentences. He carefully filled the gaps and began working the conversation round to what he wanted. First the last government instead of the present one, then Campini's exploits under de Gaulle, then the Army, then Ailleret.

'I am doing some research at the moment and I've run into a slight problem — a document I can't find.'

Campini took on a fatherly, all-embracing air.

'You have only to ask me. I can get a hold of anything I want.' The pompous streak in his character made that offer inevitable.

'It is a speech, apparently given in January 1968, by General Ailleret. Something to do with accrued powers for the Chief of Staff. I found references to it, but no more.'

'That doesn't ring a bell. But there is no problem. Absolutely no problem. Give me ten days. Come back on the thirtieth. It's always amusing to find something everyone else has forgotten.'

Campini did not spend the next ten days searching out the speech. He had other things to do. He forgot about his promise within hours of giving it. He had a Party Committee meeting followed by a Defence Committee meeting and, above all, the Prime Minister asked to see him the next day. He had once been a junior minister and hoped to be again; at least junior, if not more. And Chaban, the Prime Minister, was an old Resistance chief. They had something in common. Perhaps this time. . . .

Nine of the ten days passed before his secretary reminded him of the Englishman. She had assumed he was English.

Campini swore. He was always forgetting his unimportant promises. Whom could he ask quickly? Ah! He had a meeting that afternoon, a modified meeting of the Defence Committee. Somebody there would be able to help.

This was an unofficial co-ordinating committee made up of

five influential government Deputies and five senior officers who held important posts – not necessarily what the public thought were important posts. They were influential men in the true sense of the word, and that far outweighed any official titles the State might have given them.

They met in a rather informal manner, here and there around Paris, sometimes over lunch, sometimes breakfast. That afternoon the meeting took place across the road from the Élysée in a small committee-room. There was no particular agenda but everyone was concerned by yet another strike of young conscripts – this time not far from Paris. They were protesting against the shoddy maintenance of military equipment – two of their number had been crushed when a truck's brakes failed on an exercise. And so a hundred others had protested by blocking the road into the camp. The Ministry had decided to arrest ten and throw the book at them as an example. That had simply incited the opposition, etc., etc.; it was always the same and the problem was as much political as military. That was the difficult part of having a citizen's army.

Most of the members supported a hard line, Campini first among them. The exceptions were Cashan, an admiral who liked to make things difficult for the Army, and Dehal, a general who was simply more intelligent than the rest. He suggested they also give the two dead conscripts military funerals, ar.est the officer responsible for transport at the camp and arrest ten of the strikers. Thus everyone's complaints would be dealt with and an example would be set.

The others were at first surprised but soon fell into agreement when the Transport Officer turned out to be a nonentity without friends in Paris. They decided to recommend Dehal's solution to their ministers and chiefs of staff.

Campini chose that euphoric moment of general agreement to ask his question about Ailleret's speech. The reaction was general indifference.

'Why do you want to know?' the Admiral asked.

Campini explained briefly about Stone.

'Sounds like a troublemaker,' Dehal threw in.

'Perhaps,' Campini replied cagily, wondering if he hadn't brought up the wrong subject. 'Do any of you know anything about the fellow?' He read out Stone's name and address as part of his question.

'That speech was a bit of a boob,' the member sitting next to him said quietly. He was from the President's Cabinet Militaire. 'You know, it was never meant to happen.'

'Catton is right,' the Admiral added. 'We had a hell of a time keeping it quiet. If the President knew there was someone trying to stir up all that, he would be furious.'

At the mention of Pompidou, Campini drew his wooden hand out of his jacket-pocket. If he annoyed the President he would never see the light of another cabinet. 'What shall I tell him?'

Catton put his arm firmly on the other's shoulder and whispered in a gently way, 'Discourage him, Campini.'

'Yes, discourage him,' Dehal added. 'Put him off. You're very good at that.'

When Stone arrived the next day he was not greeted by the friendly enthusiasm of their last meeting. Campini waved him in and locked the door, slipping the key into his pocket.

Without introduction he said, 'I haven't found your speech. I don't believe it exists. You must have made a mistake.'

Stone was delighted but managed to look surprised. 'How extraordinary. My references were very specific.'

Campini leant across the monumental desk, his wooden hand in a white glove lying limp under Stone's eyes, and repeated: 'You must have made a mistake.' He was glaring now, as if any fool could see there had been an error. 'What exactly did you want it for?'

Stone took on his most naïve air. 'It would have been interesting to see what powers Ailleret felt the Chief of Staff should have. But as it doesn't exist I'd better not waste any more of your time.' He rose to leave.

'Sit down.' Campini's wooden hand motioned him down with a long mechanical gesture. 'Perhaps I can help you. Ask me some questions.'

Stone recognized an order. As the door was locked behind him, he had little choice. He began asking questions about the Army and Ailleret. To each one Campini replied either 'Yes' or 'No' or 'I don't know'. With each reply his glare magnified. From time to time he bent slowly forward over the desk, bending from the waist, and blew an imaginary speck of dust off the perfectly empty leather surface. His eyes would rise up from this occupation and catch sight of Stone as if surprised to see him still there. Then the eyes would nod to bring on a new question. And with each question new ghosts of the OAS terrorists with whom Campini had dealt from the moment of their capture until the disposal of their bodies rose painfully into the air, hovering in tortured, grotesque forms staring down.

Stone's monologue seemed to echo about the empty spotless room in a vacuum, wiping out the National Assembly and all its freely elected members who were only yards away beyond the door. He began to hear his own voice, to listen to his own voice gradually striving and faltering.

Campini's static replies enhanced the illusion of isolation. Each Yes and No was like a shot destroying the few remaining infections from the outside. The world was four walls. The world was empty.

It was a clever trick beautifully played, and Stone found himself drawn in, as if hypnotised by the latent power in the wooden hand which tapped periodically on the desk.

Twice he tried to leave. Each time he was waved down and told to continue. The questions went quickly, interrupted only by the short crisp replies. And when he could think of no more questions they fell into total silence — Campini melting his visitor into visual pulp, Stone sitting very still trying to see through the glare. All he could see was his own reflection.

In that heavy calm Stone began quietly to laugh. He laughed as if he were truly amused; and Campini, who was at first surprised, finished by joining in. They laughed like two old men who knew each other's tricks. The hatred of equals. Then Stone broke in: 'Well, I think I shall go now.'

The Deputy got to his feet, walked across the room, pulled out his key and unlocked the door, which he then blocked. When the other was in front of him, he shook his left hand firmly but did not let it go.

'There is one thing I should like you to understand, Monsieur Stone. There is no military power in France.' The tone was cold. He swung open the door and motioned his visitor to leave.

Stone controlled his smile until he was well down the corridor. He had been right. He was on the track. If there was something to hide, there was something to be found.

Campini was equally pleased. He had discouraged the fellow the way no one else could ever do. Ah, the experienced touch of a real professional.

Late the next morning Philippe Courman limped across the drawing-room of a comfortable flat in the 16th Arrondissement and seated himself well away from the indolent figure of his host. They apparently had a mutual fear of catching something from each other. They had not shaken hands, nor exchanged a word.

'It's about Ailleret.'

'So?' Courman sat absolutely motionless. Only his mouth moved. It formed a perfect O as the word 'So' slipped out.

'Someone is interested in that speech.'

'So?'

'I think we had better know why.'

'I'm not interested.'

The slouching man stiffened at Courman's reply, jumped up from his chair and went to a window. With his back turned he managed to force a smile, and then returned with a more persuasive manner.

'But I am interested and I want to know why he is. And you're the one to find out.'

'I told you. I'm not interested.'

'My dear fellow. You have become too proud in your new functions.' He expanded his smile even further. 'Don't forget. Don't forget, Courman, that people who start building their fortresses in the gutter — no matter how high they build them — have to go down personally from time to time to clear the rats out of the sewers.'

Courman remained motionless. He raised his eyes to meet those staring down and over him.

'Do you imagine that you have a hold on me for eternity?'

His host's smile turned into a laugh.

'I should have called it a two-way pact. It is in everyone's interest. The man's name is Charles Stone. Here is his address. We don't want anything elaborate, my dear fellow. Simply find out and deal with the situation accordingly.'

'I shall want a tap on his line.'

'All right. You have a young lieutenant at the Invalides who does private commissions for you on the side, do you not? There is no point in going through the regular system. Too cumbersome. Go and explain to him what you want.'

Courman showed no surprise at the revelation that his lieutenant was known of by others. He contented himself with a restrained reply: 'This is the last time.'

'I hope. I hope. There wouldn't have been this last time if Monsieur Stone hadn't come along.'

Courman pulled himself to his feet. The pain shot through

his leg. He hated period furniture. It was too low. He hated the man's smile and his easy confidence. Hate was an emotion to which he rarely succumbed. It blocked his vision.

Chapter Seven

Courman's first act on reaching his office was to organize a quick investigation of Stone. He had to know with whom he was dealing. A member of his organization ran a small detective agency in the rue du Temple. He was a vacillating, not overly successful man whose name was Peduc. Courman rang the fellow up and gave him twenty-four hours to produce something. Then he visited the lieutenant who tapped lines on the side, so to speak.

The young man was in Courman's power and therefore agreeable. But annoyingly, independently agreeable in an ingratiating, confident way. He sat in the dingy café on the rue du Commerce where they had agreed to meet, not far from the Invalides but just on the wrong side of the aerial Metro line which divides the lonely, aristocratic 7th Arrondissement from the ailing, dirty, popular fifteenth and promised everything would be installed by late that afternoon. Courman would have the first report the next evening, 31 May.

That was quick work for the Groupe Interministérielle de Control, even if this was a private commission which would be put into effect slightly outside the normal system. The GIC was an unwieldy body with too many unimportant telephones being overheard by too many unintelligent people.

That was why Courman always kept a direct contact on the inside. A few years before he had been among those invited to the official opening of the new eavesdropping centre just behind the Invalides, along with the relevant ministers and chiefs of the various official security organizations.

He hadn't been impressed.

It had been constructed in the belief that all the groups who would use it were serving a common cause – France. If that meant each department would know who the others were listening to and what was being said, it was a false belief. If it meant Courman would know what the others were up to, it was another matter. But one couldn't have one without the other. That was what annoyed army security and the Deuzième Bureau; and the autocratic Service of Documentation and Counter-Espionage, unaffectionately shorted to SDECE, who look after France's international security; and the Minister of the Interior and the Minister's agency for French internal security, the Direction for Surveillance of the Territory, the DST; and the Presidency of the Republic and all the other interested parties who don't mind finding out about their friendly competitors but insist on keeping their own little secrets to themselves.

Not that they didn't trust General Caillaut, who commanded the place. No. He was one of the boys, a former infantry brigade commander who had graduated from St Cyr. He ran things as honestly and fairly as he could, in the circumstances. It was the whole set-up which they questioned.

There was a large central hall where all the tape recorders were installed in bleak rows and branched to the taped lines. These machines were undermanned by a shuffling army of specially chosen sub-humans – mostly retired employees of the SNCF, the National Railways. The idea was that they were trustworthy because they lacked sufficient intelligence to be devious and they were too old to have ambitions. The disadvantage: they weren't terribly, terribly competent. They had poor memories. They were not very organized. And how was one to tell the difference between a stupid error and a deliberate error?

Around the hall there were a series of offices manned by each of the different departments who commissioned tapes. The railwaymen delivered their fine work into these relevant eager hands.

Mistakes were always being made. The wrong tape was always being given to the wrong man just long enough to be played through before being returned. That was why for important matters Courman had one of his own men in the administration of the GIC. Lieutenant de St Lambert was perhaps too independent by nature but he could work quickly and unofficially, backed up by one reasonably intelligent railwayman who received small extra commissions for his efforts. The commissions were paid in cash by St Lambert. It was straight piece-work and the rewards were passed unobtrusively from time to time, usually when the fellow produced a tape in the Lieutenant's office.

He also had a street unit who could almost immediately plug him in on most victims by going directly to the wires running through the sewers – those famous Paris sewers large enough to tour in Venetian gondolas and with the address of each contributor of sewage painted gracefully over the hole where his tributary joined the main stream.

Thus St Lambert avoided whenever possible becoming involved with the telephone exchange. That was the normal procedure, but was also complicated and bureaucratic. He also avoided the job being mucked up by one of the simpletons or the resulting tape being delivered to the wrong ministry because the labels were confused. Courman's client's dirty washing arriving on the desks of the Minister of the Interior could be worse than embarrassing.

For the same reason, Courman insisted that he be sent the actual tape drawn from Stone's telephone and not a typed account of it. That was one less idiot involved. And he liked to hear the voice which produced the words. There were so many nuances in the way something was said, the hesitations, every little cough.

The results of the detective's research arrived at his office the
next afternoon, five hours late. The first tape arrived at
almost the same moment. It was delivered in person by
Lieutenant de St Lambert on his way home from the GIC.
Courman began by reading the report. He slouched in a
cracking leather chair, resting the sheets of paper on his
stomach and against the desk. There were three pages
containing only the most basic details. Irish passport. Fre-
quent visitor to France. Wrote articles from time to time. A
short incomplete list of those articles. The people he mixed
with. Courman recognized most of the names. Half of them
were socialites. The other half were serious people in business
and government, people who could and might protect Stone
if ever he were in trouble. He realized he would have to go
carefully. There were a dozen photographs attached in a
folder, candid shots of Stone doing all the things he had done
that day and the evening before — which was nothing in
particular.

Leaving his flat in early evening he had gone to a café
where he met an older man, who appeared slightly seedy in the
photograph. Peduc's note on the back said they had discussed
philosophy and women for two hours. Courman recognized
the older man as a fairly well-known writer. Stone then went
on to what Courman guessed was dinner in a house just off
the Quai Voltaire. It was one of those large houses built a
hundred years before in the style of the eighteenth century.
Eight other people had also gone in. Peduc had managed to
identify one of them as a solidly established banker. The
house itself belonged to a political family who had served the
last two Republics and continued to serve this one. The next
morning he appeared at the reasonable hour of ten, drove to
the Bois, swam in the outdoor pool of the Cercle Sportif, of
which he was apparently a member, then visited a gallery in

the rue de Seine, lunched alone in a restaurant called Chez Georges, visited a lawyer and so on. All of which meant that Stone had taken two days off after his success with Campini.

Courman examined each photograph carefully. Candid shots could be both useful and misleading. He tried to balance them with the written report to make the man come alive. He decided that Stone travelled too much and wrote too little. Obviously had some money. He was a strong young man; but muscle was muscle and nothing more. Weak men were stronger-willed. Stone would probably be easy to deal with. He was a man of passing interests. A dilettante.

Curiously enough, that was exactly what most of Stone's friends had concluded. That was why many of them liked him.

He threw the report aside, drew himself upright and reached for a tape recorder sitting on the corner of the desk, then threaded the tape in himself.

What he heard first was a series of conversations between Stone and his friends. Nothing important. Courman noted down points from time to time. He liked to know the details of people's lives. So much that appeared unimportant turned out to be a key. Stone had a call from a stockbroker in England and sold some shares as a result. Then a woman telephoned, asking him to dinner two weeks later. He refused, saying he had already accepted another dinner. Then he rang a gallery about a painting he had seen — that was the gallery he had visited. And then there was a blank on the tape.

It lasted only a few seconds. It was the beginning of a conversation with another man. The Lieutenant had erased those few moments because they included the man's complete name. It was François de Maupans, and the Lieutenant knew his family. He didn't want to involve family friends in something dubious. He left the rest of the conversation for what it was worth.

Courman was furious. He played the section over twice, thinking he had made a mistake. No. It was the tape. He was yet more furious when he heard the conversation.

'— better than I thought.'

'You mean you've proved it already!'

'That it happened, yes. How and why — not yet.'

That was Stone.

'What do you mean?'

'I found the trace of a speech Ailleret made just before the end. It was covered up. I went to see Campini.'

'Campini. That old trout.'

'Exactly. He turned red and locked me up in his office long enough to explain I should clear off and leave the subject alone.'

'For Christ's sake, Charles, be careful. I told you they are a little world with their own rules.'

'So long as he thinks I've dropped it, what does it matter? I shall go more carefully now. I have no desire to finish up like Ailleret. All I have to do now is find that speech. Either along the road or when I get there the rest will come out.'

'Look, Charles—'

The tape went blank again. The lieutenant had also censored a few moments at the end. Maupans and Stone had arranged to meet each other. The details of that meeting his master could do without. If he asked what had happened, he would say one of his retired railwaymen had made a mistake; had come in too late and cut out too soon.

Courman listened to the rest of the tape, but there were no more conversations of importance. He flicked the machine off with an angry gesture, swung about and picked up the telephone. The call caught Peduc, his detective, as he arrived home.

'Get your tail back on Stone.'

'Was there something missing in the report?'

'Everything was missing,' he shouted. 'Tail him yourself if

necessary. Twenty-four hours a day. I want a progress report in my flat every morning at 7 a.m.' There was silence at the other end. 'Did you hear me?'

Peduc, who had hoped to see a film that evening and dine with his rather ordinary wife in some small restaurant on the Left Bank, pulled himself together.

'Of course, Monsieur Courman. I'll have to do it myself tonight. I'd better get on with it or he'll be out and lost.'

'That's right. Get on with it. And, Peduc, I'm very grateful. This is important, you understand.'

Courman liked to treat his men well. He liked to think of his organization as a little club.

He looked at his watch. It was 7 p.m. Perfect. He swung to his feet by putting the weight of his body on his arms and limped out of the office. His secretary was waiting impatiently outside.

'I'm taking a few days off. When you come in tomorrow morning, telephone a Lieutenant de St Lambert at this number. Tell him to deliver to my flat in the future, every morning at 7 a.m.'

He dismissed his driver, who was waiting outside, and made for the nearest taxi-stand at his sad snail's pace. The address he gave was 76 rue Taitbout, fifty yards from his actual destination.

Petit Colbert was, as anyone could see, not especially tall. He was, on the other hand, squarely built and the square was solid. He passed his afternoons and evenings in the Turkish Baths-Sauna at 80 bis rue Taitbout. It was a comfortable way to spend his free moments, though he complained periodically of the lack of sunshine.

The Baths-Sauna were opulently furnished with modern foam-rubber sofas, mauve. The air was scented by the sweating pine walls, and the sofas were filled with young men who came there on the off-chance that they might meet another young man who pleased them, at least for the evening.

Colbert was neither as young nor as lithe as many of them sought. But he received a certain admiration. Square and solid was to some men's taste. And he was by no means uninteresting or unintelligent. There was an aura of hard or, rather, undefinable experience which they seemed to find attractive. And he had a certain subtle intelligence which came more from the senses, perhaps in his case the guts, than from the brain.

The Baths were well haunted by a successful breed who hoped never to meet there anyone they knew and, with a bit of luck, never did. If you asked Colbert, he would have identified the clients as half in business and half in government. And a good part of that half were graduates of ENA, l'École Nationale d'Administration, the school which dominated the nation's bureaucracy and was gradually taking over the Government itself. If you asked Colbert, he would have told you that they were the worst – the most innocent, the most frustrated, the most vicious. 'If you ever', he once told Courman in a moment of confession, 'met a thirty-year-old virgin – I mean either way – then I'd bet my month's commission that he was an Enarque.'

Colbert worked for Courman. He was an old faithful. It was a time of relative peace and so he found himself in the Baths. There he befriended those who took an interest in his square, solid form and who were worthwhile. He became their father confessor and arranged that they be photographed in his arms – naked before God, so to speak. If possible, he won a few written words from their hearts. Courman paid him by the piece for this information – or, more accurately, by the head.

These well-placed young men were part of the new generation in Courman's organization. (He would have been horrified by the word 'blackmail'. After the first nasty reckoning they often became eager members, benefiting personally as much as they benefited Courman. St Lambert had been recruited in this way.

But Colbert was more than a stool. In difficult moments, he was also a tough, a sophisticated man. When he was called upon to use his muscles, what he might have called his physical brain, he rejoiced. Those were his weekends for exercise. More than that, he knew how to use a gun. It was he, aged scarcely seventeen, who had fired a pistol at point-blank range into the brains of the jailor who had written out Courman's charge so long ago in the Dijon jail in 1944. He was also an accomplished marksman with a rifle at more difficult distances, a craftsman exercising a very ancient craft.

He was sitting idly on a sofa waiting to make a friend, and staring pensively at a slight ripple, which had developed over the last few weeks across his normally taut stomach from lack of exercise, when the manager brought him a sealed envelope. In it was Courman's card.

'He is waiting in the office,' the manager whispered.

Colbert's heart lifted. Was there a weekend in the air?

Charles Stone had not given up the hunt. He was perhaps in less of a hurry, less agitated and nervous about taking the next step. His friends and Monsieur Courman were not entirely wrong when they called him a dilettante. Now that the suspense had gone out of his hunch, he had all the time in the world before him to find out the who and the why.

Besides, a few days' silence would help Campini calm down and forget. So Stone did nothing. He enjoyed himself and saw his friends.

For example, Wednesday of the next week he lunched in the Bois before going to the races with Maupans and some other friends. He had hoped to find Mélanie Barre in the group, but she wasn't there.

That evening Maupans gave a particularly successful soirée for important amusing friends as opposed to the lighter half of his circus. Stone was there, as always a special case, and so was Pierre Dehal, the General from the military co-ordinating committee.

Of course Dehal was not there as a general; he was there as a popular, amusing man who could be trusted to leave his unamusing wife at home. He was popular in circles such as Maupans', just as he was popular with his brother-officers.

He always had a smile on his face and a cigar in his mouth and a large glass of whisky in his hand. He called everyone by his first name, which was not self-evident in that world, and everyone was his friend.

He was a big man, a heavy man. The sort of man who had passed his youth playing sports and was now letting his muscles settle gently down into complacent mounds. That was what most people thought. In fact, he hated sports. They bored him. Had always bored him. Avoiding physical action had been the major occupation of his youth. And all that time he had dreams of growing old enough to be left alone.

There was a second reason for his popularity. Dehal was a fixer. Everyone in the Army knew that. He was ambitious. And yet no one minded. He had the same ideas as the other officers. He served their purposes. In a large group of traditional, formal men he was the one who wasn't afraid to wet his feet. They admired him. They needed him. His success was the Army's success. He would never get to the very top. That wouldn't have done. But he would get most of the way. They thought he would be Chief of the Army Staff in a year or so. And they were delighted. He was just the man to deal with the politicians and the public and the other two services.

The next evening Stone dined with a painter he admired. They were kindred spirits, friends. He put on canvas most of the doubts which Stone felt and occasionally some of the pleasures. He then went on to a late party and bored himself more than he remembered it was possible. There had been too many provincial Catholic minor aristocrats talking about cousins and uncles and nephews once, twice and three times removed, and other petty gossip of their private world.

It was one-thirty before he arrived home. He walked in the darkness across the drawing-room and into the dining-room. There, as he pulled the door closed behind, a heavy weight crashed down on to his shoulder and he fell to the floor carrying a chair with him. He lay stunned, as if it were normal that his face should be pressed into the carpet in a dark world with his legs curled over the legs of the chair. Was there any other world? Suddenly he couldn't remember. Close to the floor was a warm, safe place to be.

As if in a nightmare, he was then picked up and held in the air. A closed fist rushed effortlessly out of the darkness, mysteriously, as if attached to nobody, and sent him flying on to the table, the owner of the fist grunting when it connected.

Two hands loomed across the table to pick him up again. This time he had enough presence of mind to reach out himself. Anything to stop this game of yo-yo. He grasped on to a jacket and drew it, with all his force, towards him.

He managed to hold the man in a bear-hug and they shunted about the room knocking over chairs, dancing a grotesque dance in the shadowless night, and eventually pushing their way through the door into the drawing-room. There the man broke loose and sent Stone sliding on to the floor again with a heavy blow.

He sat twisted, still half-dazed in the darkness, his eyes slowly adjusting. Above he could make out a large square form moving towards him.

The silhouette stopped a yard away and its voice floated eerily out of the night.

'This is to teach you not to meddle where you shouldn't'

— and its leg began to draw back in an arc; the preparation for a kick to Stone's head.

In the grey contrast of the night the leg and the foot were magnified into the centre of the world and moved slowly, majestically through the air.

'Scare him!' were the words which rang in Petit Colbert's mind. It was a delicate balance to expect from a man with his nature.

In the second of that reflection the crouched man lunged. His fist rose up between the silhouette's legs with all its force. Stone heard him scream in pain. His shoulder followed the fist and sent the other man over. Stone scrambled back to his feet and, without aiming, kicked hard at the mass beneath him. It grunted, and if Stone had stooped to listen he would have heard the air running out and the gasp which followed. But he could see the other more clearly now and kicked again and again. This time at the head. Eventually the body lay still.

He ran to open the door and then back. The man was stunned. He dragged him out and pushed him on to the stairs. Stone heard the sounds of the body crashing down the first flight as he slammed the door and bolted it.

He dashed for the telephone, dialled the police. And then, and then, in that darkness, in the cool clear stillness of the empty night, he heard a policeman reply and he froze. Froze, and then hung up. Was it his imagination? Was it? He waited in a cold panic. Put his hand back down to the receiver, threw open the telephone directory and dialled another police station then listened for their reply. There was no doubt.

It had been in the back of his mind all morning. His telephone was new, had been installed two months before and was perfectly clear. And yet each call over the last few days had been slightly fainter than normal. It was a difference he would never have noticed had he not been looking for it, and had he not known about tapping phones.

In the isolated calm of that night he suddenly recognized the fall in tension caused by an extra wire clamped into his line.

He put the phone down again and sat quietly in the darkness. There was no point in calling for help. The phone and the intruder could only have come from one source. It was hardly the moment to throw himself into the hands of their police.

Chapter Eight

It was an hour before Stone moved from his chair. There was a gash in his right cheek. The blood dripped down slowly until it formed a thick scab resembling the wax on the side of an old candle. One of his shoulders ached. He did not clarify in his mind which it was. He did not feel any pain. His mind was too occupied.

His first reaction was to step back; leave for the country, or further. Not from fear. That sort of fright did not frighten him. No. But back a step from a situation out of control.

He tried to resist the temptation of an easy way out. He remembered with slight embarrassment the conversation at Noirmoutier. Was he as bad as he claimed to be?

No. Beware of dramatics. Wasn't there a way of regaining control? What frightened them? What could hold them in check?

When Stone pulled himself to his feet, cold and stiff, it was with an idea jelling in his mind.

He turned on the lights, cleaned his cut and went to the library. The desk drawers were pulled out and half-empty, his papers were strewn about on the floor. The cupboard where he kept the steel box filled with the Ailleret notes and tapes was open and empty. He looked quickly about and went back to the drawing-room. There it was, sitting close to the door, still locked, waiting to be taken away by his unsuccessful silhouette.

Stone took the box into the library, removed the Campini and Portas cassettes and played them through before the microphone of a larger tape recorder normally used for music. He placed these extra copies in a briefcase, and the originals he returned to the steel box.

There was a small table in a corner carrying a typewriter. Stone took two sheets of paper with a carbon and slipped them into the machine. He began to type. It was a summary of his presumptions, of all he had read and heard and all that had happened to him up to that moment. He typed slowly through the night, and the courtyard was a pale grey before the work was finished. He placed the originals of the seven sheets in the briefcase and the copies in the steel box.

He bathed and dressed in a dark suit and with the box in one hand and the briefcase in the other, left the flat. He did not take his car. He found a taxi which drove him to his bank. It was an American bank on the Champs Élysées. The doors were locked but he knew that the manager arrived at eight o'clock each morning and it was shortly after eight. He rang and handed his card to the porter. 'Tell him it's urgent.'

Moments later he was in Christian Smith's office. Stone gave him the iron box with concise instructions. If he had not retrieved it in three days, it should be sent by a bank messenger and handed personally to a Mr Roderick Williams in London. The address was of a large newspaper. Williams was the editor.

Before leaving Stone removed the bundle of handwritten research-notes from the box, photocopied them on the bank's machine and returned them to their place along side the original tapes and the summary. He slipped the copies into the briefcase.

The manager asked almost no questions. He was a discreet man. Even better, he was perfectly efficient.

Stone reappeared in the morning light, walked to the centre of the Avenue where the ranks of taxies waited and headed for Orly Airport. Peduc's assistant was waiting outside the bank, already bored and restless, staring about at the crowds moving over the wide pavement on their way to work. At

9.15 on any given morning there are at least three people per square yard strolling along the pavements of the Champs Élysées and at least one of those three is a young woman. The bank was now open and Stone came out at the same time as other more normal clients. As the detective's eyes were wandering, he missed the man with the briefcase who slipped through the streaming mass and into a taxi. It was another hour before he began to wonder what was taking so long.

By then Stone was sitting in a Boeing 727 waiting to take off for London. He had arrived fifteen minutes before the flight and, having no luggage except his briefcase, had walked straight through.

He telephoned the same Roderick Williams from London Airport and a short time later was in his office. Williams knew Stone well — as well as anyone knew him, if that meant anything. From time to time he published his articles. But he also knew him outside of the newspaper. When Stone said on the airport telephone that he had something important, Williams believed him immediately. He was therefore slightly disappointed when he looked up, having read the summary.

'A lovely story, dear boy. But what do you expect me to do with it? It's three-quarters presumption. There isn't a name or an organization to hang the murder on. I can't publish that.'

Stone made a calming gesture and interrupted him.

'Of course you can't. I don't want you to. Not yet. What I want are two things. You see the story. If I have the proof, will you publish?'

'That's another matter, Charles. It's good stuff. Of course I'll publish with the proof.'

'Good. The second thing is this. You noticed my summary ends on a nasty or, if you prefer, a violent note.' They both laughed. There was something ridiculous about violence discussed in a newspaper office. Was it still real, or simply copy? Had the Duchess really eaten her dog or was it suitable fantasy to put on a meagre second page? 'I don't know what comes after the threatening interview, the tapped phone and the tough sent to beat me up. What I want is quick protection if necessary. Nothing will scare people like that quicker than publicity. If things get out of hand, I want to be able to phone you and have something, anything, printed within twenty-four hours.'

'No problem. If things get that bad, dear boy, your being in danger is as good a story as Ailleret himself. The more you are persecuted, the better it is for me.'

'Perfect. I am going to leave this box with an old friend. Martin Sherbrooke. I shall give you his address and telepone number. As I progress I shall regularly send him copies of my notes and tapes, so he will always be up to date. I shall tell him you may contact him and vice versa.'

Williams was an active, middle-aged man. It was only in his pace that he betrayed his responsibilities – a careful, meditative saunter adopted unconsciously over the years in reaction to the journalists about him who walked too fast and saw too little. He led Stone slowly to the door.

'It's a funny story you've found. Why did they kill him that way? Eighteen innocent men into the bargain on an island in the Indian Ocean. It all seems so clumsy and complicated. Why didn't they simply shoot him or poison him, or something classic? If you knew that you would know the rest. Of course, nobody really remembers Ailleret, although he appears to have had a good newsworthy character. But it's all the others – the whole system perhaps – that's what interests me. Oh, and something else. You suggested some five different groups who might have done it. Surely the tapped phone allows you to narrow that down?'

'Afraid not. There are at least ten groups who have the right to tap phones and God knows how many individuals who could take advantage of that right for their own use.

Listening to people's conversations is a large profession in France.'

Stone went from there to see Martin Sherbrooke. Sherbrooke was a former parachute officer, turned magazine publisher. He lived in central London; in Hans Crescent in Knightsbridge. It was a Victorian house and the flats were rambling and pleasant. Stone found him there as his wife was away and he was working at home. He and Sherbrooke were old friends. They had met in the Far East when Sherbrooke was still a serving officer and Stone was writing his pamphlet on jungle warfare by getting involved in it. They had been sent on a small operation together, Stone theoretically as an observer. In fact, they found themselves looking after each other for three difficult days. That mutual concern became a habit, and since then they had taken turns doing one another favours. It was Sherbrooke's turn and he was delighted to do what was asked. He chafed more than he liked to admit at the bureaucratic chains which kept him in an office five days a week as his body slowly melted into commercial jelly. The only thing which annoyed him was that the action was on the other side of the Channel.

They agreed that he would keep the briefcase and add to it anything Stone sent. He also agreed not to involve himself more than as post-box for the documents and as Williams' emergency contact. Those were limitations set firmly by Stone. He did not want his friend exposed to unnecessary danger.

Sherbrooke would open a safety deposit box the next morning in the vaults of London's largest department store, Harrods. It was only a few hundred yards away, so each package could be deposited quickly. The password they agreed on for the vault was 'compass'. Stone supplied it. He did not explain about Ailleret's 'Tous Azimuts' and its translation, 'All Directions'.

In the future, any contact between them would be subject

to a disguised identification. Stone would begin any telephone call by asking for the Norwich Union.

If it was Sherbrooke who called, he would ask to speak to
Monsieur Colin. Stone would reply that he had a wrong
number, leave his tapped telephone and ring his friend back
from a café.

In the case of a total emergency Sherbrooke was to get the
documents to Williams as quickly as possible.

By three o'clock that afternoon Stone was back in his flat
in Paris, having retrieved his steel box from the bank on the
way. The manager seemed pleased to see him well ahead of
schedule. He even said as much.

Both Peduc and his assistant were waiting in the rue de
Grenelle before Stone's house, Peduc trembling at the
thought of what he would say in the report he had to write
before seven the next morning. They sighed with relief when
their subject climbed out of a taxi. As he disappeared into
the courtyard, the assistant whispered, 'He's lost his briefcase.'

'What?'

'This morning he had that box and a briefcase. Now he has
only the box.'

'Oh God,' Peduc sighed. His experience told him something important had happened. And he didn't know what.

Stone had thought very carefully about his next move. He
had prepared his protection. It only remained to inform his
enemies that they were checkmated. The easiest way of doing
this was by telephone. After all, he didn't know who they
were but knew they were listening. The only problem was to
find someone whom he could telephone to tell his story. He
didn't want to bring friends in to something unpleasant.

Then he thought of Campini. He was sure Campini wasn't
really involved. The tough had come too soon after the
unpleasant interview and Stone had done nothing in the

meantime to justify it. He seated himself comfortably in his drawing-room, picked up the receiver and dialled the National Assembly. Before him was a restful view of the garden, green in the spring air and bright beneath a gentle sun. Five minutes later Campini was on the line, obviously surprised to hear from him; surprised enough to accept the call.

'What can I do for you, Monsieur Stone?'

'Nothing. I simply wished to thank you for your help. I fear that the whole Ailleret business may be more complicated than you think.'

'Do you?'

'After you gently warned me off, I received a visitor in the middle of the night who warned me more firmly, with his fists.' There was silence at the other end. 'So I have taken precautions. I have placed a double of all my work in London. If I am warned any further, that double will find its way into the press very quickly.'

'Why do you tell me all of this? It is nothing to do with me.'

'I felt I should thank you for your kindness.'

Stone heard him hang up after a short silence. He had a second call to make. But not from that telephone. He went out and walked to a café on the Boulevard St Germain. There he rang François de Maupans. He wanted to see Mélanie Barre. She, if anyone, could think of who might be able to help; someone who had heard a rumour, someone who had an idea, anything.

Maupans was having a dinner party that evening. He offered to add Stone and Mélanie to the list, if Mélanie were free.

He had also had a visit from a vague family friend. Someone called Gérard de St Lambert. An army officer. He came to warn Maupans that his friend Charles Stone was in trouble and that he, Maupans, should stay away from him or he too would be in trouble.

Maupans had pressed him, but the young officer refused to say more. 'I've already taken a large enough risk coming to see you. How I know is none of your business.'

Stone listened to all of this in silence. At the end Maupans asked if it had to do with Ailleret. Stone said he was late for a meeting, a non-existent meeting. He didn't want any more people involved than necessary.

Peduc was obliged to abandon his coffee half-drunk to follow the quarry out of the café into the street. He adored his coffee and asked little more than to be left to drink it slowly down to the dregs. That afternoon he felt as he rarely felt — how sordid a life he led.

Chapter Nine

Like a fresh blue oyster, one side of Stone's face shone livid and swollen by the time he walked into Maupans' flat that evening. As for Maupans, he was not a man of violence, and he was always disgusted less by any vicious act in itself than by the visual after-effects. There was never time to be shocked in the midst of violence. The creative imagination was at its best in the peace which followed.

And so his stomach, gently settled for an evening *mondain*, turned acidly over as he saw Stone moving into the drawing-room, his lip carrying a vivid, multi-layered scab below the swollen cheek. A moment later Maupans had stopped him and led the way down a corridor to a small salon.

'Sit down.'

Stone found himself obeying.

'What happened?' Maupans nodded uncomfortably at Stone's face as he asked.

'That's obvious enough. I was beaten up; in fact, he was too — the other fellow, I mean — even more severely.'

'That is not a great consolation, Charles. Tell me exactly what is going on. I warned you in the beginning to be careful. You don't really understand this country, not the part lying underneath.'

Stone shrugged as he had a habit of doing when at a loss for a reply and then explained what was going on as best he could. Maupans grew increasingly impatient as he spoke and scarcely waited for the end to break in.

'So you've discovered the obvious. Ailleret was killed by one of a hundred thousand groups or individuals. In the meantime they've discovered you, little you, all by yourself.

That is not terribly brilliant. Why do you suppose nobody else tried to make this great discovery? Because it wasn't worth throwing away their skin for nothing.'

'François, François! Calm down.' He walked over to a drink-tray, poured two whiskys and handed one to Maupans. 'First, I have the situation under control. They can't move. Second, now that they have surfaced they will make a mistake sooner or later and reveal themselves. Third, there is far more than Ailleret in question. Think of what must be behind it. There is a faction in this country, paid by the outside or acting on its own.'

Maupans lunged forward and dropped his glass so heavily on to a table that it fell over and spilt.

'Oh damn!' he moaned. 'No, leave it. Leave it where it is. And for Christ's sake listen!' He was on his feet, nervously stalking about, almost in circles around the spreading stain of his whisky. Why do you imagine some faction might have been bought from the outside? Why would anyone need to be bought? There are enough people in this country who would do it for nothing. And, even if you found money had changed hands, it was surely more of a financing than a bribe.

'And where did you get the stupid idea of a faction? That is reassuring for you, isn't it? All you have to do is find the faction and expose it. Well, that isn't the way France works. Every level hides three more levels, every faction is tied into five or ten other factions, and even in rivalry they will protect each other against an outside threat.

'So, what if you found the guilty men, exposed them, destroyed them? So what? Do you suppose you would then be safe? I promise you they will see you are taken care of, and the few individuals you expose will be replaced over-night.'

'François, would you like to listen to my tape of Campini? I'll show you my notes. You'll see what an effect this could have.'

'Good God, no! Don't show me anything. I have no intention of implicating myself. I'll help you as best I can – I mean you not your ambition – but if you want to be a martyr that is your privilege. I'm not throwing my life away for nothing, is that clear? Even with half the Cabinet on your side they would crush your piddling crusade.'

Stone shrugged and climbed to his feet. As they walked back down the corridor Maupans mumbled, 'You don't understand what France is really about.'

Mélanie Barre had not forgotten Stone. She remembered him very clearly and was delighted to find him seated next to her that evening.

Delight was a rare emotion for her. A short-term emotion. She did not relish it in any way. Rather, she avoided it as she avoided anything which went too quickly and ended unexpectedly. Her life was one of muted emotions which fabricated a long, even, dull cocoon within whose soft, absorbing, protecting walls she took refuge.

And yet delight was delight. And if it could not be avoided it had to be worn, nervously like a stolen coat, until it was taken away.

Stone understood all of that. He spoke to her about everything dull that had ever happened to him; and she, sensing that he was making fun of her, began to laugh. Especially as he began to talk of the dull shoddy life he led surrounded by banality; he indicated the table and the people about it.

They were drinking a chablis, Les Grenouilles, with poached Loire salmon. The man next to Mélanie was a member of the Minister of Foreign Affairs' Cabinet Office.

He had been trying to break in on their conversation for the last ten minutes as he felt he had done his duty to the countess on his right who came from an old racing family, bred horses, talked about them and, some of her friends said, was beginning to look like one.

But he could not get their attention in any diplomatic way as they spoke quietly and turned slightly to face each other. In fact, they ignored the others through the entire dinner. She told Stone about her own life — she did research on social patterns for a research institute. It was boring, which suited her perfectly.

She scarcely seemed to notice the main course of salt-marsh lamb stuffed with wild mushrooms, known reassuringly as 'the Trumpets of Death'. And she drank the 1949 Château Margaux as if it were an insipid liquid, to quench her thirst.

That gave Stone slight shivers through his spine, but he somehow felt she avoided enjoying life more as a conscious effort than through natural indifference. In any case, he had shared more good food with insensitive tongues than he cared to remember and had learnt to ignore their crime and concentrate on his own pleasure.

He noticed that, when she listened to him or anyone else, she put her hand flat over her mouth, hiding half her face. It was a signal of constant insecurity, a small child hiding behind a door. Behind that hand she was not at all unattractive.

After the dinner he offered to drive her home. She lived in a small street near the Invalides, not too far from her father. It was a quiet street with no shops; nothing but blocks of flats built seventy years before. She asked Stone to come up for a cognac.

The flat was exactly what he expected. It was remarkably conventional. Nothing indicated that an individual lived there. It was neither modern nor old, not even functional. It contained what was necessary, nothing more.

'Have you really been so battered by life?' he asked in an innocent way.

She looked about. 'I suppose it is pretty ordinary here. I don't notice anymore. What does it matter? Come and sit down.'

He dropped on to a sofa.

'Am I so battered? I don't know. I look at myself periodically and wonder. I suppose I'm simply suffering from a terrible childhood. All it gave me was a longing for stability, and when Thomas was killed I lost even that. But, then, anyone can liberate himself from his childhood, can't he? Only I've never really felt like it. I don't feel like questioning my whole existence yet again.' She stood across the room as she spoke, pouring two cognacs, calmly as if she were talking about someone else. 'What if I got it apart, couldn't put it back together again and couldn't find anything to replace it? What would I be? Nothing. Just like my father. I would have analysed myself out of existence.' They both laughed. 'So I stay as I am.'

'That is a lot of nonsense. If you take yourself apart, at the very least you are left with the strength which made you do it.'

'Exactly. The strength and character of a destroyer. That's the same as not existing.'

This time it was Stone who looked about.

'Sounds like me.'

'I know. That was why I felt courageous, talking to you all evening and then asking you here. From time to time I do feel daring – or is it bored? The experience is usually so vivifying that I run away terrified and don't do it again for months.'

'You haven't done anything yet.'

'In your eyes. Be patient.' She came and sat beside him. 'Why did you go to Malaysia?'

He looked at her quizzically.

'What do you know about that? Who told you?'

'Ah, it is forbidden to mention you in your presence.

François committed the great sin and I tempted him to do it. Well?'

'Ah, as you say.' He slouched on the sofa and rested his head back with the cognac glass tilted gently to his lips. 'I went for very romantic reasons. It was a place where I could isolate my own existence from that of everybody else. You see, establish whether I existed or not. The surrounding war was a décor made up of a people and a world outside my reality. That friction between their fiction which could kill and my reality sharpened the eyes of my own existence. Is that a suitably obscure reply?'

'Not quite. What did you discover?'

'Vast truths beyond the imagination. Living off the land gives severe diarrhoea. Sometimes you run so fast and long that pulling down your trousers to shit is choosing to die. Pain is an antidote to fear, if you are truly egotistical. Don't ever isolate your own existence, because you don't exist. And so on.' He sipped from his glass. 'And so on.'

'And so you reject any belief.'

'Oh no. Good God, no. I believe. Oh, I believe in everything. But really. My mind rejects no ideal or hope. No angle is abandoned outright.'

She began to laugh.

'Don't. I mean it. I hold on to all the ideals to see which will survive the trip.'

'And which ones survived Burma?'

'None, dear lady. Fortunately I have a short memory and they've all snuck back.'

An hour later Mélanie lay in her bed. It was a large bed, bought for her husband and herself. Beside her was Stone, surprised despite himself to be there.

The closer he came to her the less battered by life she was. Sufferance was an air she wore to make her seem weary and childlike. Her real self was untouched. Stone had been drawn, almost forgetting why he had come. She was small and soft;

still like a child seeking protection and domination. And with a child's sense – or was it a woman's? – drawing him on, exciting him, demanding all that he could give. Stone began to wonder if she were not demanding more than he could give. That wasn't a doubt which upset him. He was too egocentric. He knew he was too egocentric to be seriously disturbed by anyone else. And any doubt could be explained away or ignored with a sufficiently strong will. It was his will which made him what he was. She wanted to be dominated, and with his will he dominated her.

He was awakened later in the night by sharp quick sounds. She was lying against, half over him, and giggling quietly.

'What's the matter?'

'Nothing. Nothing at all. It's rare that I'm so brave.'

'Why brave? This is hardly dangerous.'

'Oh, what a common definition of bravery. For me it is quite different. I consider myself brave when I do something which reminds me I must be missing a good part of life. Sowing discontent in yourself is very brave. What saves me is that I forget easily.

'The first thing which I liked about you was your distance. I noticed that at Noirmoutier. It is an apparent aloofness from the ordinary world. I think some people may hope you are a method of escape. That same aloofness frustrates me now. You made love from a distance – oh, perfectly, competently' – they both laughed – 'but I might have been anyone. You don't commit yourself even for a few seconds; you don't get mixed up in the sweat or the dirt, because you are detached.'

She pushed back up against him and made him hold her. Stone moved his hand down her body and caressed her.

'I did not forget what you told me about your husband at Noirmoutier,' he said quietly.

'What do you mean?'

'What you said made sense to me.'

'Of course it made sense. So what?'

'I had a look at the problem.'

'You what?'

'I've been looking into the whole business of Ailleret and how he was killed. And I've discovered you were right.'

He paused, but she said nothing. She had pushed away from him and was lying still.

'I know he was killed because I asked a few good questions after which my phone was tapped, and a thug was sent to beat me up. But I don't know who did it.' He began to tell her all that he had done. After a few moments she switched on the light, her breasts hard, as still as herself.

'Why did you do all this?' He was about to reply when she began again, 'Who asked you to interfere? Who told you I wanted my past ripped open?'

'It goes slightly beyond you,' he said.

'You're hardly a crusader for justice. Why are you doing it? To sell the story. It that it? You want to dig up my past for a profit. And you want me to help. Is that why you came here?' She did not move as she spoke. Stone climbed out of the bed and began to dress.

'Yes, go away. I don't want gravediggers near me. I have already spent most of my life with them. If you have ghoulish tastes, go and see my father. I'm not interested.' Stone thought she was going to cry, but she didn't.

He walked around the bed and kissed her lightly.

'I'm sorry,' he whispered, and left.

The sky was clear. The stars shone out of the blackness and doubled the efforts of the street-lights. Stone walked a hundred yards along the deserted street and crossed it to his car. He did not bother to look one way or the other. Everyone had gone to bed; not even the street-cleaners were up. And yet, as he crossed the pavement a shadow flickered into his mind fifty yards ahead.

Stone climbed into his car and drove off slowly. The shadow had not disappeared. It was sitting nonchalantly in a car. As he turned the corner, Stone noticed that the car switched on its motor and dipped headlights and began to follow.

It was the hour when Paris is truly dead. There were only three other cars in the Place de la Concorde. And none at all on the bridge when he crossed the river; that is, almost none at all.

When he reached his own flat the car was still there, discreetly stopped a few hundred yards away while Stone parked. He left his car and walked back past the other. It was the same shadow, waiting nonchalantly, slightly uncomfortable as Stone glanced at him.

So he was not forgotten. They were with him always. How clumsy he had been not to notice.

He climbed to his flat warily. Two words echoed through his mind. Care and speed. Care and speed. Time was limited.

Chapter Ten

The last thing Mélanie had intended was to give him a good suggestion. Stone shrugged mentally the next morning while looking up her father in the telephone directory. He remembered the address, rue de Constantine, which confirmed that it was the right Monsieur Rogent.

He then typed a short letter to Sherbrooke in London, with one copy; simply to say he was being followed, with a description of his shadow and his car. There would, no doubt, be other shadows and other cars, but Stone was meticulous.

A short stroll followed in the pungent, slightly humid early air, which took him past a post-box into which the letter was dropped and on to a café, not the same one as the night before, from where Monsieur Rogent could be telephoned. He said he was a friend of Mélanie's. An uneven voice said he might come later that morning.

At approximately the same time General Pierre Dehal rolled over and opened his eyes. He always opened them in that direction — the direction of his wife's bed. She was still asleep. That was a good start to the day. Not that he didn't care for her. She was a cared-for, integral, wanted part of his life; but the two beds had been his idea.

She was affectionate, and somehow he had outgrown affection — at least, the early-morning kind. Perhaps he was simply too busy and so bed had become a rare place to sleep and think. Both things were best done alone. He rolled to the other side and faced the other way on to three large jade carvings which he had brought back from the French Indo-

China war. He had been at Headquarters in Hanoi and therefore had had the time to benefit from the panicked sales made by local Chinese merchants. There was a tall woman dancing in transparent green with a thousand folds of her robe flying and songbirds holding them up as if she might fly herself.

This fluid but frozen lady confirmed that it would be a good day, as she did on every morning to which he awoke alone and at peace.

The General, without his cigar and whisky and public smile, was another man, rather unsure of himself, leaving an impression of smallness despite his generous body.

He was not frightened by his own insecurity so long as he was alone. Quite the contrary, it was his link with reality, with what he really was and wanted. He sometimes called it his soul; that is, in conversations with himself. If only in this limited little circle, he had decided not to become what he appeared to be. It was a place where, damned or not damned, he didn't believe in very much of what he spent his life protecting. Inherent contempt for the clans struggling about him was the most public sign of his soul.

Of course, that contempt was well disguised along with his insecurity behind the cigar and the other little affectations and the comfortable middle-class attitudes, and the reproduction furniture and the ideas without which they would not accept him, they his masters and his servants who would not hesitate to destroy him.

They knew he was not really one of them. If they cared to stop and look, the disguise was quite transparent. Everyone knew that Dehal came from a simple background, not a St Cyr family. He was an outsider who had been let through to the inside. Why? Because he was useful. Because he was clever and only posing. He could look after the realities of life, which his believing friends found unpleasant.

At the same time it gave them a certain pleasure to see a

clever man, cleverer than they, try so hard to emulate their way of life. He was the perfect, typical convert, usually overdoing the required public form just to be sure. He was more Catholic and minor aristocracy than any of his friends could ever hope to appear to be. They simply were.

It was a pleasure to see a clever man trying so hard to imitate; it was also gratifying in a superior way, and therefore food for contempt. Had Dehal been a Gaullist their contempt would not have been hidden. But he was an obliging servant; an obliging servant who rolled out of bed, happy at the thought of the afternoon he would spend with an agreeable lady called Agnès de Pisan. He had met her two weeks before at a reception given by François de Maupans. There was no reflection on the affection he bore his wife. None at all. It was simply a case of two separate worlds.

Stone had rung the bell beside Monsieur Rogent's door some time before. He heard no sounds on the other side. He rang again. In the silence which followed a faint noise came through to the landing. It was the sound of something being dragged and something else striking the floor in regular slow timing.

This noise grew or, rather, approached. The door eventually opened a few inches. It was on a chain. A man asked who was there. Stone recognized the uneven voice of his telephone call and identified himself. The door closed without word, then opened again, slowly, as Monsieur Rogent got out of its way.

The open space was filled by a thin man. He was perhaps tall, but the way he hunched over his two canes disguised this. The man was surrounded by a grey light. He looked at Stone and then turned about and dragged his body back down the hall.

'Would you be so kind as to close the door', he said without looking back, 'and replace the chain?'

Stone did so and followed him. There were no lights, though that part of the flat was without windows. In the obscurity Stone had an impression of papers and books strewn about. Odd bits of furniture placed without reason. General disorder.

At the end of the hallway was a large drawing-room. Or what had been a drawing-room. Rogent crossed it and lowered himself painfully into a leather armchair by a window.

'My Quartier-Général,' he announced, waving one of his canes.

Indeed, Stone wondered if he did not live entirely in this room. At the far end was a couch with a sheet, blankets and a dressing-gown spread over it. This bed was surrounded by an untidy wall of magazines, papers, books, pairs of shoes strewn on the bare parquet floor, the whole, sometimes a foot high, cutting off that end of the room from the rest. A small gap in this wall probably allowed Rogent to pass through to the centre where a desk and a table sat back to back with one chair between them. The desk faced the outer wall and a large alcove with two floor-length windows. Properly treated it would have been a light and gracious room. The table faced the inner wall which carried a cluster of photographs including one signed by the young General de Gaulle, Resistance leader not head of state, and others of martyrs captured and tortured to death – Jean Moulin, Fred Scamaroni – who had not survived to sign photographs. To one side a young woman hung in an elaborate, old-fashioned silver frame – probably Mélanie's mother.

A crystal chandelier held dustily to the ceiling, uncomfortable and out of place, left over from another life. A bottle of water sat on the table and a half-empty glass. The desk was covered by papers. Yet another untidy wall of books lying on the floor cut off that world from the near end and the corner where Rogent sat, the light from a window on his back, his face in the shadow.

'Bring a chair for yourself.'

Stone went through the narrow passageway to the centre of the room, picked up the chair between the desk and table and brought it back.

'My daughter's friends come to see me, but not my daughter.'

He waited for Stone to reply.

'Mélanie doesn't know I'm here. I wanted her help. As she wouldn't give it, I hoped you might.'

'What about?'

'The way her husband died.'

'What do you expect me to know? I never leave this place.'

'I need an opening. They know I know. They are following me, listening to me. I need an opening to find out who they are.'

'They? You mean the "they" who killed Ailleret?'

'Yes. Did they?'

He tapped his left cane on the floor.

'If you asked me to prove it, I couldn't. I wouldn't even bother. Ailleret wasn't my kind. But, yes, I suppose they did. Shall I tell you a story?' He did not ask the question. Stone could either listen or leave. Rogent was not a sentimental man but he liked to answer in his own way. 'I shall try not to make it too long. You see the state I am in?'

Stone tried to be helpful.

'The Gestapo,' he said apologetically.

'The Gestapo! Whatever gave you that idea? Do you suppose I'd be here if it had been the Gestapo? No. I'd be dead like my wife. And better off for it. Do you know how old I am? Fifty-five. Fifty-five and I look seventy, eighty, dead. Oh, I know what I am. Don't you think I look at my wreck every day. Contemplate it. Contemplate my end. No, it wasn't the Gestapo. It was the Milice.' He leant forward, supporting his head and shoulders with both his canes, and spat. 'Frenchmen!'

There was a silence. Stone continued to look at the old man, although it was painful. He did not want to turn away.

'Do you want to know about the Milice, Monsieur Stone? You don't want to know. You don't think it concerns your story. I am not so sure. You will judge for yourself.'

'They fought for the Germans?' the young man suggested.

'Not for the Germans, Monsieur Stone; they were the French Gestapo. French! They fought with the Germans, and for France — their France. We were the two extremes — the Resistance and them. Neither of us was more than a few thousand. Both of us were hated by the rest of the population. And yet now I wonder if their France wasn't closer to that of the great majority than ours. We were fighting against the whole system that had destroyed France. They were fighting to protect it because they hadn't yet had their part of the spoils.

'Everyone hated us. We were the destroyers, the traitors, the threat to bourgeois order and morality and religion and whatever else they were attached to. But we won. That was the joke. We won. Only it really was a joke; at first on them and then on us. Won? How could a few thousand ever win against fifty million? On paper we were the victors and everyone became what we were. Everyone became a resister. Everyone became a Gaullist. But the truth, Monsieur Stone, was not there. I stayed in the Army after the war. I was young and recovered quickly from my treatment. My body has given up only in the last ten years. It takes a few years, you know, but suddenly — crack! — the whole system collapses. I am a typical case. Anyway' — he waved the subject away with a cane — 'I stayed in the Army. There were thirty-five officers in my regiment. Two of us were from the Resistance. Only two! Do you know that within six months I was apologizing for my egotistical non-conformism.

'They, the thirty-three others, sang the glories of their

difficult war. We kept our mouths shut or even criticized our
own past. The pressure, Monsieur Stone, was unbearable.
You cannot survive in a closed society at the odds of
thirty-three to two. And if we wanted to get ahead we had to
be one of them – a right which was denied us no matter how
we conformed. You see, the betrayal of the class was an
unforgivable sin.

'Eventually, I gave up and went into the Conseil d'État, a
wonderful French bureaucratic invention. It was even worse.
There I was unknown so I could hide my past. Those who
didn't were shunned. People can live alone in time of war but
not over the years of a long peace. Eventually I gave that up
as well and began to mix in the fringes of politics.'

As he finished the phrase, he turned white and looked
appealingly at Stone.

'Help me, please. Quickly.'

Stone pulled him to his feet and half-carried him to the
hall. There was a corridor on the left, empty and dingy. He
indicated it, and Stone picked him up, carrying him to the
other end. The bathroom door was open. He put him down
in the entrance. The old man had forgotten he was not alone
and began to pull off his jacket and trousers with the clumsy
speed of an invalid. Stone closed the door and waited
outside. He heard an uneven voice groaning and crying. He
went back to the drawing-room and sat down, out of hearing.

Philippe Courman had been sitting pensively for some time.
That morning at seven o'clock he had received, as usual, one
tape and one report. He listened to the tape first. On it was
the conversation with Campini. He listened silently and
attentively.

He had already guessed that something had gone wrong.
Petit Colbert hadn't been his usual jocular self when he made
his report. He obviously hadn't scared the man at all. He had
probably come off worse than Stone and was afraid to admit it.

The conversation was played through a second time to be sure he had registered everything. He wondered if Stone hadn't caught on to the tapped line. There was something overly restrained about the other calls and overly clear about this one.

He opened Peduc's report and almost immediately began to swear. Peduc was less complicated or less intelligent than Colbert and had not lied. It was all there. The subject had disappeared in the early morning and reappeared at three in the afternoon. In between he had lost a briefcase. There was ample time to have gone to London.

Courman rang a contact at Air France, who checked through the passenger lists of the day before. Five minutes later the man confirmed that a Charles Stone had flown to London.

Courman read on. A telephone call from a café. He swore again. Stone was obviously on to the tapped line. And then the dinner. Stone driving a woman home, staying in her flat for several hours.

In the telephone directory of street-numbers he turned to rue Bousquet, ran through the street to number twelve, then down the list of occupants. The third name on the list was Barre, Madame T. He stopped. He knew that name. Courman did not forget names. He crossed the room and rummaged through some papers. He stopped at an old newspaper clipping containing the list of those killed on Ailleret's plane.

A moment later he rang Peduc and told him to put a tail on Barre.

Courman sat comfortably on an uncomfortable, hard chair surrounded by the papers which dominated his flat.

There was everything in those unimpressive small rooms to suggest neglect. There was no apparent pattern or decoration. Everything was old and worn and Spartan, on top of which it was in a rather grubby part of Paris at the back of the 9th Arrondissement. He lived there because he had taken the flat

from a collaborator in 1944. He had never bothered to
change or to arrange it. The hard, highish chair suited his bad
leg and the location suited his taste for private neglect and
public discretion. He had an image which began outside. And
yet order hung limply over everything.

After some time without moving, his eyes open and staring
blankly ahead, he picked up the telephone and dialled.

'I have some bad news for you.'

'What?'

Courman explained his discoveries that morning. There
was a pause at the end.

'Do we know what he has put in London?'

'Not really.'

'Then we daren't risk finishing the business now.'

'That would not be wise,' Courman replied.

'You must find the double first.'

'Exactly. The best way is to control his mail. What do you
suggest?'

There was another pause.

'I don't want to bring in more people than necessary. I
have some contacts who run post offices and will co-operate.
No doubt you have your own people.'

'All right. Get your list to me this afternoon. I warn you,
we are playing hit and miss.'

'I daren't go further at this stage.'

Rogent reappeared slowly on his canes twenty minutes later.
He apologized. The Milice had not left him everything
necessary to functioning normally. A nurse slept in the flat
and was there each afternoon, but he tried to look after
himself in the mornings.

They sat silently while Rogent settled his body and his
mind before beginning where he had left off.

'In politics I was a Gaullist. We were even fewer than

during the war. There were so many who gave in over those
twelve years of peace and joined the majority. Only the most
extreme remained. The oddballs, Debré, Chaban — you know
their names. And then suddenly it was 1958 and de Gaulle
was back in power with his marginal little band who were to
govern France for the next ten years.

'And that is where I come to Ailleret. You see, the
Gaullists didn't really govern. How could they? They needed
the population with them and the population, like the Army,
hated de Gaulle and the Gaullists. They supported him in
1958 because they were afraid of the colonels, you know, the
rebels in Algeria, and after that because they were afraid the
communists would win the election by co-operating with the
socialists. It was this fear which kept him in power. Fear and
the concession he made. The concession was that he surrounded himself with a lot of anti-Gaullists. What do you
suppose his party, the UDR, was made up of? Nothing but an
amalgam of the old anti-Gaullist forces, the middle classes
who lived on their own fear.

'And de Gaulle had an odd habit. He was hard on his
friends. They were either with him or against. There was no
compromise. With that harshness he lost half his real supporters, especially in the Army where he had so few. But for
his enemies or for opportunists he had no moral code. As he
despised them, he was willing to use them and bargain with
them the way he never would with a friend. So in the end he
was surrounded by people he despised or didn't know, while
his old friends were shunned. And that explains Ailleret. In
the beginning he was simply a pawn to control the hostile
Army. But the Army remained hostile and he became a very
important pawn, perhaps more than a pawn in the end.'

'What about "Tous Azimuts"? Did de Gaulle know about
it?'

'I doubt it. You see, de Gaulle gave a major press
conference a few days before the article was published. You

know how he kept foreign policy and strategy to himself. It seems crazy that he would have said nothing at the press conference and left Ailleret to announce a major new policy. Why don't you ask some of the people who must know? I shall give you some introductions if you come back this afternoon.

'There was something else very strange. I went to Ailleret's funeral at the Invalides, because of Mélanie and my son-in-law Thomas. Because I knew de Gaulle well from the war he made a point of talking to us. Do you know, he was furious, seething. Not everyone could tell, but I had worked with him in difficult times and could recognize the signs. He was tense, almost shivering with an expression of blank hostility which in him meant rage. He hardly noticed the people there and spoke to nobody except the families of those killed. I doubt whether he cared for Ailleret, but he was furious that the man was eliminated and he, the President, could neither stop it nor retaliate. That was the real furious frustration we had seen in him during the war. Now I think you must go.'

At the door he paused a moment.

'I know at least two of the men who tortured me. One is a banker in Paris and the other is a very successful businessman in the south. I tried to prosecute them without any success. What do you expect? They hadn't suggested bringing any witnesses into the cellar where I was to be gently questioned and then mutilated efficiently. What could I prove? Nothing. I used to think it strange to be on the winning side and lose. I don't anymore. I spend my days trying not to hate. That is a difficult challenge. Mélanie does not understand how difficult. She resents me for that. She thinks I made her suffer. It was my own suffering she couldn't bear.'

Chapter Eleven

Stone went back late that afternoon. He was given copies of four letters written by Rogent. They were handed to him by an elderly woman with strong matron's hands. She had put Monsieur Rogent to bed. He had asked her to pass on the copies.

Over the next ten days, Stone used these introductions. And by going carefully with veiled questions he managed to draw out his contacts until they passed him on to their own friends. Each one knew someone else who might be able to help. They were surprised to find a foreigner so interested in French affairs. They did not guess what he was looking for, because he managed never to reveal his exact direction to any one person. If he had, they probably would not have co-operated so willingly. It was an art to work around a question in ever diminishing circles but to refrain from leaping at the answer in the middle.

He had noticed as he went out the morning after seeing Rogent that he was now followed by two men. He added that fact to a letter for Sherbrooke; simply an additional fact, but he could not help wondering why there were two.

It was Peduc's idea. From nine until six every day he personally joined the regular tail. There were two lists in his pocket. They contained various contacts in Paris post offices. He had a total of thirty-five names. That covered perhaps a quarter of the city's total. They were, as Courman said, playing hit and miss. He wanted to be sure they hit the first time.

Among the people Stone saw were politicians, officers serving and retired, bureaucrats – in fact, anyone who had known Ailleret and had an opinion. They all had opinions. They had all seen something through the narrow vision of their own interests, either because they had suffered under him or struggled against him, or laughed at him or feared him, or envied him or despised him. Everything except liked him. His admirers were either rare or had made themselves scarce.

He asked them about 'Tous Azimuts'; about Ailleret's relationship with the Army, with de Gaulle, with anyone; about his powers; in fact, about everything except his death, because on that subject they were unlikely to help. Nevertheless, they enabled Stone to complete his picture.

He saw Couve de Murville, the thin, cold Protestant who had been de Gaulle's Foreign Minister and had so brilliantly infuriated the Americans over French independence. At the mention of 'Tous Azimuts' he interrupted with the sarcastic tone which had wounded too many foreign governments.

'Ah, that was Ailleret's idea. Mind you, I never understood why he said it. No one had asked him to.'

Stone countered: 'It really wasn't part of General de Gaulle's vocabulary.'

'Not at all,' the former minister replied.

Two days later he saw Fourquet, the general who had succeeded Ailleret after his death and one of the few who had always been near to de Gaulle. He confirmed that the idea came from Ailleret.

But the most definite was Pierre Mirabeau, who had been Secretary-General of the Presidency in 1967 and perhaps the man closest to de Gaulle. A disinterested voice of reason in difficult times. He certainly, better than anyone, knew what de Gaulle thought.

They met in the upper floors of the Counseil d'État where Mirabeau had been relegated by the new regime after his perfectly loyal and intelligent service. He had been too honest, the only man to cry the day de Gaulle left power.

How could the others, ambitious and jealous, forgive him his simple loyalty and his undemanded power?

'Those weren't General de Gaulle's words. Not at all!' he said of 'Tous Azimuts'.

'Perhaps de Gaulle found them useful on the political front,' Stone suggested.

'Quite the contrary. General Ailleret's extreme words brought on unwanted and irrefutable criticism of the Government.'

'Why didn't de Gaulle refute him?'

'It would have been too complicated. It would have required firing Ailleret.'

And to fire Ailleret, Stone thought, would have meant replacing him. But de Gaulle was alone and hated. Ailleret was his only bulwark against the officers.

A clearer picture gradually formed of Ailleret reaching for power against the Army and, in the end, beyond de Gaulle. Stone drew the only possible logical conclusion: de Gaulle had known nothing about 'Tous Azimuts'. He had been faced with a *fait accompli*.

The few who said he had known claimed the President's approval had been passed on orally. But Stone spoke to the man who was meant to have done the passing and he could remember nothing. Perhaps he had forgotten. It was hardly the sort of thing he would forget.

Each new piece of information was sent off to London on tape or by letter. From time to time he added a new summary to make the mass comprehensible. And Peduc followed unhappily behind, waiting for the right post office to come up. When finally it did he almost failed to react. It was Friday morning. Stone sent off his report from a main branch in the west of Paris near the Palais de Chaillot. Peduc checked the lists and to his surprise found it was run by a retired Major Foullement.

Peduc leapt out of the car, leaving his companion to follow
Stone. He rushed into the cavernous, depressing hall and
pushed by two old-age pensioners waiting for their cheques at
the first gate. 'The Director's office?' The girl behind the
counter pointed towards a door at the other end of the hall.
He walked quickly across the grey-yellow tiled floor and
pulled open the door without knocking. Foullement looked
up annoyed at the intrusion but after a few words of
introduction was ready to co-operate. He was a large grey
man, almost indistinguishable from his surroundings. He had
always held staff positions and had transferred from the
Army to the Post Office as if nothing had changed, not even
his inbred respect for the authority of superiors.

He led Peduc down some stairs to the sorting-room, but
when they arrived the overseas mail was being collected and
stuffed into a bag. They looked at each other. There were
five employees staring at them, wondering what the Director
wanted. Foullement stepped forward.

'Hold on a moment. My friend has just thrown a letter in
by error. Luckily he knew me, as it's rather important.'

He picked up the sack and dragged it to the side of the
room.

'It should be there.' Peduc began picking the letters out.
There were several hundred. Very quickly he had found seven
for London. Was it one of them? He noted down the
addresses as best he could. But the employees were still
watching, and Foullement was becoming nervous.

'Haven't you found it? I'm afraid we shall have to let the
sack go.'

Peduc had ten addresses by then. He found an eleventh.
'Ah! There it is!'

Thanking everyone like a small boy given a chocolate, he
escaped as quickly as possible. Outside he pulled open the
letter. The wrong letter. It was from a student to her parents
in Kensington. He revenged himself by ripping the sheets into

small shreds and throwing them into the gutter. Courman would have to check the ten addresses he had noted. It was better than nothing.

The next morning Stone had a new opening. An outspoken and therefore backbench Deputy offered him an unexpected introduction. It was to a close friend of Ailleret. He had had so few. This friend was an officer who had been 'voluntarily' retired after Ailleret's death. He had chosen self-imposed exile in a small château east of Paris. Apparently he had taken a large part of Ailleret's private papers into exile with him.

Stone telephoned immediately and arranged to be there the same evening. It was two hundred miles from Paris. The line was bad and the voice faint. The only advice Stone's Paris contact gave was to take along a bottle of Ricard. There was a rumour that drink had helped to soften the man's frustrating existence.

The château was in fact a large farm-house surrounded by woods. The woods were rich in wild boar and stocked with pheasants around the edges. Colonel Gigotte spent his days in the forest shooting game. He sold his kill to a local merchant, who shipped it to Paris. Gigotte himself hated game or anything rich. He preferred soup and potatoes. It was a diet he had adopted after being retired, as an illustration of his monk-like exile.

Stone knew none of that when he arrived alone, in early evening, on the edge of the forest. He had left his tail on the outskirts of Paris simply by accelerating.

The house at first view appeared sinister. On second view, simply abandoned.

It stood in a large clearing. Untended grass ran like an overflow of the forest up to the stone walls. They were a soft cream colour, but against one side was a sprawling tin hangar without doors. Various jeeps and rusted farm-machinery were arranged inside in a disorderly way. One roofless jeep was sitting outside before the main door on a muddy patch of earth. Stone drew up beside it and climbed out. There were three floors of large high windows, most of them dark or shuttered.

As he stood outside an untidy middle-aged man filled the door and then opened it. 'Hé! Monsieur Stone?' Stone nodded an acknowledgement and stepped forward. The Colonel was average in every way except that neglect had made his insides swell as if to escape their covering and his skin was tight; his features stretched out into hard rounded forms behind the resistant covering like a stuffed bladder.

To his abandonment Gigotte added a constant nervous excitement. It was the loss of power badly digested. His remedy for this indigestion was drink.

He was only too happy to see Stone. Even more happy that Stone had come to listen. They sat in an old-fashioned drawing-room, unchanged for fifty years.

The house had been inherited from an aunt ten years before and he had had neither the money nor the inclination to tamper with it. It was furnished with a mixture of light marquetry tables, stained or damaged, faded chairs and rugs, depressing portraits and the typical bric-à-brac that an old lady collects around herself. Three large dogs were given free run of everything and lay either on the furniture or partially on Gigotte himself. He was constantly slapping them and pushing them off the sofa across which he sprawled. There was a bottle of Ricard by his side. Stone's contact had been right about the man's tastes.

He poured two half-tumblers and left Stone the choice of adding water or not. To his own glass he added a drop, just to turn it cloudy.

He then began to talk about Ailleret. Most of it the same old stories, told from the other side by an admirer. More emphasis on his role in the Resistance and his deportation to

Buchenwald. Ailleret's originality in going home for the weekend by parachute. His desire to shock the desk-ridden officers by coming to work in battle-dress. The traditional Army's hatred. They wouldn't accept their century or atomic warfare. The only difference in the stories was the accent.

Stone reflected that he wasn't there to choose sides but to learn something new. He tried to steer the monologue on to a more profitable line — Ailleret's struggle for increased power. Gigotte followed his lead and began to recount their battles with the other generals and with Pierre Messmer, the Minister of Defence.

'He hated Ailleret as much as anyone. His power was the Chief of Staff's weakness. When Ailleret gained a step, Messmer was one of those who lost.' He continued describing the rivalries, the infighting, the jealousy, the. . . .

At a certain moment, fifteen minutes later, even Gigotte suffered a surfeit of invective. They fell silent. Gigotte emptied his glass, then stared at Stone, his eyes burning. His eyes burnt permanently; like the Tomb of the Unknown Soldier he could not extinguish the flame of his anguish at remaining unrecognized. And, of course, there was the alcohol to help it stay alight.

'Hate is a tonic. It is the tonic which keeps most men alive. Either because they are hated or because they hate.' He drew a hand across his body as in the horizontal half of a cross and it continued on until it pointed at the now empty bottle of Ricard on the table beside him. 'It is of no importance which. Would you like to see the forest?'

There was an open window through which the night air flowed. Stone looked out into the darkness.

'Will we see much at this hour?'

'Now is the best time. Come on.' The Colonel walked out of the room leaving Stone no choice but to follow. He switched off the tape in his pocket. It would be no use outside. He would simply have to remember what was said. The Colonel pulled on an old parachute-jacket hanging in the hall and threw another one to Stone. He picked up a rifle lying against the wall and led the way to the jeep outside.

The motor turned over reluctantly. Stone sat beside him holding the rifle as the other fiddled with the ignition until the jeep burst into noisy life. He turned across the grass in no apparent direction, heading for the dark wall of trees. As they approached, the small black hole of an opening appeared. It was a mud-track and as they bumped down it, ducking every few moments to avoid low branches, the Colonel shouted above the noise addressing all of the trees and the animals cowering beneath.

'We almost won in the end, if only' – he raised his eyes to the hidden sky, letting the jeep swerve momentarily out of the deep mud-ruts – 'there hadn't been that accident. We had won against all of them – the generals, Messmer, we even managed to carry de Gaulle with us. Except that dead men don't win.

'Six months before, or was it. . . ? Yes. In June 1967 Ailleret told him what he wanted. He told de Gaulle, "Give me the powers or you can't count on me anymore." Oh, he didn't say it that way. He wrote a report. Couched it in recommendations. But de Gaulle understood. Christ-forsaken machine!'

The motor began to cough. He pushed the accelerator to the floor and it lurched momentarily forward, bouncing almost in the air. The sweet smell of the pines mixed with the humid air and the petrol fumes pushed into Stone's nostrils.

'Either he gave Ailleret the powers', the Colonel shouted, 'or Ailleret wouldn't stay on. You see, officially he was up for retirement in March. The old man wanted to keep him. But he wouldn't stay under the same rules – bowing and scraping to the generals and admirals and ministers. That fool Messmer.

'Ha. Talk of hate. Nobody hated that man. He was
Minister through the entire Algerian disaster and he didn't
make one enemy. You have to be pretty useless to leave that
shallow an impression. Look! Do you see that?'

A dark form blocked the track ahead. Its eyes were shining
at them. 'Un sanglier!' Gigotte brought the jeep to a halt and
switched on the fog-lights. The wild boar stood frozen in the
glare. It was a large male, at least three feet high. Gigotte
grabbed the rifle and stood up in his seat, resting the barrel
on the windshield. The shot exploded into the night and the
animal literally leapt into the air at the impact. It hit him in
the shoulder and he came back to earth facing them again,
frozen in a blind stare for another moment. Then he began to
move forward as if to charge their open jeep. 'Merde!'
Gigotte murmured and fired again. He missed but the shot
stopped the boar, who turned and began running.

The Colonel began clambering over Stone. 'Come on!
Come on! You drive. Follow him!' Stone managed to crawl
under him and get into position. He pushed down the
accelerator and started after the loping form ahead. Gigotte
wedged himself into an upright position with the rifle over
the windshield, holding himself almost steady as they
bumped forward.

Each time the sanglier veered towards the edge of the path
to escape into the forest he fired a shot on that side to scare
him back on to the track.

'Shoot at him, you fool!' Stone called out. 'Not around
him.'

'No. They can take twenty shots if you don't hit them
right. It'll just make his direction more erratic. Faster. Get
closer.'

They pounded through the mud, branches whipping across
their faces, the wheels slipping in and out of the ruts and
trees suddenly appearing before them as the track changed
direction slightly. If they were able to keep up at all it was

thanks to the track being cut straight, the way only the French love to cut them, applying logic to disordered nature. From time to time Gigotte fired another shot and it echoed in the eerie silence beyond the jeep with its exploding motor and the grunts of the fleeing pig.

'Soon now! Soon! You'll see,' Gigotte called out. 'Watch for it.'

The silence redescended for another thirty seconds, then a solid row of trees appeared ahead. It was a T junction. The animal, stupid and panicked, stopped dead, unable to decide which way to turn, then faced about and stared at them, intellectually cornered.

'Stop at fifty feet', Gigotte called out, 'and cut the motor. We shall give him his chance.'

Stone did as he was told. For perhaps ten seconds the animal waited for the silent but glaring jeep to come back to life. Then he moved forward into a charge. Gigotte waited until he was at twenty feet, then fired. The bullet caught him in the head just below the eyes and rose up to shatter his tiny unimaginative brain. The form stopped, then dropped, almost in mute tribute.

They climbed out of the jeep and approached carefully until sure that it was dead. The yellow teeth were bared, ready for the fair chance of battle which it understood. They took two legs each and dragged the still weight up to the jeep. Limp and unwieldy, it must have weighed almost five hundred pounds.

Gigotte took the wheel and turned the jeep about. He drove back slowly and began on Ailleret again as if nothing had happened.

'De Gaulle understood we were on his side, but we wanted the rewards, the normal rewards' — he repeated the words doggedly — 'of loyalty. And what did he reply? Nothing. Not a sound. For six months he made us sweat. Finally, Ailleret had had enough, so he published that "Tous Azimuts" business. He thought he was on the way out, so why not? Why not shake them all up? He loved to do that.

'But when de Gaulle kept silent even then we knew we hadn't completely lost; we realized de Gaulle hadn't replied because he didn't know what to say. You see, Ailleret really had become indispensable, more than he realized. And do you know how the old boy gave in? It was at his New Year's reception. Normally he wandered about, towering above the mob like a demi-god and bending his head from time to time to drop a word in an ear. Instead he addressed Ailleret in a loud voice, asking him what his plans were. Ailleret replied he was going to retire to the country as he was worn out. De Gaulle replied that that was no reason. He was worn out himself.

'God only knows why he decided to announce it that way. In any case he had given in. That was it, you see. We knew we had won. Ailleret confirmed the victory by making a speech calling for all the powers he had always wanted. That was just to be sure his position was clear, but it caused a lot of jumping about in the Government.'

They drove out of the forest into the clearing around the house. The sky appeared above them, almost luminous after the long cavern through which they had driven. Gigotte pulled up before the front door and leapt out. He motioned that they should leave the boar in the jeep and banged into the house; Stone followed, stopping just long enough to grab the bottle of Ricard from his car. Inside he offered it to the Colonel, who accepted with almost childish thanks. 'Would you like some dinner?' He led the way into the kitchen where he poured two large glasses from the bottle, then turned to light the stove under two large pots. After a few moments he produced two bowls of soup and a plate of potatoes, mixed with milk and overcooked. They ate in silence, Gigotte swallowing the food in large sucking mouthfuls as if it did not exist. He took up his monologue again, without intro-

duction, except to say that the bottle was a kind gesture
while he poured out another tumbler for each of them.

The purpose of the visit was to make the man talk. But
Gigotte, who normally drank alone, insisted that his guest
drink as much as himself. He insisted yet more firmly as the
bottle was a gift.

'Then, a week before he was to retire, they reappointed
him. In the circumstances, he accepted gracefully.'

'But he was dead!'

'That's right. Dead!'

'Did they kill him?'

'Yes. Of course they did!'

'Who?'

'Who? How should I know? The fucking Americans, I
suppose. He always said they would get him. I suppose "Tous
Azimuts" was too much for them to swallow. Anyway,
Ailleret knew what was coming. He told me the day before
leaving on that trip to the Indian Ocean that he knew a plot
was in the air and that I should get his papers in order just in
case. He was so worried he didn't want his family to go with
him. Then someone must have reassured him, because he let
them go.'

'They tell me you have some of the General's papers.'

Gigotte looked up from the table. He was at the end of the
Ricard and his burning stare had become a leer.

'So that's why you came?' It was a bitter question.

'They could help me. I am trying to find out who might
have killed him.'

'What do I care? You want them. All right.' He lurched to
his feet and out of the room, shouting over his shoulder, 'If I
could publish some of them, I could leave this hole in
comfort. I won't show you those. I have his reminiscences on
Algeria. Do you know what they would do to me if I
published? They would shove me into Third Category. You
know what that means? I'd lose most of my pension. But the

rest you can see.'

He came unsteadily back into the room, kicking a cardboard carton before him. It slid heavily.

'There you are.' He kicked it a last time. 'A great man's legacy rotting in a soup-box. That is power in its finite form.'

Stone waited.

'Examine it. Read everything. Pay your respects and put it all back. I'm going to bed. Stay as long as you like.'

The Colonel stumbled back out of the room, leaving Stone alone. He switched off his pocket tape recorder for the last time. He had had to change cassettes twice during the evening.

His head was throbbing from the alcohol. He went out to his car and fumbled for a small leather box which held a precision camera with a highly sensitive light-meter. He brought it back and began to photograph the documents.

It was four in the morning before Stone had finished. He left the box in the centre of the room and drove to Paris where he slept until midday, then developed the photographs. It was another twenty-four hours before he had examined them all.

In those documents he found everything he wanted. Ailleret's suggestions for new powers, sent to de Gaulle in June 1967. A rough draft withdrawing his "Tous Azimuts" proposals, obviously scribbled out in a moment of lost nerves, but never used. And, above all, the famous speech which Campini had said did not exist. It was dated 15 January 1968. In it Ailleret called for total control over the other three chiefs of staff. He called for war-time powers in peace-time. He defined the powers by citing Marshal Joffre's responsibilities at the most difficult moments of the First World War. 'Un véritable Généralissime.'

Stone made two copies of each document, prepared a summary and put one set in an envelope for London. Finally, he collapsed into bed. He now held proof of too many motives. All he needed was a murderer.

Chapter Twelve

The catching of a murderer, Charles Stone reflected lying on his bed, was a matter of detail.

And yet he was drowned in detail — all of which he had managed to discover without approaching one inch nearer to a name.

Would it not be simpler to walk down into the street, pick up one of his ridiculous shadows and beat him till he revealed something or, more to the point, somebody? The villains were, after all, not mysterious beings. They were on his tail, for all to see.

But what was the point? The idiot in the street was a mere nothing. The man he worked for was probably nothing. How many steps up was the man in command, the man who had ordered the elimination of Ailleret? If he began to climb the chain, they would quickly cut off the link in danger. No. There was no point.

Documents and conversations with important men had given him everything except a name. They were too important, too caught up in their Olympian feuds to worry about who might have killed nineteen people. Anyway, most of them didn't like Ailleret. Alive he was a factor of power. Dead he was dead, non-existent. Only their hates and loves remained, superficial, ephemeral, vicious.

But if he reversed his tactics. Yes, Stone thought, if he came down to earth, abandoned his ministers and generals and treated the case as a common murder.

So what if the murderer turned out to be a minister or a general, or a government, or even a common criminal? It was down on the ground that he would have a clear view up their skirts to judge the real state of their virginity; down on the ground where things happened.

Yes. There he might find his man.

Of one thing he was sure. For the same reason that an important man would have him followed by a nobody, an important man wouldn't have the Chief of Staff murdered by a nobody. He would want to control it closely without actually wetting his feet.

The next day, Tuesday, 20 June, Philippe Courman was busy organizing an investigation. Before him lay the ten addresses noted from the ten unopened letters to London. The telephone rang. It was Peduc, nervous. He had had a call from an assistant – the one tailing Stone that morning. The assistant had been in a panic. He had communicated his panic to Peduc. And Peduc felt obliged to communicate his own to Courman.

'What is the matter?'

'He's going away.'

'Away? Where?'

'La Réunion.'

'Where?'

'La Réunion.'

There were moments when Courman would have liked to panic, like most men. Like Peduc, or poor Albert Duschêne. But no. That wasn't his role. His was to calm the others. To get what he wanted.

'When?'

'Now! In forty minutes. He's a nut. He dropped off that steel box at his bank and drove on to Orly with nothing more than a briefcase. Bought a ticket on the spot. People in their right mind don't fly to the other side of the world with a briefcase. What is he going there for anyway? Do you want me to go with him?'

Courman thought for a moment. Peduc would be useless in

La Réunion. He was already lost in the suburbs of Paris; he would only be a burden.

'No. Wait until he has taken his plane. Then go home. Oh, and while he's away you might have a look through his flat. Neatly. Don't disturb anything.'

As he hung up, Courman reached for an address-book. He dialled the international operator and asked for a number in St Denis, the capital of La Réunion.

Robert Tocqueville was one of those rare Réunionais who had spent more than a year off the island and out of the Indian Ocean. He had been fifteen years in France; long enough to gain the distinction which marked him as more than a *petit blanc*. And yet he had been exactly that. His father was one of those 'poor whites' who slaved out their lives on a small sugar-cane plantation; poorer than the Indian or Chinese merchants in the towns and not much better off than the black peasants who worked for him.

'Had been' because Tocqueville had abandoned his class. The Second World War had taken him to France, and in the general collapse and disorder of 1940 he had opted for de Gaulle. Not because he was less bourgeois-minded than those who didn't. No. But he was far from home. He had come this far to fight. And it wasn't in the pitiful ranks of Marshal Pétain that he would have a chance. So he left for London with two friends and was sent back only weeks later to join a Resistance group in the Jura, that hilly region of good wine near the Swiss border. There he amused himself to no end until the victory; playing boy scout and appearing out of the woods from time to time to attack the Germans, who took their revenge by collecting hostages in the nearest village and shooting them.

Tocqueville belonged to the cavalier part of the Resistance. Nevertheless, his chief managed to get himself shot in the last days of the German retreat. That was how the rest of the group came to be gathered up by Philippe Courman, who suddenly appeared as a guardian angel out of the disorder and promised to look after them, find them jobs, employ them, feed them, anything. A boy scout needs a father.

Until 1955 the young man served well, here and there helping different causes which Courman took in hand. He did not have any political beliefs except one: action. He was not remarkably intelligent. He was a man suited for what he liked and Courman ensured that he was kept active, not simply as a strong man, but as an organizer, an encourager, an active worm in the woodwork.

In 1955 he went home, richer, with introductions, a new social status, a man 'respected' in the plantations when political options were to be taken. La Réunion suited his style. Personal force was more easily used. There was a long tradition of violence and of clan rule which stood far above the law. Thus, at the age of thirty-five he discovered Caesar's adage and became with delight a big frog in a small pond. Or perhaps a medium-sized frog. He was, after all, still a persuader, not a creator.

Courman's call came through late in the afternoon. Tocqueville was overwhelmed to hear his boss on the other end of the line. It was rare that he was given a specific job as La Réunion was too far away from France to need more than general housekeeping. The order to meet and watch Stone was a simple task; too simple. He and an assistant were waiting at Gillot Airport when the Air France jet curved in and down from over the sea.

Stone was seated on the right side of the plane, before the wing. During the landing that was the island side. They came down in the same direction that Ailleret's DC6 had taken off. He could see St Denis below, and behind the town mountains rising up.

The flight had lasted fourteen hours. He had slept from

Paris to northern Africa, where they stopped briefly at Djibouti, and then had slept again until the last hour when they flew south down the Indian Ocean within sight of the African coast. He caught sight of La Réunion toward seven in the morning. The light was a different light, soft and hazy. The Poets' Island, he reflected. The mountains followed the coast a few miles back. They were hard and barren in the distance; a barrier without faults. No pilot having seen them once could have forgotten and turned his plane into their rock. Somewhere in that mass Ailleret had died.

The airport itself was small, surrounded by a simple barrier. There was one plane a day from Paris; not an international traffic which required great bureaucratic control.

From the tiny terminal it was a ten-minute drive by taxi to central St Denis. There he checked into the best hotel, La Bourdonnais, a new cement block with air conditioning and all the other characteristics of modern banality.

Stone lay in his bath for an hour and then telephoned the Prefecture. He had a name, a young Enarque who was beginning his career in this colony which was legally a Department; an integral part of the French nation just five hundred miles away and dominated by a not overly Westernized population. Stone introduced himself and offered to pay a visit to the Prefecture. The young man was delighted to hear a voice which came from Paris, even if it belonged to a foreigner.

Twenty minutes later Stone was strolling the few yards which separated his hotel from the Prefecture. He noted with relief that he was not followed. He did not notice Robert Tocqueville because Tocqueville was a local worm and knew how to slide unobtrusively through the local woodwork.

The Hôtel de la Préfecture was a columned colonial residence. As for the young Enarque, he was inoffensive, just as Stone had imagined and hoped. He had only one all-consuming desire and that was to talk about Paris and everyone there. About all his fellow-Enarques who were closer than he to the seat of power. About who had replaced whom in what committee responsible to which minister and why. And all the other essential questions which decided the future of France without the ignorant voting public being any the wiser.

Stone had constantly to turn him back to La Réunion, a subject which bored the fellow, and to the Réunionais whom he held in contempt.

'They only survive thanks to us. The economy is completely artificial, because everything is imported from France at controlled prices. We call it a department but anyone can see it's a colony, with one difference: they exploit us. We take 230,000 tons of their sugar every year at triple the world price.'

Later, he conducted a short tour of the building, showing the room where the Governor, Monsieur des Brulys, had cut his throat in 1809 when the English took the island, and on the first floor the dining-room where official dinners were held. It was there Ailleret had dined before taking his plane. Beside it a ballroom with Venetian crystal and furniture left from the building's first owners, the Compagnie des Indes. It was there that Ailleret had met the ruling class of the island at the reception which followed his dinner.

With persistence Stone managed to find out which of the staff had been there for the last ten years. The young man pointed out some of them, only half-registering his visitor's unusual interest in the servants. When the tour was finished, they lunched together.

That evening, Stone waited discreetly outside the Prefecture. He had taken note of three men during his tour and was waiting for one of them to appear. Two of the three were *huissiers* and one was a senior waiter. It was the waiter who appeared first, from a side door. He was no longer in uniform and was apparently on his way home. Stone fell in behind and Tocqueville, like a third blind mouse, followed in his turn. The waiter walked along the main street, rue de Paris, toward the mountains. Stone hesitated, hoping for an opportunity. He wanted a long quiet talk with the man, who stopped periodically to chat with friends, or simply to wave to them. He was half-breed, as were most of the people he greeted.

Then suddenly he disappeared. Stone ran to close the gap and discovered a small alley off to the left. The waiter was before him, disappearing again into a bar. Stone waited a moment before following. It was a small bar, more a back room. The man was standing talking to the barman, yet another "half-breed. Stone placed himself beside them, ordered a punch, and then with surprise recognized the waiter, who himself remembered the foreigner being shown around the Prefecture.

Stone bought him a drink and began talking about La Réunion, or rather asking. The waiter was delighted. It was rare to find someone who knew none of the local stories; a virgin sponge ready to absorb whatever was said.

With application, the sponge brought him round to the Prefecture and the servant's gossip. From there to Ailleret's visit was only a step.

Louis — that was his name — had been on duty that night. They had all been on, including part-time help from the town. Ailleret wasn't the only visitor. Michel Debré, Deputy for La Réunion, former Prime Minister, Minister of Finance at that time and one of de Gaulle's senior barons, had arrived the same day. Guichard, the Minister of Industry, arrived a few days later. And Bettencourt, the Secretary of State for External Affairs. For once the island was crowded with important people and with all their aides and associates. The Government was holding a major political fête, and Ailleret was almost out of place.

He remembered the evening perfectly. He had rarely met such a difficult, authoritarian man as the Chief of Staff. 'Met' was perhaps not the word. He had served him and also carried two telephone messages which arrived in the midst of the dinner. Ailleret had begun the food in good humour. He finished it furious.

What were the two messages?

They came from the pilot of his plane, who didn't want to leave that evening. But Ailleret insisted.

Why didn't they?

The weather, their messages said. The politicians around the table encouraged him to stay.

And why was Ailleret in such a hurry?

How was a waiter to know? After the second message he had almost given in. But when they went into the reception he changed his mind again and insisted that they leave.

Why did he change it again?

The waiter had noticed him talking to a senior officer just before he sent a last message. He was furious and left for the airport alone.

What senior officer?

He couldn't remember. One of the many outsiders who had appeared in La Réunion that week.

What about his wife and daughter?

They followed afterwards. They didn't want to go either and had an argument with him. They were having a good time.

What a strange story.

The waiter smiled knowingly. They had all been having a good time, including the pilots. Too good a time. That was the rumour. That was why the local papers had dropped the subject so quickly.

Had they?

Oh yes. Very quickly. It didn't do the island's reputation any good. Or the armed forces'. It was the first accident there had ever been on La Réunion.

That evening, Stone slipped his tape into the mail. It was addressed to Christian Smith, his American bank manager in Paris, who once again held the steel box in his own safe hands along with its growing collection of tapes and documents.

Tocqueville also reported that evening. By the time the call was through he caught Courman in mid-dinner, half a world away and four hours earlier. The dinner had been sent up from a restaurant below — an old habit for the rare nights when he worked at home, refusing invitations to political meals. The restaurant was mediocre, which suited him perfectly.

He was home that night because he hoped to hear from Tocqueville. But also because he was slipping behind in his normal tasks as a result of concentrating on Stone.

A small problem had come up that morning. His secretary had telephoned him to say that a government supporter, a UDR mayor in the Auvergne, had defected and was reorganizing himself as an independent. The town was fairly large; large enough to have a representative of the central administration — a Sub-Prefecture.

Courman was known to have a certain influence in that district, and a message had come from the Party's Secretary-General asking him to deal with the situation.

He had already discovered who would be the most logical and loyal local party man to push the defector out and take his place. He was now arranging the details which usually made that sort of push successful.

Someone would visit the local printer, who leant his presses either free or at reduced rate in return for tax considerations. The printer would quickly realize that the Mayor should no longer have access to the presses — at least, not at the same price.

The same person would visit the publisher of the town

newspaper. The publisher was assured of a certain quantity of advertising from businesses run by UDR supporters in return for reasonable support. He would want to keep that advertising.

There was also one of Courman's young men in the regional Prefecture. Courman would have to speak to him personally to ensure that in the future all building projects supported by the Mayor were refused permits. That would soon scare the promoters and constructors out of his camp.

The young man could also begin going through all the Mayor's official acts while in office. He was bound to find something unpleasant: a municipal action approved without a quorum or town council minutes tampered with after signature. That they always found. It was a national habit.

On a slightly higher level Courman had found out who was responsible for the credits or loans made to the town by the Government or indirectly by the banks. They would be cut back drastically, if not cut off.

And so on. Each negative act was balanced by a positive act to create a new power centre around the Mayor's chosen rival.

At that point Courman was interrupted by the telephone ringing. He left his more legal, sophisticated work to return to the man in La Réunion. On a surprisingly clear line Tocqueville recounted Stone's conversation with the waiter. He had been seated at another table in the bar.

Chapter Thirteen

The next morning Stone took a taxi, again down the rue de Paris, left on to the rue du Grand Chemin and out of the town on to the Route Nationale past the airport and along the coast to the small town of Ste Marie. Shortly after Ste Marie the taxi turned left on to a small road, and CD51. There they began to climb into the hills which eventually led into the mountains. Four kilometres up he told the driver to stop and wait. They were on the edge of a village. Beaufond. It was there the plane had come down, five kilometres in direct line from the airport.

Stone walked through the sugar-cane up to the village, brushing the swarms of flies away from his face. At the first line of meagre houses he looked about for signs of life. A dried and tatty white man appeared from behind a wall. Stone walked up to him. Was Monsieur Georges Baray there? It was on Baray's property that the plane had come down. The villager looked about, surprised, as if he expected Baray to appear out of the air. No, he wasn't there. The dialect was thick, and Stone understood with difficulty. What did he want?

Wasn't it here that General Ailleret had died?

The man's eyes lit up. There were very few exciting moments in the history of the village. That had been the most remarkable.

Would he show Stone where it had happened?

The man led him to a clearing. He showed him the trees half-destroyed by the plane on the way down. There was still a slight trough in the earth. It had become a sacred spot for the village. Something had happened there which they did not understand. It was a place to come and talk.

The peasant had been there that evening. They had all been there. Where else would they be? They had been thrown out of bed; come out of their houses in the rain to see a yellow flame shooting up only yards away.

He had not gone into the wreckage with most of the villagers. The wisdom of age told him it might explode again. Waiting on the side he had seen the poor young girl they had cut from a seat. They had carried her by. And he had seen the ministers and the Prefect and the generals. They had all come to see the hole. That night. That very night. It was the only time they had ever come. There had been hundreds of officials and soldiers. Not to mention the inquisitive populace. They had destroyed the sugar-cane tramping through the fields.

Had he seen anything peculiar?

The whole thing was peculiar. They had never seen anything so curious. All those important men running about in a panic. Not simply the corporals and sergeants; but the officers, the politicians, the Prefect standing there lost. Some were running through the wreckage looking for survivors. The old man could remember every detail. It was a poem, a song floating in his mind. It was a view on to the outer world. Everything beyond the island had been defined for him on that muddy, grotesque night. It was his one experience.

Was nobody calm?

He thought. Calm was something he knew; it was his world. There was one man. A young soldier.

In uniform therefore? Stone had withdrawn beneath a tree, out of the sun, and broken off a branch, which he waved periodically to discourage the flies attracted by his unbitten skin.

Yes. In uniform. An officer, he thought. He was one of the first to arrive. In the second car.

What did he do? Stone asked his questions gently but

quickly. He did not want to panic the man but he did not want to give him time to stop.

While the others stood around the edge of the fire or ran about, he stepped into the centre of the wreckage and lit a flashlight.

What was he looking for?

Like everyone else – survivors, he imagined. The soldier had walked slowly with his head down, picking up pieces of metal from time to time and throwing them away. The peasant remembered because he had been tall and thin, and the flames reflected on his body in the black clearing.

Did he find anything?

The peasant thought not.

Could he remember him in any more detail?

No. Especially as he disappeared from the centre when the others arrived and waited at the edge in the darkness while the official search began. A nice-looking young man with a decisive air.

Stone began to draw away from the conversation.

They hadn't been properly compensated for the damaged sugar-cane. The man looked at him as if he represented the Government. Anyone educated who came to the villages was certainly from the Government. A taxman probably. Stone's foreign accent for him was indistinguishable from the accents of those who came from mainland France, known locally as Z'oreilles. They had lost a lot of money that year.

Stone offered a ten-franc note and left him with apologies.

That evening the old man received a second visit from a second outsider with questions. Tocqueville he knew by sight. It was a face which normally appeared during the election campaigns. He answered the questions with care, as he had Stone's. And he was rewarded with a five-franc coin. Local tipping was not so generous.

From Beaufond, Stone started back in the direction of St

Denis. Shortly before the town he made the taxi turn off to the right toward the sea on the road to the airport. A few hundred yards from the terminal he got out and walked, asking the driver to wait for him before the main door.

The mountains stood out clearly, stark and beautiful, towering up, dominating the island. Sinister if one remembered the rainy night and the flaming wreckage. He could distinguish Beaufond in the distance. The choices open to the pilot when seen from the flat coast were so obvious; it seemed insane to believe that a man had actually turned toward his own death.

He walked on past the terminal, quickly in the midday heat, until he found a service gate. A sign indicated NO ENTRANCE. He entered and crossed the tarmac toward the technical sheds, simple metal hangars thrown up beside the runway. In the second shed there was a Dakota and two men working on it. He pushed open the plastic double doors and strode in.

'Good day,' he called out. 'Is there a senior ground engineer here?'

The mechanics in overalls pointed to the back of the shed. There were three more men he hadn't noticed, one of them visibly in charge. Stone strode up and shook his hand.

'They said I might find you here.'

'Who?'

'Control,' Stone replied, waving behind him. 'I've just come from the Prefect's office.'

The chief engineer smiled.

'What can I do for you?'

Mention of a superior with the right tone of assurance always had a marvellous effect. That was something Stone had learnt late in his childhood. All that remained was to put them at ease.

'Nothing complicated. A bit of information. Old history really. Has anyone been here permanently for the last ten years?'

'I have, for a start,' the chief replied. 'In fact, I think we all have. This is the sort of place you either stay a long time or you don't come.'

The others nodded. The chief was a heavy slow man – a colonial type, Stone thought, like everyone on the island who was there by choice.

'This airport has changed in the last decade. Up until eight years ago it was hardly safe to land, the runway was so bad. Just like a roller-coaster. Now we have jets.'

'Tell me about the runways and landing directions. Has that ever changed?'

'Not much. There is one runway. You've seen it if you came here by plane. It has always been the same one – narrower and shorter, but always the same one, parallel to the sea. As for landing directions, they are the same as taking off. There is only one way to arrive here and the same way to leave: with the sea on your left and the mountains on your right. As soon as the plane is in the air it turns left to avoid the mountains. It's the winds, you see; they never change. Everything has to happen in the same direction.

'Well, what happened to Ailleret's pilot? Did he get mixed up?'

The chief stopped and looked at Stone.

'So that's what you've come about. I wondered. I always said we hadn't heard the end of that business.'

The others nodded.

'You'd like to hear the whole story, would you? You won't be much wiser in the end. We aren't. The investigating team wasn't, either. Come and sit down.'

The four of them walked to the back of the shed where there were folding chairs around a battered desk. A photograph of the chief's wife sat on its wooden surface. She wasn't pretty and she was half-breed. Perhaps that was why he had never gone back to France. She would neither like it nor be liked, while on La Réunion he was something, somebody. As an outsider her husband could speak his mind the way no islander would care to do. The chief sat heavily behind his desk, put the photograph face down as if to protect its purity and looked up at Stone quizzically.

'What I don't understand', he asked, 'is why wait four years to pick over the bones? It won't help anyone now. I ask you that, but truthfully we knew someone would appear one day and start nosing around. It ended all too quickly.'

'There weren't enough questions asked,' one of his companions said earnestly. The others laughed.

'Poor Leclerc,' the chief said, indicating the man. 'He always claimed he had something to add to the business. But nobody asked him.'

'What was that?'

'Let me tell the story first. Don't be impatient after all this time. Ailleret arrived in the morning in his DC6. He was to leave the same evening at 23.15. In fact he left ten minutes late. While he was enjoying himself at the Prefecture, the crew had its own party. We were there with the junior officers based on the island and some others who tagged along; all the visiting firemen. There was a strong punch, a local speciality, and the crew tried it. All twelve of them.'

'Twelve?' Stone said, surprised. That had never struck him before. Too obvious. Why twelve men? 'You don't need that many men to fly a DC6.'

'It was a long flight out and back so they had a double crew, heavy on the steward side. I heard he was a demanding fellow.'

'And all twelve of them got drunk?'

'Well, let's just say they were drinking. All except one. He said he didn't drink.'

'But why?'

'They didn't think they were leaving.'

'What do you mean they didn't think they were leaving?

The flight was planned. What was there to stop them?'

'I don't know. The captain announced early on that they were staying the night. By the time they found out the General wanted to go it was too late. They were already well into their party.'

'And then?'

'And then they said they wouldn't go, stalled for time and, of course, put away the punch. They tried every excuse, including the weather.'

'And?'

'It was raining, foul weather. Not a night for walking, but nothing to stop an airplane. In the end Ailleret went to the plane without them and waited in it alone for thirty minutes — furious. I saw his face just before the take-off. Well, you can imagine. The others were obliged to follow. The captain made a last attempt to convince him to stay but he couldn't really say, "Look, I'm tired and a bit tight." A perfect way to ruin a career. Ailleret said that if the control tower gave permission to take off they would go. And it did.'

'Was the plane overloaded with fuel?'

'No. Where did you get that idea? People print a lot of rubbish. The truth is their flight was 2500 miles and the plane's normal range was 3800 miles; if necessary almost 5000 miles. They had room for another seven hundred gallons. I should know. I had it fuelled.'

'Did you check it over?'

'When it arrived. We should have done it again when it left but there wasn't time. After the captain announced they weren't going until the next day, we didn't bother to do our normal pre-flight checklist. Then suddenly they were leaving. There wasn't a moment to do anything. All we had done was refuel her during the day. Anyway, she had been examined nine hours before on arrival.'

'Was the plane guarded?'

'Of course it was. The way all planes are on the airport. No one unauthorized is allowed to come into this area. It is written up at the entrance.'

'There was no special guard?'

'I should think all the spare policemen were busy', the third man answered in the silence, 'keeping their eyes open downtown. It's pretty rare that so many important people come here.' They all laughed.

'And what was it that no one wanted you to add?' Stone asked, turning to Leclerc.

'Ah. Now, it isn't what you'd call fact,' he began slowly, 'but I never enjoy myself at parties here. Everyone always drinks too much as there isn't much else to do. So I noticed that officer in their crew who didn't drink. He was clean sober up till eleven o'clock, after they had put the punch away, and he was the one who kept telling the captain they shouldn't go. Then five minutes later I saw him again and, by God, he was tighter than the others. Now, that was strange to see, I can tell you. And the others all teased him, and he kept saying he hadn't drunk a thing and they all laughed. He was fit to cry trying to be sober and the others forced him to go back to the plane. They didn't want to go themselves, but him the least of all.' Leclerc sat up straight, tensely, while he spoke, then relaxed again as he finished.

The others listened to his tortured speech in a half-respectful, half-mocking silence. And when he finished no one spoke. There was something grotesque about dragging a drunk man to his death.

'Was there anyone at your party who did anything strange? Anyone who had come specially for that day?'

'No. We knew all the fellows who had come from Madagascar with the plane.' The chief paused. 'There was a young officer. But he had already been here for a couple of days to check the airport. The military capabilities, you see. They send someone periodically from the big base in Madagascar.'

'Who was he?'

They all shrugged.

'I'm not sure I ever knew his name. He was nice young man but just another tourist for us. He was thin, I remember.' The chief fell silent again. 'A funny business.'

'What do you think happened?'

'Oh, they were drunk and they crashed the plane.'

'Do you really believe that?'

'I don't know. Nothing else was ever suggested. Not to me. But the boys in the control tower told me what they heard on the radio.'

'What?'

'Nothing. Silence. Now, that was strange. They kept telling the pilot to go left instead of right, and he didn't even answer until the last second. Then he screamed.'

'I understand he had begun to turn back to the sea but it was too late,' Stone added.

'That's somebody's imagination,' the chief retorted sarcastically. 'How could anyone see what the plane did in the middle of a rainy night at two hundred metres' height five miles away?'

'It wasn't very high?'

'You have forgotten perhaps. Passenger planes with propellers don't climb very quickly.'

They waited for him to ask something else.

'You were right. I'm not much wiser.'

'I'll tell you what I'd do, young man. Go and see General Elestre. He was Commander-in-Chief of the area. He arrived on the plane with Ailleret and stayed behind. But, more important, he was the one who carried the enquiry team's report back to Paris. And this I know. He refused to go back on a military plane. He took a regular flight and they tell me he put the report directly into de Gaulle's hands. That's what his assistant told me, and we've never heard a word on the subject since.'

Robert Tocqueville knew he couldn't march in and ask what they had been saying to Stone. The chief engineer would have thrown him out. The chief wasn't from the island and he didn't like political organizers.

But Tocqueville had a friend in every organization or a friend who had a friend. That was his job. In this case he knew the third man in the conversation, and with a little coaxing later that day he pushed him to repeat what had been said.

Tocqueville wasn't a man to panic. That was a lesson he had learnt from Courman. But what he heard worried him. He had known the young officer who had been twice noticed – once at Beaufond and once by the engineers. Tocqueville had carried a note for him the day Ailleret was killed. He didn't know what was in the note or what had happened to the plane, but he didn't want things to go any further. Something somewhere told him that things had gone far enough, and he had a good nose for approaching disaster. He would tell Courman his fears when he reported to him.

Unfortunately he couldn't get through to Paris that evening. The local lines were blocked, or down, or something. They were like that half the time, and nobody knew why. His worry grew into a nervous worry when the man on Stone's tail reported that he had arranged to see other airport officials the next morning and two of the more difficult prying island journalists in the afternoon.

His orders were to follow, but he was the man on the spot and he knew La Réunion. It was a bad thing to start people talking. There was no stopping them afterwards.

Stone dined with the young Enarque from the Prefecture. They drove out of St Denis on the west side and up a difficult road into the mountains. Twenty minutes later they came to a hotel with a large restaurant overlooking the sea. It was almost empty. Stone's friend explained that that was

because few tourists came to La Réunion. It was too
expensive. Air France had a monopoly and they used it to
soak the islanders to the maximum. He also explained how
justice worked on the island. Most intelligent criminals
disappeared behind the volcanoes and were never caught by
the police. The police didn't like going up into the mountains. Besides, they were all more or less related to the men
they chased or didn't bother to chase.

He also explained all the other disagreeable things which
he felt about La Réunion as they ate an imported, col-
onialist's dinner over the forests which plunged down the
hillside into the coastal towns and the sea.

It was midnight before Stone arrived back at his hotel. He
opened the door to his room and switched on the light.
Before him were his few belongings spread across the floor.
The bed itself was stripped. It went through his mind that he
had done well to send off his day's tapes before dinner.

The door into the bathroom was closed. He stepped
forward to open it. On the other side was Robert Tocqueville
with a pistol pointed at his chest. 'Turn around.' He did so,
and Tocqueville grasped both his arms just below the
shoulder. As Stone turned, another man came in from the
hall, closed the door and approached. His fists were covered
by kid gloves and one of them rose quickly to Stone's
stomach.

He tried to protect himself by kicking out, but Tocqueville
pressed a knee hard into his spine. The other man hit him
again in the stomach, then in the face, then in the stomach
and then again and again.

When Stone awoke his briefcase was beside him. He was
stretched out on an uncomfortable foam-padded bench. He
opened his left eye slowly; but around the other the skin was
too swollen to allow vision. It was 8.30 the next morning and
he was in the departure lounge of the airport. The daily plane

for Paris left at 9.30.

A woman's voice came out of the haze. A nasal voice trying to be agreeable, but fundamentally disagreeable. Trying too hard. Or was it the pain which raced in a jagged line across his head and down through the body?

'They brought you half an hour ago. They were worried you might miss your flight.'

'They who?' Stone asked in semi-blindness. He ached, oh, in such a detailed way. For once he was conscious of his entire body, of every little bone and muscle.

'Your friends. The men who brought you.'

'What friends? What happened?'

'Apparently you enjoyed yourself too much last night.'

Stone had let his left eye slip closed again. He forced it back open to look at her. Was she serious or sarcastic or lying? She was smiling and pleasant and inoffensive in an Air France uniform.

'You are not from here?' he asked.

'Oh no,' she replied in a relieved voice as if Stone were joking.

'Then you wouldn't know my friends, would you?' He tried to climb to his feet but fell over backwards. The hostess was obliged to support him on to the airplane.

Chapter Fourteen

'I want to speak to Mr Sherbrooke of the Norwich Union.'

'I'm sorry, sir. This is not the Norwich Union.'

'Look. Your Director is called Mr Sherbrooke.'

'Yes, sir.'

'Well, tell him Mr Charles Stone is on the line and mention the Norwich Union and be quick about it. It's urgent.'

'Yes, sir.'

Stone stood in a telephone booth at Orly Airport. He was propped against the glass wall trying to keep on his feet. Nothing was broken. He was simply thoroughly battered. They had given him some treatment on the plane and he had managed to open the other eye. He knew he could not go to his flat and telephone. He could see Peduc further down the corridor. Paris had obviously been advised on which plane he would be back. The comedy was no longer a comedy.

'Hello, Martin.'

'Charles! At last. I've been trying to phone you for two days. I thought you were dead.'

'Martin, listen. I'm giving up. I wanted to tell you I've had it. I've been beaten up again. The double system obviously hasn't stopped them and I've been to La Réunion and I'm still not much closer.'

'Charles, you can't give up.'

'What do you mean? I want to! Do you understand?'

'Charles, listen. I had a telephone call two days ago. Somebody who said you had asked them to phone.'

'What!'

'Yes. They wanted to know if I'd received that last envelope.'

'What did you say?'

'I said I didn't know what he was talking about and didn't know a Charles Stone. He didn't mention the Norwich Union. I've been trying to get hold of you ever since. I thought they'd got you. I was on the verge of asking Williams to publish.'

Stone was waiting at the other end. He felt himself locked in the glass box waiting to be delivered to the shadow waiting down the hall. All he wanted to do was walk away and forget the whole story.

'Do you understand, Charles? This means you can't give up. If they've gone to the trouble of tracking me down they won't let you drop it now. You know too much. There is only one way out. You must find the answer first before they confirm I'm your man and try to get the duplicate. If they do, Charles, you're dead.'

He was still silent.

'Do you hear me?'

'Yes. Yes, I hear you.' He shifted his weight to the other shoulder on the other side of the box.

'Charles, from now on send the stuff to my secretary.'

He read out the name and address. Stone took it down resignedly on the back of his ticket; then hung up in silence.

He limped out of the terminal into a taxi. On the Autoroute into Paris he glanced back at his tail a hundred yards behind, then sank into a morose coma. Was it simply exhaustion and pain or was it what he had called fear?

Not until the next morning did Stone feel strong enough to leave his bed. Perhaps he simply didn't want to feel strong enough. Perhaps he was still looking for a way out. But the night brought only one truth: that he was cornered and hadn't much time.

It was with a feeling of being hunted instead of hunting that he went down into the street, past his tail who was unobtrusively gazing into a pastry shop. He drove to the Invalides and the rue de Constantine. He was sure Rogent would be there.

Half an hour later he left the sick man's flat with an introduction to General Elestre and a promise that Rogent would telephone ahead to prepare the ground.

Elestre was at home when Stone rang. He was leaving for the country that same day to join a salmon-fishing party and then going on alone to a quiet week with other friends. As a matter of fact, Pierre Dehal was going on the same fishing party. They were not old friends, or even good friends. Inevitably they knew many of the same people and Dehal loved fly fishing. It was a gentle, fine, unathletic sport. One for a delicate soul.

Elestre suggested Stone come to see him immediately. He lived at Neuilly in a comfortable building looking on to the Bois de Bologne.

He was a small, alert man, very old and very slow. He motioned Stone toward the salon and then to sit down. Stone threaded his way through the décor of period furniture and thick nineteenth-century carpets, dominated by dark reds and blues.

'I have just returned from your old command in the Indian Ocean,' Stone began. 'La Réunion to be specific.'

Elestre ignored this opening. He was staring at the bruised face before him, with compassion perhaps. Curiosity, certainly.

'Rogent tells me you are interested in the Army and that I should help you. What is it you want?'

It was the voice of a man who understood the limits and responsibilities of command. More than that. It was the voice of a man who accepted to choose. Later in the conversation he said: 'We Gaullists are all politicians, not bureaucrats, thanks to our original decision to disobey and enter into sin in 1940.'

'I am trying to find out who killed General Ailleret.'

'I don't know that I can help you on that.'

'You must help me. I have no other possibility. I have not found them, but they have found me. You see my face. The rest of my body is in the same state. I would willingly drop the whole business now but I can't. They wouldn't let me forget.'

Stone himself was unsure to what degree his plea was natural and to what degree a premeditated gamble.

'You've been beaten up, have you?'

'Twice.'

The General looked at him with commiseration. He abhorred violence. It was the privilege of someone who had seen too much.

'Rogent said I should help you. But there isn't much to say.'

'You saw the report by the enquiry team?'

'Yes, but there wasn't that much in it. There were certain implications, certain sentences which did not come to the end of their thought. I think there was even disagreement among the team as to what they should write.

'In any case, there was more than the report; there was also what people said and didn't write because they couldn't prove it.'

'What?'

'Oh, that the plane had been tampered with – which it probably had, but that is not easy to prove. I shouldn't tell you this, but General de Gaulle is dead now and so is everything he stood for. His world evaporated like a mirage and behind it appeared the same old desert we had always known. I sometimes think he might have done better instead of covering up the affair, to publicize it and crush whoever ... you know, there were too many worms tolerated in his day, just to keep the peace. Now that he is gone the worms have become snakes.'

'And who tampered with the plane?'

'That was the problem. That was why I came back alone on a regular flight and handed the report directly to General de Gaulle. There were flies swarming about my head so long as I had the report in my hands. They wanted to know what was in it. They warned me to be careful; to think of my future, etc., etc. The finger pointed in a dangerous direction. The Army was in question. Suppose we had pushed things further and proved that most of the military élite were involved, imagine the consèquences.

'De Gaulle was furious that they should butcher his Chief of Staff as if he were powerless. But he *was* powerless. He didn't dare admit that, so many years after Algeria, the Army was still out of control. So we dropped the subject. Dropped it flat.'

He got up and walked to the windows facing on to the street and the Bois. Somehow, he needed light and air in the middle of this claustrophobic subject. The older Elestre grew the less he could tolerate being closed in by the vicious cobwebs. He swung open a window and put his head out for a moment. Then turned about and called Stone over.

'I suppose those men are following you?' He pointed at Peduc and his assistant waiting a hundred yards down the street.

'Yes, you are very observant.'

'Experience. Nothing more. Those are worms who haven't become snakes. I can smell them from here.' He swung about, closed the window and drew Stone back to their chairs. 'It was a great victory for the mass of the officers – the old Vichy army. It was their final revenge.

'Oh, de Gaulle in his fury named a few more Gaullists to command posts. Fourquet replaced Ailleret. He was a good airman and a good Gaullist. But the officers hated him. He wasn't one of them. He had disobeyed in 1940 and obeyed in 1961. The wrong choices in their view.

'But that didn't change much. There aren't many Gaullists left. They are growing old like myself. And we are a sterile band. There is no second generation. There couldn't be. We are marginals, you see – individuals who know how to say "no". That sort of animal doesn't reproduce. It simply exists or doesn't exist.

'So de Gaulle's fury could only have short-term effects. And the others knew that. They knew they had won. In fact, they were never worried about us. They counted us out almost the day the war ended in 1945. What worried them were men like Ailleret; what you might call the new school. A school which hadn't sinned as we had in 1940 and didn't give a damn for all the class interests and negative traditons which bound the old officer corps together. You might call them opportunists or modern or anything your particular prejudices led you to call them. But two truths everyone had to admit: they were ambitious and they could multiply. So the traditional army put all their effort against that new prolific breed and they won. It was the mass and weight of the old clique.'

'And you said nothing?'

'General de Gaulle wanted silence. I followed his example. I never liked Ailleret, but that wasn't the reason. There didn't seem to be anything to gain by a general blood-letting in those days. I suppose there still isn't.'

'Unfortunately, I have discovered too much to avoid that blood-letting. Theirs or mine.'

'And what is stopping them, Monsieur Stone? Why do they gently beat you up and then follow you meekly about?'

'I have some documents which will spring into print if I disappear. They must find those first. And they are fairly close.'

'Very clever.' Elestre spoke in the same quiet controlled tone. 'I can only make two suggestions. Go to see the members of the enquiry team. One of them – I can't remember which – was much more eager than the others to push things further. I think he did some research on the side. The others were worried about their careers.' He climbed to his feet and left the room. A few moments later he reappeared with a sheet of paper. 'Here are their names. I'm afraid it isn't secret information.' He smiled ironically. 'I believe it was published in a newspaper short of copy. Most of these men are probably in the same jobs, so you should find them easily.'

There were eight names on the paper. Stone folded it and pushed it into his pocket.

'And what is the second suggestion?'

'Ah, now we enter the field of supposition. There is a man called Philippe Courman. He is a prosperous-looking fellow, engaging, with a club foot and a beard. He is also a worm. A worm become a snake. A phoney. He has a certain amount of power in political circles and he carries the credentials of a courageous past which is wholly fabricated. I am one of the few people who know what he is. But you understand that there wasn't much point in my going for his throat. There are too many people like him in power in France.

'The war seemed to throw up a lot of rubbish. Perhaps wars always do. Anyway, Monsieur Courman is what we call in French *un homme de main*. You understand? An executor by force of other men's wishes. Of course he is a very sophisticated specimen. Other men do the work for him. Philippe Courman was at St Denis the day Ailleret died.'

'And?'

'That's all. He had every reason to be there. He's a pillar of the party in power which calls itself Gaullist. He was simply one of many on the island that week. But I know his style. He doesn't cross the world to do minor political fence-mending.' Stone opened his mouth to interrupt, but the General pressed on. 'He was there; that's all. And he employs worms like those two men waiting for you in the street.'

Stone retrieved his steel box from the bank and immediately made copies of General Elestre's tape and of the conversations which had arrived by mail from La Réunion. He sent them and the names of the enquiry team off to Sherbrooke's secretary. The less time lag there was in London the better. He was also more careful about choosing post offices. He went to a large branch on the Champs Élysées to ensure that there were a mass of letters going abroad. He also dropped his envelope in half-way between collection times to ensure it was well buried and, by waiting a moment, in the midst of a group of English tourists who each mailed their words for the family at home.

Chapter Fifteen

In the basement of the post office on the rue des Saints Pères there is a telephone room — a large room walled by booths and dominated by an impatient woman seated majestically in a raised glass box from which she distributes jettons, metal slugs which bring the telephones to life. She is hot because there are neither windows nor fans and the air lies still and stale and heavy. Inside the booths with the door closed the atmosphere is still worse. That was a calvary Stone imposed on himself for most of the afternoon.

He chose a booth with a view on to the stairs. From there he could see whether his tail had or had not dared to come too close. Even so he kept the door closed. It was impossible to judge how far his voice might travel across the murmur coming from the other callers.

There were eight names on Elestre's piece of paper. Five were officers and three were civilians. The civilians were from SLA, the company which did the regular maintenance of the DC6.

Stone wanted to know what each of them was doing four years later. Undue success or undue failure — in fact, anything out of the ordinary — might mean something. He began a series of phone calls to the Ministry of Defence information service and SLA's central office in order to track them down.

At one point in the afternoon his tail came down the stairs, worried by Stone's long absence. Peduc looked about to see if there wasn't a second staircase up which his quarry might escape and then walked across the room glancing into the different phone booths. They caught each other's eye inadvertently and Peduc averted his stare jerkily, nervously as if the man inside was the last man he had expected to see. Stone stared out from his dim coffin at the weedy man, who paused momentarily, then turned about and left.

He had automatically hung up when the other appeared. He now telephoned again, complaining that he had been cut off. A minor clerk at the other end in the Army's information service replied painfully, at first denying that he had been speaking to Stone a few moments before. As always, the simple questions were the most difficult to have answered, and the minor official withdrew within his shell repeatedly as if Stone were after state secrets. For the clerk in question they were state secrets – the secrets of his small private state. Somehow releasing the public information confided to his information department devalued its importance, reduced the securities which it held. Yet by the time the post office closed Stone had found his eight men and by double checking in Paris phone books had found where they lived.

That evening he lay on his bed studying the old list and the new, looking for an indication. The military members had advanced as one might expect. Regularly. Of the three civilians he was less sure. It was extremely difficult to judge, but the second in importance on the list of 1968 had apparently dropped to third position by 1972. His name was Ardant.

There was no guarantee that he was the man for whom Stone was looking. There was only the possibility.

The following morning he went out early, his bruises tender and delicate in the cool air, having swollen to a coloured ripeness which made them sensitive even to the clothes he wore. He carried in one hand the metal box holding all of his papers and tapes and in his left breast-pocket an envelope containing an updated list of the enquiry team. That was to be mailed to Sherbrooke's secretary. He drove slowly across the river under the arcades of the Louvre and dropped the envelope into the box of a post office near the Opéra.

He did not notice that the tail stopped momentarily behind him while one man left the car.

Peduc had begun his morning in a reasonable state of mind. His wife had lain serenely naked beneath the sheets when he awoke at 6 a.m., and resplendent in her plumpness she had not woken while he dressed and slipped quietly out of the bedroom. That was somehow a comforting image to send him on his way, an almost unreal image in the soft early light. Even better, everyone had smiled and been polite in the café across the street when he went in for his breakfast. Days could be made or soured easily at that delicate hour, but it was left untarnished as he stood at the zinc bar drinking a large black coffee and dunking the buttered half of a baguette into it before each mouthful. He liked to watch the globules of melted butter which, as always, soon began floating about on the surface of the coffee. Best of all, he liked to count them, on the understanding that the more globules there were the better his luck would be. This exercise was a daily reminder of the basic precepts of self-control — how difficult it was not purposely to leave the bread longer than usual below the surface in order to help the globules along. That morning there were ten, and ten was a reasonable score.

His luck was confirmed when, sitting in the car beside Marcel Montesquieu, his associate, he looked down at the papers on his lap and saw that Stone was pulling up in front of a post office which appeared on the list. Its director was a former civil servant and black marketeer who was now simply a civil servant. He had joined forces with Courman during the war. Or, rather, had joined Courman's force.

There were six hundred letters in the box that morning. Two hundred of them were addressed to England. Peduc and the Director closed themselves in the latter's office with all of these and began their task. Each envelope had to be opened carefully and quickly resealed to avoid complications later on. It was a long ordeal and only they could do it. As Peduc was ham-fisted most of the job was done by the Director. It was an eight-hour job. That was what the man said, grumbling. Was it really so important?

That Saturday morning Stone's exhaustion caught up with him. If his bruises had not gone away it was because he had tried to ignore them. He decided to disappear for the rest of the weekend to gather the strength he felt he would need to deal with what lay ahead.

But there was something more.

Stone believed he had reached a stage when it was dangerous to let the men who followed him know whom he saw and where he went. He wanted to disappear from their view — in fact, from their existence. He wanted to reassure them or confuse them or at least to get them off his back. He turned behind the Opéra on to the rue Lafayette and headed for the Autoroute to the North.

It was difficult to lose a tail in Paris without a thousand acrobatics and risks. But on the open highway there was no problem. He accelerated as he rolled across Porte de la Chapelle and down the ramp on to the Autoroute. Then he watched in his rear-view mirror as the insistent Peugeot slipped gradually further behind.

The Autoroute was half-empty. He pulled into the fast lane, left his indicator on and pressed down on the pedal until the speedometer read 190 Km/h. He continued past St Denis and the airport of Le Bourget on to the exit at Survilliers, half an hour out of Paris. There was no sign of the Peugeot.

At the exit he cut west on a small road until it crossed a main highway. This he took back toward Paris, leaving it only shortly before the ring road to cut west again just in case his friends were waiting at Porte de la Chapelle. Two exits further on he turned into the ring road itself, the Boulevards de Maréchaux, and drove around Paris to the south. There he found the Autoroute to the South and headed out of the city.

He aimed for a village called St Benoit-sur-Loire. He knew a hotel there run by a young woman. It was a little more than a hotel because the young woman had a certain appeal and a soothing way with a few of her customers. Stone remembered that clearly and felt that soothing was exactly what his body needed to mollify the bruises.

L'Hôtel de la Bienfaisance was not a brothel, not in any way. Odile, the owner, was a lovely girl. She had inherited it too young and been forced to abandon Paris for a population of old men and monks who sang Gregorian chants in the Romanesque monastery which dominated the town. And so from time to time she made a guest more welcome than he expected to be. That was how Stone had discovered her, welcomed into her arms the year before when he stopped for an evening on his way back from a wine-tasting trip in Burgundy.

It was one of those nineteenth-century country hotels, rambling and comfortable and out of date. Odile greeted Stone as if he had left the day before and installed him in a large room overlooking the Loire. It was early afternoon, but he lay back on the bed and tried to draw himself into this tiny world where he might forget what had brought him there and what was waiting in Paris. He could feel that his will was on the verge of giving up, and he knew he couldn't. Oh, he could always escape by going somewhere so far away that they would leave him alone.

No, he wouldn't. He would not give up. Not this time. He would finish the business. He drew down his eyelids and tried to push everything out of his mind. But he could hear his mind whirring, ticking over, going over and over what had been done, what had to be done, how to do it, looking for something he might have missed.

He jumped up from the bed and pushed the two double windows open wide. He could hear the birds over the river as they swarmed and dived or waited on the sandbars which lay tranquilly in the middle of the flowing water. He threw off his clothes and lay back on the bed. There was a high ceiling moulded in plaster and culminating in a simple grapevine, running around the edges with bunches of grapes hanging in each corner. His eyes took in the room. The walls were covered by an old-fashioned flowered paper — faded pink and green. There was a heavy chest of drawers between the two windows.

On the left wall a closed door lay in the centre. He jumped up again and pulled the door open to discover an antiquated bathroom with a long cast-iron bathtub. He twisted the hot tap fully on and added a small measure of cold before dropping into the steaming water, then stayed there for an hour until Odile appeared.

The restaurant was closed downstairs and she brought him a tray with cold asparagus and smoked ham and cold duck beside a large bowl of wild strawberries and a bottle of Pouilly Fumé.

She came into the bathroom and looked at him with a smile. The smile slipped away momentarily at the sight of the battered body with its bruises magnified under the water, then came back. She walked forward, got down on her knees and began to wash him gently as if her fingers might make the blue marks go away. Her hands were not as fine as he remembered, but perhaps that was his imagination. In any case, they were subtle and warm and her breath was tinted by strawberries.

When she had finished she brought the tray and placed it on a wide board over the bath, then disappeared. Stone stayed there for another hour eating, adding more hot water from time to time as he cooled off, absorbing the heat, pulling the duck apart with his fingers and chewing the bones obsessively until not even the hint of a scrap of meat remained on them, dipping the wild strawberries individually into a pot of cream and squashing each on his tongue against the roof of his mouth and drawing the dry white wine down into his system, relaxing muscles and cooling ideas and soothing the edges of his nerves and of his mind. He was beginning to feel better, and as his mind emptied from one side it filled up from the other with Odile. She was a peculiar being; apparently meek and silent, she knew exactly what she was after and took it. It was the meekness of someone getting her way. She wanted Stone in exactly the same way she wanted other men who periodically passed through.

Late that afternoon she came and ministered to him. He had imagined something soothing and discreet, but she came and stood before one of the large open windows, silhouetted by the light coming in low over the water, and in the fawn-shaded atmosphere removed her clothes nonchalantly, dropping them on to a chair. Her skin was white, milky. She did not colour it in the sun like the middle-class sun-worshippers. And her flesh was opulent, rich in the moist air of the low Loire valley. She walked across the room towards his bed, blocking out the sun as she approached. He fixed his view on her navel slightly buried in the flesh like the eye of a storm growing larger until only the eye could be seen and he reached out to pull her down, cupping his hand around her buttocks where it slid over an invisible layer of velvet fur. Like a storm she gyrated about him and he at first lay back surprised — then began to fight to assert himself against the wind.

She became a symbol in which to empty the tension of the last weeks and she asked nothing more as he brought some tension into her banal existence.

She was with him again that evening, and when he awoke late Sunday morning she was gone, organizing the cook and the servers for lunch.

He had thought of going for a walk on the grass-covered dikes of the river. They stretched for miles protecting the rich low farmland behind. He had often stopped to lie on their slopes between St Benoit and the moated château of Sully-sur-Loire, usually with a woman who had come along for the weekend. It went through his mind that Mélanie would enjoy the calm movement which he found there.

In the end he moved no further than the restaurant. Odile suggested he go back to his room after each meal, and he found it difficult to disagree. Like the room, she was ample and warm, and he did not find he could maintain his false sense of inner calm if he stayed alone for very long. In fact, he seemed to lose some of his balance and control in this cocoon.

'So you want me to mend you,' she repeated periodically. 'And how did you come to be knocked about like this?'

She ran her hand over one of his bruises. It was Sunday afternoon.

'What do I care about that? What do I care about my skin?' he almost shouted, suddenly, and rolled over crushing her hand under his side.

She winced and pulled it away in silence.

'What do I care?' he began again after glancing at her freed hand as if surprised that it still existed. He slapped at a thick scab on his chest, surrounded by blue skin, winced at the pain, then looked contemptuously down his body and suddenly with his fingers ripped off the scab.

She gasped and put her hand over the sore where blood ran out and rose between her fingers. She pulled her hand away, looked at the blood on it and then put it back gently.

'Don't,' she said.

'Why do you suppose I came? For my skin or my soul?' He laughed as he asked, but painfully.

She drew her hand away again, got up and crossed the

room.

'Why should I care why you came? Do you suppose I have the space in my life to care about sadistic subtleties? You've come to find a reflection. No, isn't that it? I am a comforting reflection. Allow me the same privilege. I care what I find in you; not what you find in me.'

Stone was staring absently at her and then looked back down at himself. The blood was hardening but still running slowly in two trickles down his side on to the sheet.

'I suppose. And yet the skin and the soul are the same thing; there is no wall of separation. This pain is nothing — only an outer covering to the rest. Why does the rest hurt, I'd like to know.'

'Because you're a fool and a loner,' she said somewhere outside his dream. He looked up and she was sitting in a chair by the window, a sheet or something wrapped around her. 'Don't you suppose I know about that feeling, living my life? The only men I want and get are men I don't know.' He was about to break in, but she continued, 'It's the same fear. You don't realize but you said yourself the skin doesn't count; it's being alone, living in a vacuum. That is the real fear which counts.'

'Is that peasant wisdom?' he said.

She laughed.

'Do you suffer not knowing us? Is it so bad to be alone if you can stand it? Perhaps it's better not to know.'

She shrugged as he finished and came back to the bed.

'Then you must care about your skin.'

'A wrapping to be written upon,' he murmured to close the conversation.

A few moments later she asked: 'Who did it? Why didn't you stop him?'

'He wasn't alone,' Stone replied bemusedly, kissing her brown eyes and then her rather large, soft lips.

'He wasn't alone. That makes more sense.' Odile ran a

hand over his chest muscles. 'He wasn't alone. Were they policemen?'

'No.'

'At least that's a good thing. I had been wondering about that. And why do you want to go back to Paris? They might do it again.'

He reached out and pulled her against him, almost violently.

'I am sometimes a solitary person. Perhaps. That is what you said and that is why I am going back.'

'Do you think you can be a loner sometimes and sometimes not? I think you must be one or the other all the time and anything in between is a pretence. That is why you want to go back, because you pretend badly.'

In the end he lulled himself into staying on Monday and left early Tuesday morning. She woke up as he was dressing, but he pushed five hundred francs into her hand and kissed her and told her to stay in bed.

He drove along the river bank for the first forty minutes. The sun was rising gently through the clouds of river flies which swarmed over the road, filtering his vision and committing suicide by thousands against his windscreen. It was ten o'clock before he was close to Paris and Orly Airport.

Chapter Sixteen

Stone parked his car in a slot marked 'Directeurs seulement' and left a note referring anyone who read it to the office of the 'Directeur Général'.

The technical and maintenance section of the Sociéte des Liaisons Aériennes, known as SLA, was housed not far from the cargo sector of Air France in a large cement hangar. It was built in the severe style of the 1950s, and the offices were stuck on to one wall of the hangar.

The atmosphere inside was bleak as if bleakness were a quality in the world of technicians. The offices either looked on to the inside of the hangar itself or, for more important employees, on to the outer world of unending carparks.

Monsieur Ardant's office gave on to the hangar from the fourth floor, as did that of the secretary he shared with three other engineers; all of them younger than himself. They belonged to another generation which was overtaking him. His secretary was ageing and frustrated, the sort of woman who ends up as secretary to unsuccessful men.

She looked up, surprised to see someone she did not know come through her door. It was rare that men came to see Monsieur Ardant or his colleagues. More often it was they who walked down to the executive offices on the second floor or went out to their appointments.

'What can I do for you?' she asked suspiciously.

'Is this Paul Ardant's office?'

'Yes. Do you have an appointment?' She knew Ardant had no appointments that Tuesday. Nor the next day, nor the next. He was busy checking over the charts of an old Caravelle which had been brought in for a check. If 'busy' was the word. She knew her boss was not an important man. That made it all the more essential to protect him.

'Is he there?'

'Is he expecting you?'

'My dear lady' — Stone leant over her desk heavily with as long a smile as he could manage — 'I asked if he was there.'

She shrank back.

'Yes, but. . . .'

'In that case tell him I have come about General Ailleret. It is important.'

She disappeared in confusion through a door beside her desk and reappeared seconds later.

'Monsieur Ardant will see you.'

She waved him into the next office and slammed the door. There was a tall, nervous man waiting on the other side.

'Sit down,' he ordered curtly. 'What do you mean by barging in here and threatening me?'

'I didn't threaten. I simply wanted to see you.'

'Then why announce that bastard Ailleret's name at the top of your 'voice? Everybody in the bloody office will be talking about it tonight. I share my secretary. Didn't you notice? As if my position isn't bad enough.' He was pacing back and forth before the wall of glass which separated them from the hangar below. The noise of men stripping airplanes came through as muffled background. He spoke quietly without lessening his anger. His voice was controlled to avoid it carrying to the outer office.

'Who sent you? What do you want? Haven't your people done enough harm?'

'I saw General Elestre on Friday. He suggested you might help me.'

'He did, did he? Why didn't he help me four years ago? Why did he leave me for the hatchet-men? It's a bit late now. And how do I know he sent you? Who are you? Show me some proof.'

'I am nobody in particular, Monsieur Ardant. My name is Charles Stone. I represent no one but myself and at the moment I am trying to save my skin. Now, if you will sit down I shall tell you what I want.'

Stone recounted all that he had seen and heard, and all that had happened to him. It took thirty minutes, at the end of which he added: 'Of course, you don't have to believe me. All I might add as proof are my bruises. You can see that they are real. And my story is a bit long and complicated to be an invention. And why should I bother?'

Ardant sat upright behind his desk, apparently thinking. He stared at Stone's right eye, which was still swollen and bloodshot. Stone smiled and pulled up his shirt to reveal a blue patch just below his ribs.

'What do you want from me?'

'The rest of the story. I believe you know it.'

'Not quite, Monsieur Stone. Not quite. I knew and know where to look; but I never looked, not up to the last stage. I was discouraged. You see this stinking little office. That was the reward for my curiosity. And it isn't simply the guilty who keep me here. It was everyone – even de Gaulle and his friends, who wanted to close the affair. They didn't want to know the answers to the questions. They imagined or feared what they might be.'

Ardant had prominent cheek-bones and a wide jaw. His skin was stretched tightly over them and it twitched noticeably on the left side, creasing from the jutting corner of his jaw to the high point of his cheek. Each time he finished speaking his lips appeared to pull down the skin on that side in order to stop it moving. Instead that effort caused a second twitch which distorted the lower half of his face.

'I was an idiot. I didn't realize until it was too late that no one wanted the truth. I went on digging long after the signs to retreat had gone up. I was a bit naïve, a bit young. Justice is not the protection of the honest man in this country.

Silence is his only protection. Discreet silence. This isn't a police state; it's worse. It's a democracy controlled by people who think it's a police state.

'You must learn to shut up and remain unnoticed, do your job and take no responsibilities, drown yourself in the mass. You understand? That is the rest of the story.'

'No. No. You owe me more than that.' Stone leant forward from his chair in the centre of the room and grasped Ardant's arm lying on the metal desk, as if to wake him up.

'Me? What do I owe you?' He tried to draw his arm away.

'I picked up your robe of justice, perhaps for the wrong reasons and, somewhat like you, innocently. Now I can't get the thing off. It has clung to me, tied itself around me for all those interested to see, and so I have to finish the job. Your career was at stake, Monsieur Ardant. It is my life they want.' He released the arm and sat back himself. 'Don't you think that one day they will come back for you? This sort of thing doesn't really die completely. Never. One day it all comes back. By then I shall be gone one way or the other and you will be the only rough spot in their design.'

'Shut up,' he barked in a whisper. 'Shut up.'

He got to his feet and walked over to a small safe flush against the wall furthest from the glass windows. From the bottom of the safe he drew a file, then returned to his desk, sat down and opened it.

'I shall give you some facts,' he began in a neutral voice. 'The plane was a DC6-B. It was the most sophisticated version of the DC6. The unofficial explanation for the accident was this: the plane was overweight and unwieldy in bad weather.' He looked up from his notes. 'The weather was not good, but it wasn't particularly bad' — then lowered his eyes again. 'As for being unwieldy: the DC6-B is designed for a maximum take-off weight of 106,000 lb. Normally that is made up of:

– the airplane empty	54,148 lb
– a fuel capacity of 5,512 US gallons	32,151 lb
– cargo or passengers, normally 64 passengers at, say, 250 lb, baggage and meals included	16,000 lb
– a crew of four, say	1,000 lb
	Total 103,299 lb'

He pushed a chart over to Stone. 'There are still 2,700 lb to spare. Now our airplane took off carrying this:

– the airplane empty	54,148 lb
– 4,755 US gallons of fuel	27,737 lb
– 20 passengers and crew, say	5,000 lb
	Total 86,885 lb

As you see' – he handed him the second chart – 'she was well underweight even if my calculations are conservative.

'Second unofficial argument: the crew was drunk. Now, you may have noticed that there were twelve crew members. That is a very generous double set. How did twelve experienced airmen serving in the special section formed to fly VIPs come to be drunk the night they were flying the Chief of the General Staff?

'Of course there is the great confusion, which you brought up, as to whether they thought the plane was leaving or not. That is hardly an explanation for all twelve of them being incapacitated. And incapacitated to what degree?

'They were sober enough to be considered fit to fly and to actually take off. And yet they were drunk enough to turn the wrong way and commit suicide. You saw the airport. A pilot would have to be blind drunk and a fool to make that mistake. These men were neither.

'So what happened? That was what I asked myself. That was what we all asked. A technical fault? Impossible. That plane is brilliantly simple. In fact, perfect simplicity was the dominant characteristic of all Douglas aircraft in those days. There is nothing which could go wrong or break, causing them to turn the wrong way.

'There is only one other possibility: someone tampered with the machine. All of that we put in the report. But the report stopped there. Or, rather, the other members of the enquiry team stopped there. I went a bit further. All the bits of wreckage were collected up so that the plane could be reconstructed on the floor of a hangar in the Guillot Airport and examined. But I was interested in one piece only, the aileron cross. The ailerons are the flaps on each wing which make the plane tilt and turn. When the aileron on one wing goes up, on the other wing it goes down. They are controlled by cables which run from the pilot back to the aileron cross, which is a small mechanism midway between the two wings, below the cabin floor. The cross in turn feeds out other cables which control the ailerons themselves. That was the piece they had to tamper with.

'I personally searched that sugar-cane field the first day we arrived. The local troops had almost finished clearing the mess by then, but I still found bits and pieces everywhere, including small bits of the passengers which I imagine the others hadn't thought it worthwhile to pick up. When I found what I was looking for, half-buried in the earth, I took it back to the airport. The half which I found was in a terrible mess. It had been twisted out of shape at the moment of the crash. To my eyes it was twisted the wrong way.

'I wanted to show the piece to the rest of the team the next day. Unfortunately it disappeared overnight. The others didn't want to put anything about that in their report. They said it was hearsay. But I told Elestre and I imagine he told de Gaulle.'

Ardant stopped talking and closed his file. Stone waited, then couldn't wait any longer. 'Is that all?' His voice rang in the sparsely furnished room, bouncing off the metal filing cabinet, the cheap tiles, the metal wall partitioning.

'Not quite. To tamper with an airplane is not a common criminal act. You have to know how to do it. Almost by curiosity I was drawn to find out who on that island could have done it. There weren't many. I made a list.' He pulled a sheet of paper from the back of his file. His cheek was twitching violently and he managed a small tortured smile. 'No one else has ever seen this list. No one even knows about it. Nevertheless it was my prying into how many technicians there were on the island that very special day which started the trouble.

'Suddenly people began to notice me and take an interest in me. I was warned off by the other team members in a friendly way. Oh, in a very friendly way, brother to brother, professional to professional, the initiated to the initiated, nervous bureaucrat to nervous bureaucrat. Then I was cautioned by a few officials on the island. Discreetly, you understand. And then I received two threatening notes. Would you like to see one?'

He drew out a piece of paper written on in an untidy scrawl of black ink. The message was unsophisticated and clear. There was a small drawing of a man with his head cut off. Beneath it the name PAUL ARDANT was printed in capital letters. Stone handed back the note.

'But who exactly warned you?'

'Don't worry about them. They were simply passing on the message. Telling me not to play detective because they wanted to keep the hypocritical peace. It was something for the police to deal with, not me. When we got back to Paris I noticed that the police weren't looking into anything, so I asked some questions. That was when they gave me this nice

little job. It had its desired effect. It helped me to understand.'

'But who demoted you?'

Stone leant forward again, then stood up and placed his
back against the glass pane which stopped him from falling
four floors on to the wing of the Caravelle below. He began
to tap the glass with his fingers, and it shuddered slightly at
each touch. Ardant ignored this and remained at his desk,
looking past Stone out into the empty rafters of the hangar.

'Oh, my superiors, my friends, nobody in particular. There
is no need to dramatize. Whether they were pushed by fear or
specific threats from the Government or from the Army or
from I don't know who. . . . A mystery. But I understood
and I shut my mouth. I wasn't quite alone. The deputy chief
of army security in Paris was close to Ailleret. He would
automatically have known what was cover-up and what not.
One week after the crash he was fired from his job and sent
to command a reserve depot in Normandy. Poor fellow. I
suppose I should be grateful.'

'Why didn't you change companies?'

'Oh, I tried that' — Ardant laughed weakly — 'last year and
the year before. But my reputation had arrived before me, so
to speak. I was not a desired piece of merchandise. So I
remain in my impressive office, protected by the gentle
dragon you met outside and forgotten. I always hoped they
would completely forget and let me escape, but you are right.
I am the rough spot in somebody's view of the world, even
up here.'

He was much calmer. That was the way he passed his time;
resignation was an acquired taste.

'What does this paper mean?'

Stone was standing over the desk and holding up the list of
fifteen names.

'Every one of those men would have known how to switch
over the aileron cross. I imagine that one of them is the man

you are looking for.'

'Which one?'

'I don't know. Myself I should eliminate the first four. They were on the airport staff. They are nice old boys, probably the same ones you met. I don't believe it was them, or any other local. Nor these officers.' He indicated two names. 'They are too important and too senior. It is a young man's job, climbing quickly into a tiny compartment, then using both his muscle and his skill.'

'Which one do you think it was?'

Ardant paused, bent over the list like a child playing a game. With quick short jabs he put a cross beside three names.

'Why?' Stone asked.

He pointed at the first name.

'This one arrived on the plane that morning with Ailleret and Elestre and all the others. He had arrived from Paris at our base in Madagascar a few days before. There didn't seem to be much reason for his being brought along to La Réunion. And he certainly would have known what to do.'

His hand slid down to the second name.

'This fellow arrived on La Réunion a few days before. He also came from the base on Madagascar. I found out he had been in Paris for two days the week before. He had come over from Madagascar to do a check of the airport.'

'What did you say?'

'He was sent to confirm Guillot Airport's military capacity. That is a regular formality. Only it usually happens in June, not March.'

'How do you know he had been in Paris?'

'He told me. I met him before he went back to Madagascar. He was quite eager to meet me and to hear about our investigation. It was professional interest. I told him about the twisted aileron cross. He was one of the few people I told. He seemed to know what he was talking about. A very nice young man, if he wasn't the one.'

'What was he like?'

'Pretty average. Thin. Perhaps a bit tall.'

'That's him. I'm sure. It fits in with what I was told on the island.'

'Well, there you are. Unfortunately, there isn't much reason for him to admit it. Or, more important, to tell you whose orders he followed.'

Stone remained silent. Eventually Ardant pulled himself together and got to his feet.

'Good. Apparently you don't want to know about the third, so you now have everything. Go away and leave me alone.'

'I may need your help again.'

'You forced your way in. I've given you what you want. Now leave me alone. If you stay much longer I shan't have any job at all.'

Stone did not go home that evening. He checked into a large new hotel near the airport. It was perfectly anonymous in its plastic majesty. He asked nothing more. There he began looking for the man on the list.

Chapter Seventeen

Courman's Saturday had been an uncomfortable day — a worrying day, and worry for Courman was a more uncomfortable sensation than for most men. It was a sensation he had banished from his world years before, or at least he had consciously pretended that it was banished. The question which dogged him that morning was where to find his subject. The germ had jumped from the microscope slide and, focus as they might on the world under examination, the germ would not reappear.

Peduc's assistant had reported the blue Alpine missing after watching it speed away beyond Porte de la Chapelle. And then nothing.

Shortly afterwards there had been a slightly cheering call from Peduc himself to announce that they had stopped a letter. All they had to do was find it in a sack of several hundred.

Unfortunately that took a full eight hours, exactly as the Director had feared. It was one of the last envelopes they opened. There was one sheet of paper inside and on it was a list of eight names followed by addresses. It was headed 'Enquiry Team Status as of 1972'. There was no signature and no covering note. Simply the paper. Peduc jumped into a taxi and delivered it to Courman.

Courman guessed without great difficulty that Stone had gone to see one of them. But he decided to wait before finding out which one. He didn't want to approach them directly over the weekend. If someone was helping Stone, he would hardly admit it. On Monday they could begin checking the members without their knowledge to see what they had been up to.

In the meantime he concentrated on setting the London end of the operation in motion. The intercepted letter was addressed to a Miss Margaret Cotter in north London. It seemed unlikely that she was the real destination. He therefore concluded that hers was a covering address. She was being watched within a few hours, and Courman had a general biography of her by late Sunday evening.

All that time, Stone's disappearance was nagging at him. On Monday they began to investigate the enquiry team. They began with Le Bourget Airport because Stone had disappeared towards the north. By the end of the day Courman's men had discovered nothing and he redirected them towards the other members. Ardant had been on his mind since Saturday, but no more than the others. They had all been troublemakers in one way or another and Ardant, who had already been beaten into obedience, was a less likely suspect than someone who had escaped lightly in 1968 and could therefore afford the easy moral compunctions of a later day.

It was mid-Tuesday afternoon before they had any luck. Courman had a friend who worked for SLA at Orly. He had asked questions and listened carefully and had soon come upon a talkative secretary who confirmed proudly that she had seen Monsieur Stone. What was more, he had seen Monsieur Ardant.

Early Wednesday morning Courman paid a personal visit on Ardant. It was the first time they had met. He explained that Stone was a troublemaker and therefore the authorities wanted to know what they had been talking about. He insisted in his most vaguely sinister way.

Ardant didn't lie. He knew that anything inconsistent would only make them more suspicious. He said Stone had come about the Ailleret accident, but he hadn't been able to help him. Their enquiry was still classified material.

When Courman left, repeating firmly that the subject was

considered dead and anyone who stirred things up was asking for trouble, Ardant agreed wholeheartedly. He waited a few moments, then looked up General Elestre in his address book and telephoned. There was no answer. He could think of no other way to contact Stone. He tried again an hour later and regularly through the day. Unfortunately, Elestre had gone to the country for the week.

Pierre Dehal would have loved to do the same, but he was not retired and had already extended his weekend longer than intended. He drove back to Paris that Wednesday morning, rested and contented and generally pleased with life. On arrival he telephoned Courman, just to see if there was anything new.

Stone spent his morning in the airport hotel, trying to trace Roland Bertiaud. He might even, had he glanced from his window at 8.30 a.m., have noticed Courman's black Citroën rolling silently out to Orly, Courman in the back meditating over a sheet of paper.

If he did not, it was because time was short. There was no R. Bertiaud in the telephone directory. He made a series of calls to telephone information asking for the number of Monsieur Roland Bertiaud in Montrouge, Vanves, Malakoff and so on through all the suburbs of Paris.

There was no guarantee that he lived in the Paris region; any more than not finding him in the directories meant that he didn't. Half the telephones in Paris were listed under incorrect names.

He tried the armed forces information service. They passed him to a sergeant who had the lists of retired officers. He confirmed that there had been a Roland Bertiaud in the Air Force until 1970. He had resigned in the middle of that year and had not even maintained his 2nd Category status. He had cut all ties with the forces. They had no address.

By the end of the morning Stone had exhausted his

imagination. He checked out of the hotel after making an arrangement with the desk to leave his own car in their garage. He told them it was running unevenly and he didn't have time to take it in to a specialist garage that week. They accepted his story sympathetically and rented him a Renault 16. He wanted to remain anonymous.

That afternoon he tried a series of sources in Paris, most of them were associations of retired officers. He also asked François de Maupans to check the common lists which passed through the Company Directors' Organization and himself tried the different Caisses des Cadres which offer Executive Benefits. There was no indication to that effect, but perhaps Bertiaud had become a businessman.

Just before 4.30 he called on a group called the Association of Officers in Civilian Life. It was a private group which welcomed retired officers and helped them find jobs in civilian life. In return each new member helped the following crop to find places. In fact, they generally patted each other on the back whenever it could be useful.

Many of their members had had contacts with the OAS and had been 'retired' early by Ailleret. There was a distinctly anti-Government air about the organization. That Stone knew. But they were not openly political. They were everything except that. Difficult circumstances had taught them discretion. Discretion and secrecy.

Stone knew one of their five hundred members. By uttering that name he gained entrance to their central office in a turn-of-the-century house on a small street in the 17th Arrondissement.

The house had been built after the style of a miniature German castle on the Rhine by a biscuit manufacturer in private atonement for the French defeat at the hands of the Prussians in 1870. He had made his money selling *biscuits fins* to the occupying enemy army. Stone was met at the door by what could only be a retired sergeant. He was led up

a badly painted staircase to the first floor and into a large
office. There were no furnishings. Only bare floors and walls
with a few old desks and chairs pushed into each corner as if
to get them out of the way. Stone found it hard to believe
that these retired officers wielded as much power as he knew
they did.

Before him were two middle-aged men, both with closely
cropped hair and the uncomfortable air of having taken too
much exercise for their age. Their suits lay nervously over
their bodies, pushed out of shape by dry muscles bulging
unexpectedly. They were discussing a member who had a
good post in the largest of the French banks, the Crédit
Lyonnais. He was having difficulties finding a spot for a
young, recently retired major sent to him by the Association.
They broke off as Stone appeared.

He explained that he was looking for an old friend, an
officer he had known abroad. He had lost all contact but had
been told that the fellow might be a member of their group.
Neither of the men recognized the name. They checked in
their annual. He wasn't a member. They checked in their
files. No, he had never applied for membership. There were
not too many airmen on the list. Being technicians they had
no difficulty looking after themselves in civilian life without
any brotherly help.

'We do have a former pilot on our staff. Now, he might be
able to help you. He knows everyone in the Air Force. They
are a snotty little closed shop. If Georges joined us it was
because of his politics, because he wouldn't sell out. Wait
here while I fetch him.'

The man who had spoken disappeared with energetic
strides through a door and reappeared a minute later with
another man. He was younger, in his late thirties and wearing
a shabby dark suit which made him resemble an unsuccessful
businessman.

The new arrival looked at Stone with curiosity. 'You want

to see Bertiaud?' he asked rhetorically, then fell silent before beginning again. 'I knew him. In fact, I served with him. A bit different from the others. He was one of the rare Algérie-Française officers in the Air Force.'

'Apart from you,' one of the others remarked.

'Most of the pilots were with de Gaulle and Fourquet, but Bertiaud didn't give a damn about being with the majority. He even got involved in the active groups. The OAS, you know; they were the ones who weren't going to be cheated by de Gaulle and his politicians. The Secret Army. They tried to assassinate the bastard and unfortunately missed.'

Stone indicated that he already knew about the OAS.

'Funny, really. Bertiaud was younger than most of us. He had only just got his commission when he arrived in Algeria − let me see, it must have been in late 1960. Funny he got so excited about things. Most of the army officers were against de Gaulle because he wanted to destroy all they had built in Algeria. But Bertiaud hadn't built anything, he hadn't even been there until he was sent by the Air Force that year. Typical. You know the sort − only virgins understand love, only civilians really want war and only intellectuals really know how to hate. He was a bit of an intellectual. He talked a lot about people's rights and how de Gaulle was a traitor. A bit of an idealist, I suppose. Talked too much.

'I saw a lot less of him after that. Different paths. All I know is he never got caught, but his career sort of dried up. I guess he had talked so much that Ailleret and his boys were on to him, although they didn't kick him out. He seemed to be fairly well protected. I used to see him from time to time until he quit in 1970. Then I lost track.'

Stone shrugged in disappointment.

'Well, not completely. I ran into him about six months ago, here in Paris. I wouldn't have recognized him if he hadn't come up to me. He had completely changed. The little intellectual had become a successful man. You could really smell it – the money, I mean. I tried to get him interested in our association. A guy like that could do us a lot of good. But he wasn't interested; he wouldn't even tell me what he did. Just wanted to talk about old times. I haven't got time for that kind of useless sentiment.'

'You don't know where I can find him?'

'He gave me his address, wrote it on a bit of paper, said we had to get together. He was just as big a mouth as ever. Let's see.' He began going through bits of paper in his wallet: old cards, scraps. 'Yes, there you are. No. No. Take the paper. I don't want it. He's no use to us.'

Stone bowed out as quickly as possible.

The Place des Victoires is a particularly good address. Not far from the Louvre and the Palais Royal and the Banque de France, it is an example of eighteenth-century architecture at its best. Graceful and balanced, the circle of stone façades glance down on a statue of Louis XIV waiting on a rearing horse.

By six o'clock Stone had discovered that Bertiaud lived on the third floor of Number 13. The concierge had told him that, and also by inference that he lived alone. It was apparent she did not like Bertiaud. He was difficult. Uncommunicative – a terrible sin in the eyes of a concierge. All the more so as she implied that he definitely had things to say. Was he in? The concierge looked out into the Place. Yes, his car was there. She pointed. It was a silver-grey Mercedes sports model.

Stone placed himself in a café next door and waited. He was in a hurry, but it would do no good to go too quickly at the last moment. The sky was cloudy and he could see the lights burning on the third floor.

After an hour, the windows darkened. A few moments later a man appeared on the street. Stone thought at first it was the wrong man. He was waiting for someone thin and agile. Instead a fat, heavy form filled the entrance, walked to the Mercedes, put a package in it, then returned to the pavement and headed for the café where Stone sat.

No, he wasn't so much fat as dissipated. His weight hung on a thin man's form. His face was unhealthy — white, and yet dominated by a smile as he was greeted by the staff of the café. The owner automatically poured him a double Armagnac; a good Armagnac. They began laughing together. Bertiaud was obviously considered a jovial man, a classically jovial fat man.

Stone watched him in the reflections of the mirrors which lined the walls. The lines on his face were at odds with his smile. They were sad and grotesque. It was a clown's face.

He was dressed in a heavy, blue wool suit. His shirt was silk. He wore a dark cashmere coat, long and double-breasted. It was scarcely the picture of a retired officer. He had, as his former friend had pointed out, a prosperous air; the air of a man fifty years old. He was at most thirty-five.

From the café he drove to a florist's on rue St Honoré and bought himself a rose for his buttonhole. And then to the Crillon bar where he drank another Armagnac and stayed talking to some journalists who hung out there. Stone followed carefully behind. At the Crillon, Bertiaud gave the doorman one hundred francs for the privilege of leaving his car on the kerb and his shadow was obliged to follow suit.

From a corner of the room Stone guessed that the journalists were bar-friends and not Bertiaud's real friends. Half of Paris knew that they had long hung out there, fashionable ageing bar-flys, in order to talk about horses, the mention of which seemed to bring a faint glimmer of light to Bertiaud's eyes. An hour later he left his immovable acquaintances and walked around the corner to a restaurant where he dined. From there he drove on to a nightclub at Montparnasse. He was given an elaborate welcome and led to

a comfortable seat in the centre of the room. There he sat, a
wax effigy examining everyone, even Stone, who was obliged
to submit to this stare. The girls, whom Stone guessed were
the club's regulars, apparently knew Bertiaud. They came
over with enthusiastic greetings, sat down for a few moments
chatting until they saw he wasn't going to buy them a drink,
then went looking for new customers.

Stone peered about himself. He was in a corner to the side
of the room. The walls were lacquered deep red and the
lighting filtered through cream-coloured naked glass ladies
fixed here and there against this pure background. Most of
the tables were crowded, occupied by a mincing crowd,
slightly overdressed.

After half an hour a feeble cabaret began on a small stage
raised a foot above the floor. The nightclub was meant to be
lesbian and each little act had a woman in the man's role.
Nothing very exciting, a bit tatty and vulgar, the highlight
being an Othello-and-Desdemona death scene with a very
chesty red-head. As far as Stone could see she smothered
Desdemona with her breasts.

After that there was some dancing to a three-man band.
The vacated stage became the dance-floor, and Bertiaud
wallowed around it twice with two different girls. They hung
gratefully to him and gyrated their abdomens against his
loose form dutifully before being dismissed one after the
other. Without changing his bored expression he then
wallowed back to his place. One of them came over and sat
down with Stone. At first he thought Bertiaud had sent her;
but, no, she simply wanted a drink, and Stone bought her
one to pass the time. She was from Lyon and told him about
life at home with her father in the police and her uncle a
pimp. It was a comfortable situation but a bit claustrophobic.
That was her word. She had read an article on the psychology
of girls in the public eye. That was also her phrase.

Bertiaud didn't seem to enjoy himself and yet it was two

o'clock before he went home. Stone followed him back to the Place des Victoires and then himself checked into the Hôtel Meurice, which had been German headquarters during the Second World War occupation of Paris. It was too late to find a small hotel and he did not want to go home.

He was sure that Bertiaud would be a late riser so he slept deeply, calmly somewhere in another world, until the desk woke him at 7.30 as instructed. He had time for a leisurely breakfast in bed surrounded by plaster wood panelling before going out to take up his position again below Bertiaud's flat.

It was a cloudy Thursday, 29 June. The Mercedes was still parked outside Number 10. Stone waited in his car on the other side of the Place. He tried to follow more discreetly than those who had followed him. His only desire was to be an obsequious shadow.

Philippe Courman was up well before either of them. He had a series of conferences that morning. His quarry had disappeared on Friday, and that was a long time ago. All they had discovered in the interval was Stone's visit to Orly.

His London agents were getting on well with tying up the letter. That was all very well, but where was Stone?

In his frustration Courman had asked Dehal to pay him a visit. Dehal had been particularly agitated. He paced about the paper-laden room, and each time he was behind Courman, who could move only with difficulty, he would repeat, 'Well, find him for God's sake!' which Courman found tiring and not very helpful.

The other conferences he held were with the leaders of the different branches of his organization. He was bringing them into his search. A nightclub-owner succeeded a Deputy who succeeded a pimp who succeeded the Mayor of an arrondissement and so on. Like an unofficial cross-section of society, they followed each other into the flat. They were given descriptions and photographs of both Stone and his blue Alpine.

They did not constitute a police force, although they included certain sections of the police and other control agencies, both legal and illegal. If they found nothing by the next morning, Courman had decided to set the DST, the State's internal control agency, and the Préfecture de Police in motion. Dehal would help him with that.

Chapter Eighteen

At precisely eleven o'clock, Bertiaud appeared in the street and climbed into his car. He was dressed in grey and shone with the same elegance as on the previous day. He drove out of the Place and headed across Paris toward the Bois de Boulogne. Stone shook himself out of a bored stupor and followed.

There was racing that day at St Cloud, and that was where Bertiaud was going. He lunched alone at the course and then wandered over to the paddock where he seemed to know most of the attendants. He talked to them about the horses running in the next race – it was the second – then placed some money and wandered back to watch it. On the way he began running into friends. No, they were acquaintances, as in the Crillon bar. This time they were race-track regulars who had nothing else to do. The first was an old woman in a flowered hat whom he called Duchesse and who floated about like an ancient butterfly, refusing stubbornly to turn back into a caterpillar. The next was apparently an owner who measured his words in order not to waste too much wind on a mere placer of bets. Bertiaud went with him to the owner's enclosure and stayed there until the last race at five o'clock, making only quick sorties to place more money. He bet heavily and appeared to win moderately.

From St Cloud he drove back across the river to the Bois de Boulogne. Half-way through the woods he turned off to the right on to a small road. A few hundred yards along the road he stopped before a small red-brick house with 'Café – Restaurant' written up on the outside. There were several like it in the Bois, hidden in the trees; country inns except that they were on the walls of Paris. Stone left his car a short distance away pulled up among the trees.

Their clients were not passing strangers. There was no reason for anyone simply to pass through those parts of the woods. They were regular customers who found there a small world of their own.

This particular restaurant was a favourite of the prostitutes who worked in the forest. There they met their customers or came to warm up on a cold afternoon or to celebrate at the end of a good day. Their pimps dropped them off outside its door in late morning in time to catch the lunch-hour trade and came to pick them up in the evening, often staying long enough to drink a glass of cognac.

They were a special brand of girl; figures from a grotesque fairy tale, strolling through that rural scenery in tight leather boots, plastic raincoats and false eyelashes.

Perhaps it was the 'amusing' contrast which drew Bertiaud. He could have afforded better but he obviously preferred these tough women with character to the much more than pallid nightclub version of the night before. Half their work was done outdoors, often standing up. Clients who would pay for a room were rare.

Madame Montjoie, the café-owner, kept a room on the first floor for such rare occasions. She was reimbursed by the girls' pimps at the end of the day on the basis of fifty per cent. As far as she was concerned, that service was a sideline, a small extra which she offered to please her customers. Her main profession was restauratrice.

Stone glanced through a window from the garden. He could see a woman sitting behind the bar on a very high stool. It was Madame Montjoie. She wore a coral-coloured dress which matched the coral-tiled floor and coral-painted walls. She was taller seated than standing and she therefore passed the days seated to maintain such dominance over her clients as she apparently felt a hostess should have. Beside her, also behind the counter, stood her daughter who was plump with short legs and muscled calves. She was born for the trade; that is, her mother's trade of running a bar.

Madame Montjoie was also short of leg, as her tall stool suggested. Her calf-muscles had untensed over the preceding ten years. Her legs were now relaxed, extremely relaxed, even limp. Her face was one of innocence – professional innocence and perpetual interest in what everyone had to say. That was the summit of her trade: listening to excerpts from paying clients' lives.

There were perhaps a dozen people spread about the room. Stone could just hear the conversation of four women at a table near the window. One of them was saying loudly: 'I've had my arse tattooed.'

There was a minor uproar among her friends.

'Shall I tell you what they put? "BITE ME"!'

There was general laughter, and someone called out: 'Which cheek, Pauline?'

'Both, and it tickled when they did it. But, you know, it was a butterfly I had always wanted.'

There was more laughter. Bertiaud stood at the bar finishing a glass with a black-rooted blonde who was caressing his arm. A few moments later they disappeared through a door which Stone guessed led to the stairs.

As he walked away from the window to wait at a discreet distance, one of the girls appeared out of the woods. She noticed Stone. She thought she recognized his face. She had seen it only that morning in a photograph when her pimp came back from a visit to his boss. But, no, it probably wasn't him. He should have had a blue Alpine; she had also been shown a photograph of the car. This man was walking toward a very ordinary grey Renault, so she put it out of her mind for the time being. It was far more important to find another client.

*

There was warmth in the air that evening and Stone passed the next hour walking under the surrounding pines. He felt he was now beginning to understand Bertiaud. The man had been lean and no doubt tough. Now he was fat and bored and, more important, had probably been untried for the last two years. Whatever he had done in the past had earned him his comfortable retirement, but comfort weakens the spirit and the reflexes.

Stone knew that to get what he wanted he would have to break the man and the only way to do that was to do it quickly, suddenly. If the fellow had time to think, he would resist. That Stone knew from Malaysia and from close observation in other colonial wars. The same man could either be broken in five minutes or five days, but rarely in between. Surprise was the key, and in Stone's case five minutes was a necessity.

He turned this over as he inhaled the evening air and scuffed his feet against the scrub grass. The light was beginning to fade when Bertiaud reappeared.

He pushed open the door with an over-eager thrust and strode out as if he had lost a heavy load. Stone waited in the distance while the man came down the steps, then hesitated momentarily. Instead of heading for his car, he turned left from the bar and walked through the prim little garden surrounding it toward the woods.

Stone could only guess, but he imagined that this was one of Bertiaud's habits. It completed his amusing contrast. Having left the heavy clutch of the cheapest, hardest, most urban-waste girl in the bar, he liked to lose himself suddenly in the surrounding nature and breathe in a measure of fresh air.

He strolled down a dirt pathway, flicking with his hands at various overhanging leaves, flicking them back, flicking back the world. Stone followed cautiously behind. Beneath the trees the remaining light was severely shaded. The body before him rolled on, a contented darkening elephant.

At a certain point it stopped. One of the large hands already extended toward a leaf was brought back and held beneath the nose. In the silence Stone could hear him sniffing at his fingers, smelling the woman — mm, crusty, eh? — he laughed gently as he whispered almost to himself. Then he walked on, sniffing, waving his fingers in the air, smelling again.

There was a small stream before him. He put his perfumed right hand in the air and with his left drew the rose from his lapel. He sniffed it, a long deep breath as if he wanted to inhale the entire flower, then held the rose away and brought the other hand back to test his fingers again, delicately. He smelt each alternately, comparing them, mumbling, and eventually threw the rose into the stream.

With long silent strides Stone came up behind him in the semi-darkness.

'Bertiaud!'

The man twisted his head about without moving his feet and Stone struck him hard twice. The pallid face collapsed without further coaxing, a sinking formless balloon. The fragrant hand fell back into the stream where it bathed in the cloudy water. Stone heaved the weight up from the dirt on to his shoulder and made through the trees to his car.

Chapter Nineteen

Bertiaud awoke in darkness.

He was seated, his hands tied behind his back. His jaw ached. He tried to move. Immediately a light burst into his eyes and he shut them in pain. He sensed that there was someone beside him and then realized that he was in a car.

'Bertiaud,' the shadow whispered.

'For God's sake!' he managed to say.

'I've come about Ailleret.'

'For God's sake,' he began again, the voice trembling. The flashlight moved closer again as he tried to open his eyes. 'Who are you?'

'Courman sent me.'

'Courman? He must be crazy.' There was a hint of relief in his voice. 'I've still got the paper. I'll fix him, by God! He knows that.'

Stone tried to fathom the meaning quickly. If he lost the initiative, the other would realize it was a bluff. He plunged desperately.

'We've got Courman too.' There was a gasp from his prisoner. 'Why do you think I'm here? We've got him, but he saved his skin.'

'What? He put you on to me? That won't save him.'

Stone moved his flashlight to within inches of the other's eyes and slapped him hard on the face. There was just enough room in the front of the Renault for a little swing and Fontaine's nose began to bleed.

'No. It won't save him. Nothing could save him. But it won't save you either.' He spoke in a cold whisper.

'Oh, listen—'

Stone slapped him again.

'What do you want? I can defend myself. Just tell me what you want.'

'Start with the details.'

'What?'

'Everything.'

'But if you—'

Stone slapped him a third time, harder. The blood was dripping down from the nostrils to his lips and rolling slowly to each corner of his mouth before sliding down to his chin and neck.

'Please. All right.'

Stone pulled a handkerchief out of the man's pocket and wiped the face.

'Start with Courman.'

'Yes. Yes. All right, I . . . I went to Algeria in 1960. I was against the Government; I believed we ought to keep Algeria. In 1961 I . . . I joined the Secret Army. That wasn't very difficult. Anyone could do that.'

'Come on. Come on. If you think I'm going to wait while you stall.'

'All right. Don't hit me.' The large silhouette tried to edge away while turning its face in appeal to the invisible threatening voice. He smelt of a sweetish eau-de-Cologne, mixed with a sour odour of sweat and his breath which was tinged with the whisky he had obviously been drinking that afternoon. His breath came each time he spoke. 'I met a man in the OAS. Another officer. I didn't know then, but his real boss was Courman. We mounted an operation together. Four of us. We shot General Castal and two other bastards with him who had sold out to de Gaulle. They were minor political hacks.'

Stone placed the tape recorder on the dashboard and switched it on. He had pulled the Renault up into the trees in a deserted part of the Bois near Neuilly.

'Three months later Courman changed sides. He arranged for my friend to be shot. The poor fellow was too compromised in too many things. And he kept my friend's papers. There was enough there to cut off my head three times, do you understand? I only discovered all of that afterwards. At the time I didn't even know Courman existed.

'One day an army goon squad picked me up. We were all caught sooner or later. I was dumped in a cell in Avignon for a week, in the dark most of the time with a bit of basic food pushed through a slot in the door and not one visitor. Then Courman appeared. He showed me the documents scavenged from the loyal supporter he had murdered. They were my death warrant. He offered me a deal. I would be freed, and evidence of my being picked up would be destroyed, if I agreed to work for him.

'What do you expect? By God, I was even grateful that he paid me well. In the next three years I did a few illegal jobs for him, so when all the amnesties came for Algerian offenders I was still in his power.

'That was his method.' He coughed. 'For God's sake, I've got blood in my mouth.'

Stone shoved the man's head down between his knees, heard him spitting and left him like that for a moment before jerking him back up. He had drawn the light away but now shone it close again to get Bertiaud talking.

'That was his method. Nobody works for Courman purely by devotion or for money. He always gets something on them for extra security, and he usually needs it because he doesn't believe in anything. He changes sides as regularly as most men piss.

'Then he left me alone a bit and let me get on with my life. But I always knew he was there. He and his friends kept me in the Air Force. My career was dead, but I was more useful to them there.

'In 1967 I was sent to the Indian Ocean, to our base on

Madagascar, a bloody good place. It was a long way away from Courman and there were plenty of planes I could take up whenever I wanted. In February the next year I was ordered back to France for a few days. In Paris I saw a general in Personnel who said I was to be promoted and asked me where I wanted to serve. Supposedly that was the reason I had been brought back. It was pretty strange, but I understood the next day when Courman paid me a visit. He told me they were planning to do in Ailleret. I asked who "they" were, but he wouldn't say more than that. I was to be his man. Ailleret was coming to Madagascar and maybe La Réunion. They wanted me to provoke an accident, an accident, you see. And they wanted it done out there where things aren't quite so closely watched.

'It was up to me to choose the method and the moment. I wasn't especially eager, so I said: "And if there isn't an opportunity?" He told me to find one. I couldn't understand what his real interest in the affair was but I found out afterwards. There was a general who had stuff on him. Funny, eh? The blackmailer blackmailed. He was forcing Courman to help because he and his friends were a bit reticent. They didn't have his fine touch for crime. Courman agreed on one condition. He wanted to equalize their positions. He wanted a letter from this general setting out their deal – a sort of order to execute Ailleret. The general agreed in the end because Courman wouldn't budge. Anyway, the paper could never be used. His name was on it. So was Courman's. It was a double death certificate.'

'Who was the general?'

'Ha!' The pasty cheeks rose in a mock laugh cracking the blood dried on them. From the side Stone saw a large slit open up in the front of the silhouetted head. The faint light of the night shone through so that it resembled the head of some prehistoric animal. 'Is that what you want?' 'That's right, Bertiaud.' Stone slapped at the face. 'If you are very

clever, you might just save yourself. You don't think we want
little rats like you.'

'Stop it. Please. Pierre Dehal. Dehal.' The voice was a
whine. 'Ha!' The jowls rose again. 'I hear he's up for Chief of
Army Staff. Ha! Reward of the just. But he's not your man.
He's just a mouthpiece for the rest of the bastards. You
understand that. You can't hang an army, or even half the
senior officers. You don't imagine he thought the thing up on
his own.'

'Just let's start with Dehal. We'll look after the rest.'

'Ha! I'd like to see. . . . A colonel representing Dehal
arrived on the same plane as Ailleret from Madagascar. I told
him my plan and he showed me the letter just to prove that it
existed. The deal was that he would hand it over the moment
Ailleret was dead, and the guarantee was that if he didn't I
would kill him. It was hardly a foolproof set-up but it was the
best each side could get. Courman arrived half an hour later
on the same plane as the politicians. It wouldn't have done
for me to be seen with him, so one of his local thugs, a fellow
called Tocqueville – can you believe it? – carried the message to him that everything was all right.

'The Colonel made sure no special guard was placed on the
plane. In France it's automatic, but out there the occasions
are so rare that someone has to order it. All he did was make
sure the order wasn't given. As soon as night fell I went to
the airport. It was foul weather. Dark, raining. I got into the
plane and it only took a second to get the carpeting up and
the opening into the compartment over the wings unscrewed.
You want to know about that?'

'The exact details.'

'That's the only good part. In the compartment there is
the aileron cross. It controls the ailerons, therefore the
direction. Two cables come back from the pilot. That's his
control. They are half a small finger thick and under about
eighty pounds' pressure. They have screw joints which you

loosen to take off the pressure; all you need is a ratchet. Then I unhooked the two cables, loosened them off their maximum and inverted them. There is just enough give in the joints to do that if you add a bit of muscle. Then I tightened them back up to a decent pressure. The whole thing took twenty minutes. After that I went to the party given for the crews. The Colonel had arranged for them to think Ailleret would be staying over. All he wanted to do was to get them a little loosened up, dull down their reactions.'

'And what was his name?'

'Oh, that doesn't matter. Dalbot. He's dead now. Was killed in a shooting accident two years ago. Funny thing, eh? Anyway, the party was his idea because he didn't believe my plan was sure. He thought the pilot might save the situation – a lot of rubbish but, then, he wasn't a pilot. So I went along to encourage the crew to have a few drinks. As they thought they were staying, they got a bit carried away and drank too much. All but one of them, who stuck to fruit juice. Then the word came through that Ailleret wanted to go. There was a panic and they sent a message saying the weather was too bad.

'Apparently, Ailleret almost gave in, although he was eager to get back to Paris to claim his new powers.' Bertiaud sensed the other tense. 'Yes, I know about that. Even a rat like me knows the reason why. But the Colonel got to him and hinted that the three Chiefs of Staff were putting pressure on de Gaulle not to come through with the new powers.

'That was it. He had to leave straightaway.

'Trouble was, the crew wouldn't give in. The worst one was the sober fellow. In the end I actually stooped to the level of spiking his drink. Can you imagine? Like a fucking gangster movie.

'Even so, they made the General wait thirty minutes alone in the airplane. Then they tried to convince him again; but he appealed to the control tower, and our colonel was up there with the other big shots. He quietly told the people on duty it was a matter of national security that Ailleret get back.

'It goes without saying that there was no last-minute check of the plane. Even if there had been, they wouldn't have noticed. You see, the ailerons worked, only backwards. But the pilot can't see them from his cockpit. And the communications between the pilot and the ground crew in a place like that aren't very precise, especially at night. So they took off. Bang!'

'But, surely, the pilot could have reacted?' Stone had almost lost his threatening tone. The other surged back quickly, leaning towards the shadow beside him, his heavy cheeks shining in the dull light with fresh blood.

'You asked me for the story. I gave it. If you don't believe me, that's your problem. You're obviously not a pilot. Listen. The plane was in the air for eighty seconds. The pilot probably started turning after thirty seconds. He has fifty left. He's flying away from the town over fields, so he has no natural orientation, just darkness everywhere, like this bloody car. Don't you understand? Look at me. I hardly know what way up I am. Add to that a plane which is climbing fast. So there is already an angle. The pilot turns left. All the machinery works as it should. The correct lights. Twenty more seconds have gone. Somewhere in the back of his mind he begins to realize he's going right and not left. He hears the control tower telling him he's going the wrong way. He doesn't understand, but his logical reaction, as any pilot will tell you, is to turn still harder to the left. He looks down again. Nothing wrong with the machinery. He has turned the correct way. No lights outside. Maybe if he's quick. There are ten seconds left. He doesn't even know that, because he can't see a thing. So what does he do? Panic? Turn to his co-pilot? Try to pull up steeper? Don't forget, he is in the middle of the plane's most dangerous manœuvre: climbing and turning

at a slow speed. He's terrified of going into a stall. Bang.
Time's up. I'd say the chances are ten thousand to one
against him swinging the stick back right to try to turn left.
He still would have been too late.'

'And then what happened?'

'I collected the letter from Colonel Dalbot as he came out
of the control tower and then hitched a ride up into the hills
with one of the ground crew. I had an unsuccessful look
around the wreckage to see if I could find the aileron cross,
just to be sure it was destroyed. They found a small part of it
when they collected up the wreckage next day.'

'Which you stole.'

'That's right. But walking around in the burning wreckage
I went a bit funny. Seeing those bits of people everywhere,
you know. Hands, legs, heads. It wasn't the first time I'd seen
things like that, but it was the first time I'd killed eighteen
innocent people. Don't count Ailleret. I was there to kill him.
So I went kind of funny and I decided to keep Dehal's letter.
I'd already thought of keeping it. But then I decided
definitely. I'd earned my freedom at the price of damnation.
That's what I told Courman the next afternoon when he
came to collect. He almost had me shot, but I said I'd sent
the sealed letter that morning to a notary in France with
instructions to open it if ever I died suddenly or disappeared.'

'Was that true?'

'Of course. I'm not a fool. So Courman left me alone after
that. Only thing was, I started thinking. I thought for six
months and then I went to see him and started blackmailing.
All I wanted was to have a regular income and eventually to
retire. He saw I had gone a bit funny and would do what I
threatened to do. An independent income, that's what I
wanted, a big lump sum that I could invest and so be free of
the bastard.'

The fat man fell suddenly silent as if he were unconscious.
Stone waited a moment to see if he had finished, then leant

across and spoke almost against his face.

'Now, listen carefully, Bertiaud. I'm going to let you go. Tomorrow morning you will see your notary and get that bit of paper. It will be picked up at ten o'clock precisely. If you are not there you are a dead man – in which case we shall have what we want anyway, because your notary will publish. And if you are a good boy we'll leave you alone.'

'The others won't.'

'I told you. We've got Courman. And Dehal never knew you kept the letter, did he?' Stone was guessing, but he had begun to understand the mentality of this enemy he had never seen. 'Courman had to keep it quiet because that was his control over the General. So Dehal will think we got it from Courman's papers, just the way we got all the papers on you.' Bertiaud froze. 'That's right. Now you understand why it was a good thing you told the truth.'

Stone turned on his motor. He lit only the small lights outside and left the dashboard in darkness. They drove back to the restaurant in silence. It was much quieter, and Bertiaud's car was one of the few remaining. Stone pulled up beside it and kept his motor running. He pushed the fat man forward to get at his wrists, cut them loose with a small knife, then opened the door and pushed him out. Bertiaud stumbled as he tried to land on his feet, failed and lay in the damp grass.

He got up slowly, rubbing his wrists, looked back at the car but could see only a silhouette inside. The silhouette spoke to him in the same cold whisper.

'Ten o'clock, Bertiaud. And don't bother running. There are men watching you all the time. If you do, you'll be dead tomorrow at eleven.'

The Renault drew away into the night.

It was another hour before the girl, who had noticed Stone earlier in the evening, was picked up by her pimp. She was one of the last to leave. Nevertheless she asked him to show her the photograph once more and realized immediately that it was the same person. Unfortunately she had not bothered to write down the number of the Renault.

Her man called Courman, who told him to find out why Stone had been hanging around the café. That would mean finding all the girls who had been there during the evening and questioning them. Most had either gone home or were out with other clients.

Courman told him to stay up until something had been discovered and to telephone the moment it was. He himself called a few key people to spread the word that Stone was now in a grey Renault 16, then exercised the privilege of a master and went to bed.

Stone drove out of the Bois and waited in the service lane of the Avenue Foch to be sure he wasn't followed. No, it had worked. The man was terrified. He would do what he was told.

Stone wanted to laugh or shout. Anything. But he couldn't. There was a dirty taste in his mouth and, swallow as he might, it wouldn't go away.

Chapter Twenty

He did not go home that night. It was eleven o'clock – not too late to check into a small hotel. He found one on the rue Pergolèse, discreetly retiring, comfortable and unremarkable, reeking of family dedication to the small, desirable, middle-class things in life. It was just off the Avenue de la Grande Armée, not far from the Étoile. He was as sure as he could be of running into nobody there.

The next morning he drove his rented car to the rue de la Banque near the Place des Victoires, parked it and placed his metal box in the rear after removing two tapes. From there he took a taxi home.

That was something he had been considering all night. At first glance it seemed a far too risky idea. But the more he considered it, the more it seemed a reasonable decision. Courman apparently knew nothing of what he had been up to. In a sense, reappearing might allay their doubts and fears. Had he found something he would hardly go home. And he wanted to arrive at Bertiaud's looking authoritative. That was the last thing he looked, not having changed since Saturday.

In any case he would have lots of time to lose their tail before ten o'clock and time to make copies of both the Ardant tape and the Bertiaud tape. More than anything he wanted to see those in the mail.

It was seven-thirty when he arrived, approximately the same hour that an ageing black-rooted blonde came home after spending the night with a client who had rented for their pleasure a small hotel-room. Waiting at her door was a young man whom she knew to be one of the other girls' pimps. He had some questions to ask.

Stone did not bother to examine the street. He knew someone would be there waiting. The door into his building was locked. That was unusual. He rang. More quickly than he expected, the concierge appeared and nervously waved him in.

'Why is the door locked?' he asked, excusing himself.

'She wanted me to,' the old woman replied, indicating the entrance to her lodge. 'I let her sleep in my parlour.'

Mélanie Barre appeared in the doorway. Her face was red. She had obviously been crying.

Stone was surprised and annoyed. 'What are you doing here?' Without waiting for an answer he grasped her arm and half-dragged her up the stairs.

'What are you doing here?'

She looked up at him resentfully. They were sitting in the dining-room. He had pushed an apple into her hand as he was hungry and had one in his own. She bit into its skin and said nothing at first.

'I told you to leave me alone,' she eventually snapped.

'I did. As alone as you bloody well like to be.'

'That's not true.' Her voice rose. 'That's a lie. I told you to stay out of my affairs and you've done nothing but stir them up. I know you've been to see my father twice. François de Maupans tells me you're still searching about. I know all that.'

'You don't understand, Mélanie. There was a point when I could have dropped the subject, but beyond that point I knew too much. They wouldn't let me drop it.' Then he lied slightly, moving the crucial moment forward. 'When I saw you that night it was already too late. Do you know there was a man waiting for me downstairs. Since then they have simply been looking for their chance to get me. Give me the right to save my skin, even if it does disturb the dust you like to live in.'

'So you disappeared.'

Stone looked at her surprised.

'Yes, I disappeared. It was too dangerous to have them tailing me everywhere. It was involving too many people.'

'It didn't matter that you involved me.'

'I didn't know I was being followed then. I didn't realize how dangerous the situation was.' The last thing he needed that morning was a woman slowing him down. 'So you came to find me?'

'No,' she replied quickly. 'They came to find you.'

'Who?'

'They! How should I know? Some men. They pushed their way into my flat last night. They thought I knew where you were. They insulted me. Said I was your tart. I told them I hadn't seen you since that night, but they wouldn't believe me. They said I was in a lot of trouble for stirring up the mud with you — a lot of trouble, and it would get worse if I didn't help. They said I should tell them the moment you appeared. They gave me a number where I could leave a message and warned me that it was a police-station number.'

'So you came straight over here to help them as quickly as possible?' he replied sarcastically.

She leant across the table in a rage and tried to strike him. He caught the arm quickly and pushed her back into her chair. She stared down into her lap. Stone noticed a fresh bruise on the side of her neck.

'What's that?'

She looked up, her voice filled with spite.

'Just one of their friendly gestures of persuasion that went off target.' As he looked at her horrified, she burst into tears.

'They beat you up!' He leant in his turn across the table and shook her to make her stop.

Trying to control herself, she replied: 'That's hardly surprising. Beating up a woman is nothing. They also killed my husband.'

He went around the table to comfort her, but she pushed him away. 'No. No. You're right. I must be hard like you. That is the way to survive.'

He left her sobbing, set his tapes to rerecord the Ardant conversation and went into the kitchen.

In London, Martin Sherbrooke was awoken by a persistent ringing of his door-bell. He went to answer, thinking that his wife, who still lay asleep, must have arranged for work to be done in the kitchen. He had been pushing her to get on with it. But the two men on the other side of the door were not in workmen's overalls. Their only uniform was a stocking stretched over the head with holes cut for the eyes, the nose and the mouth. Their only tool was a pistol which each of them pointed at Sherbrooke's head.

Ten minutes later Stone appeared with coffee and toast. She had pulled herself together and was sitting silently in the same place, waiting, her spine arched slightly away from the back of the chair and her face soft and flushed after the tears, staring ahead at nothing in particular. When she had a cup in her hand and had sipped it carefully, he began talking, calmly, quietly.

'I'm sorry, Mélanie. Not simply for you. For me and everyone else who has been involved. But apologies aren't going to change anything now, so you might as well convince yourself that what's happened is for the best. It must be for the best to find these criminals and expose them. This morning at ten I pick up the last key document and then it's over. I'm leaving for London on a plane this afternoon and everything will be in the newspapers tomorrow.'

He began to tell her all that he had discovered, the different people he had met, what they had said. He hid nothing. It was better that she understand what was in question. He explained how her husband had tried to stop the crew and had finally been drugged. He described Bertiaud and their conversation in the dark in the Bois de Boulogne.

When he finished it was after nine and the Bertiaud tape was not yet copied. He said he would have to leave. She said she wanted to come with him, and after a short hesitation he agreed because he was afraid to leave her alone. His idea was to take her to London until the game was played out. Stone shaved, changed quickly, shoved the two original tapes into one pocket and the one copy, packaged and addressed to Sherbrooke, into another.

They went down into the street. He pointed out his tails waiting a short distance away. They were talking to a third man who had probably followed Mélanie there the evening before. They strolled quickly through the busy streets with the Peugeot following discreetly behind. It was a warm day. Friday had brought the sun.

Outside the pharmacy on the Boulevard St Germain they climbed into a taxi. Stone asked for the rue Cambon entrance to the Ritz. That was in the right direction, fifteen minutes away on the other side of the river. When they were half-way he leant forward and handed the driver a fifty-franc note over the back of the front seat.

'I want you to do me a favour. After you drop us off drive slowly around to the Place Vendôme and wait for us at the other entrance of the hotel.'

The driver took the note and looked back with a smile. 'That's an old trick. I've seen it done many a time.'

Stone laughed.

'That's right. It's an old trick, but it still works. You see that Peugeot behind us. We want to lose it.'

The driver probably imagined there was a jealous husband following. He did not see that there were two men, both armed.

'Give us exactly six minutes to get from one side to the

other, neither more nor less. If you're on time I'll give you another fifty francs.'

The driver laughed.

They climbed out calmly in the rue Cambon and entered the hotel slowly. The Peugeot drew up as they disappeared inside. One of the men jumped out, the other waited. Stone and Mélanie passed the bar and the reception, Stone talking loudly and making her laugh. They paused at the beginning of the long carpeted corridor which joined that half of the hotel to the other half where the restaurant opened on to the Place Vendôme. There was an elegant news-stand on the left, and they glanced at the papers before strolling on, peering as they went into all the cases displaying jewellery and porcelain and clothes.

It was Peduc who followed. He knew most of the dodges in Paris but he was half-way along the corridor before he remembered this one. He wasn't sure what to do. They might simply be going to the restaurant for breakfast. If not, he should try to run back to the car and get round to the other side as quickly as possible. He followed in indecision through the twisting salons at the other end of the corridor until he saw them heading for the door. There was only one thing to do. He turned about and ran. There was no point in going out after them because there was never a taxi at that entrance. That was the key to the dodge.

Stone told the driver to head up toward the Opéra, where he dropped the copy of Ardant's tape into a post-box, then along the rue du 4 Septembre and down the rue de la Banque. There they got out and recovered his car.

It was shortly before ten when they arrived outside Bertiaud's flat. Mélanie waited downstairs in the Renault while Stone climbed to the third floor. The stairs were covered with a heavy green carpet which absorbed all sound.

There was only one door on each landing, a large double

door painted the same green as the carpet. He paused on Bertiaud's floor and was about to ring the bell when he noticed the door was a fraction ajar. He pushed it open. The carpet was yet thicker on the other side. A solid mass of period furniture lay before him, lining the hall under the blessing of the sun which streamed in from a courtyard. It was, like the nightclub, all slightly vulgar. There was too much. Bertiaud was a man alone with nothing else to spend his money on.

Stone pushed open two successive doors which led finally into a square mirrored antechamber with a door in each wall. One of the doors was open. It gave on to a drawing-room where white curtains shaded the furniture from the strongest light. The result was a milky filtered atmosphere which made everything richer and softer. In the centre in a Louis XV armchair sat Bertiaud. He was smiling and held out his hand in an expansive gesture along the arm of the chair.

He was dressed in dark-grey suit and there was a fresh rose in his buttonhole. The rose was an Alexandria Autumn.

Stone approached and was about to speak when he realized the man had not moved. He stopped. Bertiaud's cheeks were paler, more unhealthy than he remembered. He approached slowly. The smile was in reality a grotesque gasp for air. He walked round the chair. The fat man's neck bulged over a thin necklace. From the rear Stone saw more clearly. It was a wire twisted tight, biting into the skin.

Stone continued his circle back to the front. He looked down at the body. The letter? He slid his hand between Bertiaud's shirt and suit. The soft fatty flesh gave before his touch. The body was still warm. He had only just been killed. Stone felt in the left breast-pocket and pulled out the contents. There was a thin lizard wallet and an envelope. He wiped the wallet with his handkerchief and put it back, then ripped open the envelope, unfolded the paper inside and saw at the bottom a signature, 'Pierre Dehal'. Holding tight to that, he retreated from the room, glancing once behind him at the last moment. Bertiaud sat still balanced on heavy silk upholstery, smiling welcome.

He left the latch ajar as he had found it, stopping only to wipe each door where he might have left fingerprints. On the landing he paused, listening for any sound. There was no one on the stairs. He started down them quickly, glancing to the left into the concierge's lodge at the bottom. There was no sign of her.

Mélanie was waiting in the car. He climbed in, unfolded the paper and gave it to her. There was a short, handwritten text. It began, 'My dear M. Courman,' and contained such phrases as 'In the interests of national security' and further on 'essential the elimination of General Ailleret over which you have agreed to co-operate'. He took it back and folded it into his breast-pocket.

'Bertiaud is dead.'

'What?'

'He's been strangled. I want you to go into that café and telephone the police. Simply say there is a man strangled on the third floor of 13 Place des Victories and hang up. Then buy a coffee and wait for them to arrive. I want to be sure he is found quickly. That will give Courman something else to worry about and perhaps divert his attention from us. I shall wait for you at the Place de la Bourse on the corner of the rue Notre-Dame des Victoires. It's only five minutes from here on foot.

The interior of Harrods basement vault is painted in turn-of-the-century Egyptian. This vivid though slightly yellowed decoration is all the more strange applied to gigantic safes assembled inside a room like a ship in a bottle.

Sherbrooke's companion was there for the first time and his eyes were continually wandering away to their surroundings. Sherbrooke thought of taking advantage of this and attacking the man. But he could see the imprint of the pistol in the other's pocket and, even if it missed, he could imagine the effects of a ricocheting ball let loose in this confined, metal-lined space. They were not the only customers. There were three others in the wooden booths next to them.

He would not have given in had there been another solution. He had denied everything at first, but they had intercepted an envelope to his secretary and had been following him for two days. They had seen him go down into the vaults and had guessed why.

His two captors were French. The man who had accompanied him spoke English badly. He was an ex-Legionnaire sent over earlier in the week to direct the operation. The other was a commercial attaché at the French embassy.

They were impatient men. When they saw Sherbrooke was going to be difficult they made him telephone his office to say he wouldn't be in. They then ripped out the line.

Their orders were to get the documents, burn them, then inform Paris and hold their captives for twenty-four hours. A third colleague was holding Sherbrooke's secretary, the innocent post-box for Stone's letters. They had to stall long enough for Courman to deal definitively with Stone himself.

What had broken Sherbrooke was not the blows he received. Pain left him indifferent; that was a victory of his mind. He had won it in Malaya when he was badly wounded and lost for ten days in the jungle. The two men who struck him seemed to understand this indifference. The man in charge recognized it from his own experience of torturing rebels in Algeria. He knew he did not have enough time to break the man. He therefore turned to the other solution. Sherbrooke's wife. It was only a matter of moments before her husband gave in.

The commercial attaché was obliged to be discreet and so he remained in the flat with his mask and the woman while

Sherbrooke and his companion went to collect the briefcase. It was not far. They were gone not more than twenty minutes.

It was another half-hour before they had burnt everything. It is not easy to destroy papers in London. The fireplace was blocked off and the kitchen extractor had to be used slowly to avoid attracting attention. The smell of burning tape was nauseating, so they took turns; one in the kitchen and the other standing with a gun over their captives in the next room. They were in too much of a hurry to bother to tie them up.

Almost everything was destroyed before Sherbrooke got his chance. The commercial attaché was in the kitchen finishing the last tape. The other turned his head for a moment, distracted by a noise outside on the staircase. A second later the ex-parachutist had lunged on to him with his whole weight, throwing him literally across the room into the kitchen, knocking the other off balance in the process as he came out to see what had happened. Sherbrooke slammed the door on them and turned the small key in the latch. That was one of the few advantages of the number of burglars in London. Even the kitchen had a lock.

He drew back, glanced momentarily at the kitchen door separating him from the two men, grabbed his wife and dragged her behind him out of the flat and down into the street. There he forced her to run toward the police station in Lucan Place beyond Sloane Avenue, praying he would see a patrol car on the way.

He did not and it was fifteen minutes before they had arrived and explained themselves to the desk sergeant. It would be another five minutes before a policeman arrived at the flat. Sherbrooke was sure the toughs would be gone. At least he could describe the one who had been forced to take off his stocking when they went into Harrods' vaults.

Simultaneously two things broke into his mind. His

secretary — they had told him she was being held to prove their control of the situation. He gave her address to the sergeant. And Stone — he was without a double. His protection was gone. He had to be found before the Frenchmen rang through to their boss.

Sherbrooke sat fidgeting in the police station thinking about all this while a young man in uniform began dialling Paris. It was the worst hour of the day to get through.

Stone waited thirty minutes before he recognized her walking quickly toward the car. So far as he could see, no one followed. She dropped into the seat beside him and he drove off.

'There was nothing.'

'What do you mean?'

'Nothing. I waited for them as you said. They arrived five minutes after my call. There were two police cars. Everyone else in the café and on the Place crowded up to see what was happening, so I joined them. It would have been suspicious not to. The police disappeared upstairs for fifteen minutes. When they came down I heard an inspector tell one of his men to radio headquarters that it was a false alarm. Another hoax. There was no one up there.'

'But I saw him.'

'So you told me. I suggest you forget what you saw. You have the paper. Now, let's go.'

Stone was inclined to agree. He had what he wanted. The rest was superfluous drama. They would return to the flat, make a copy of the Bertiaud tape from the night before, then a photostat of the letter, and send them off before taking a plane to London. He was in danger so long as he held the only copy. This was not the moment to be clumsy.

Chapter Twenty-one

Petit Colbert was a man in a hurry. He didn't know why, but he had a feeling that something was wrong. He wanted to know what it was.

His Baths—Sauna opened for business at 11.30. Colbert arrived only moments later. He had already telephoned Courman and fixed a meeting there without explanations. Courman had not been alone that morning. He kept the pimp from the Bois by his side in case an extra hand was needed. The young man was now left there to relay any message which might arrive.

Colbert undressed as he always did, and wrapped a large towel about his waist. To have done other than the normal might have drawn attention. He sat on a foam-rubber sofa and waited for Courman to arrive.

It was ten minutes before the manager approached, whispering that he was wanted in the office. Courman waited. He was annoyed and scarcely hid it. That was rare.

'Where is he?' he began abruptly.

'I'll tell you. Sit down.' Colbert's order was more an entreaty. Courman accepted because his leg hurt. 'I did what you said. I went to Bertiaud's place this morning early. He greeted me like an old friend, and waved me into the parlour. I said I'd come from Monsieur Courman and he smiled again and told me to sit down and did I want some coffee. Funny, like I was expected. Then I said no I wanted him to come see Monsieur Courman, and there he seemed surprised. "Why?" he says. "I thought it was understood. I've given you all you asked for and I don't want to be involved anymore. Listen, I've got the paper." '

'He went on like that for quite a while until I began to see he thought I was someone else and he wouldn't move. Pretty soon I was sure he had already spilt whatever you wanted me to stop him from spilling and all he had left was that paper. So I killed him.'

'Why?' Courman looked up calmly.

'Seemed like the only thing to do. I guess it took me too long to see he was waiting for someone, so he got suspicious and then frightened. He wouldn't budge. I tried threatening him but he just sat there like a lump. There was no way I could get him out of the building alive without being noticed and, anyway, he had already talked. So I killed him and went to look for a backstairs entrance to get his body down.'

Courman cut him off.

'Give me the paper.'

'Wait. When I came back from the back door – and that took a while because it was double-locked on the inside and I had to find a key – I heard a noise. So I went carefully. But when I came into the parlour there was no one. Everything was as I left it. Bertiaud hadn't moved. I searched him for the paper he was talking about. Couldn't find anything of interest. Then I searched the flat without much luck. I've brought you everything that seemed worthwhile, mostly business stuff.' He pulled a large brown envelope out from under his towel.

Courman snatched it from him, looked through the contents in a matter of seconds as if he knew he would find nothing, looked up without showing any disappointment before asking quietly: 'And nobody?'

'Nobody. The only unusual thing I discovered was the main door ajar.'

'What!'

'That doesn't necessarily mean anything. That idiot was so excited when he let me in that he could easily have not closed it properly. I tried it myself a few times afterwards, just to see, and it needed a good push. So I dragged the body down to the basement. Just in time, because the police arrived ten minutes later.'

'The police?' Courman had gone cold and was tapping a finger on the knee of his bad leg. 'And why, Colbert, did the police come?'

'That's what I couldn't figure out. Anyhow, they went away because there was nothing to be seen.'

'And that's all?'

'Isn't it enough, for God's sake? Now all I have to do is get the body out of the cellar.'

Courman had struggled to his feet. He had lost his calm again.

'Colbert, you're a fool.'

Surprised at himself, Colbert sprang forward to vent his frustration.

'That's not fair. Christ! That's not fair! You send me to get a guy. You don't tell me anything about it.' He was towering over Courman. 'You don't tell me what might happen. You don't tell me about any documents. Christ, what do you expect? I play it by ear and I do my best. And the best thing, the first fucking thing to do, when you have a body on your hands is figure out what to do with it. And if I'd searched for the paper first the police would have càught me. What then, eh?'

'All right. You did your best.' Courman turned away from him and said quietly and slowly, more to himself than anyone else, 'I can't wait any 'longer,' and then to Colbert, 'Get dressed. I need you.'

Stone was in the process of setting up his tape recorder when the telephone rang. He hesitated before answering it. There was no time, nothing to be said. Mélanie had stayed behind in the drawing-room. He arrived to find her standing over the telephone, listening to it ring. He walked up to her and took the receiver in his hand. He said nothing, simply listened. There was a strained voice at the other end.

'Hello. Monsieur Colin, s'il vous plaît.'

Stone did not understand at first. He had forgotten the sign. The voice began again.

'Monsieur Colin. C'est très urgent.'

Stone recovered and replied.

'Vous vous trompez de numéro' — and was about to hang up when the other voice began again.

'Vous êtes sûr? C'est très urgent. Ce n'est pas 584.23.16?'

Stone reacted slowly, then caught on.

'Quel numéro?', he asked. The voice repeated the number. Stone wrote it down and replied, 'Non,' then hung up.

Without a word he ran out of the flat and down the stairs two at a time. He didn't know the people on the second floor. They were a young couple he had seen periodically in the distance. He put his finger on their bell and pressed solidly.

After a moment a woman opened. It was the wife. Stone pushed his way in, excusing himself. 'I'm sorry. It's very urgent. I must telephone. Where is it?'

The woman remained transfixed and then asked weakly: 'Don't you have one of your own?'

'Mine is tapped,' Stone replied. 'This is a matter of life and death.'

He caught sight of a machine at the end of a hall and rushed for it. The first time he dialled too quickly. He swore. It never worked if one did it too quickly. He took his time. 19-44-1-584-23-16. It rang twice before answering.

'The Norwich Union?'

'Charles. Thank God! I'm ringing from a police station. No time for talk. They have the double. It is destroyed. Their people in Paris either know already or will know in the next few minutes. Run for it.'

There was a pause.

'Are you all right, Martin?'

Sherbrooke glanced at his wife, her face and arms bruised.

'Just, old boy. Just. They are a vicious lot.'

'I've got the stuff, Martin; I have everything. Go straight to Williams. Tell him I shall be there this afternoon and he should be ready to publish tomorrow. It's very important. They killed my contact this morning and there are other people in danger.'

'Don't carry the stuff with you,' the voice came back faint and excited. 'Dump it in the mail.'

'I daren't.'

'The police. Take it to the police.'

'You don't understand what I'm dealing with. Which side are they on?'

'Stash it somewhere.'

'I don't even know how closely I'm watched. I must bring it with me. They'll kill anyone who has it. Do you understand?'

They fell silent, then Sherbrooke's voice came back 'It's your game, Charles. Get moving. I'll wait at the airport.'

Stone heard his friend hang up. He turned to find the young woman standing behind him, frozen. And behind her was Mélanie.

Two minutes later they were in the Renault driving down the small streets of the 6th Arrondissement at the maximum speed Stone could risk. He had been stupid bringing the Renault back to his flat, but he had thought the game over and won.

He was sure he could lose his pursuers. All he really wanted was to lose them long enough to get rid of Mélanie. He had changed his mind. It was too dangerous taking her with him. She said her father had a house in western Normandy. She would go there.

Stone told her to take a taxi to the hotel near Orly where

he had left his car, pay them and drive the car down to the country. From the hotel she could phone François de Maupans and insist that he and his wife join her for the weekend. Maupans knew enough. A few words of explanation would make him understand the necessity.

As soon as everything was published she could resurface. It was a question of two days.

Near the Luxembourg gardens he lost them momentarily by weaving in and out of the complicated one-way streets. He headed for the Place Denfert-Rochereau and stopped long enough before its Metro station for her to leap out. She would take a train back toward central Paris, and then a taxi out to the hotel.

A few minutes later Stone saw the Peugeot back on his tail. It was difficult to manœuvre quickly. The Friday traffic was already building up. He turned west into that part of the 15th Arrondissement which has been completely pulled down and partially reconstructed since the war. There was more room for acrobatics and fewer jams. After ten minutes of turning and twisting he thought he had lost them. He pulled into an open carriage-entrance and waited. Nothing. Peace.

From there Stone headed for Orly Airport. The time was one o'clock. There was a flight for London in thirty minutes. All he asked was to catch it.

He suffered from a strange sensation as he drove, difficult to identify at first. What was it? He settled finally on satisfaction, a deep satisfaction. He had won. It was over now. He could come out of this wonderland and stop looking behind. He had got them. Not all of them, that he realized. Courman and Dehal were only the signs of a greater sickness. But he did not want to go farther and did not have to. He would settle for these two superficial cancers. The others . . . as for the others, he knew he couldn't do better than de Gaulle, who had fought them and wooed them from 1940 on and had only succeeded in increasing their hatred and their power to act as a world apart.

No. It was satisfaction he felt. He thought back to Noirmoutier and their conversations. Satisfaction was a middle-class emotion, a boring emotion. It was not banal. Banality could not imagine or conceive a feeling so oppulently fat with ego.

He arrived fifteen minutes before the plane was to take off, left the car with its keys outside the doors of Orly Sud and ran for the ticket counter. He pushed by a few people and called out his flight. A girl tapped it out on her machine. The answer flashed back. It was fully booked. 'I'm afraid it's Friday,' she smiled. There was another flight thirty minutes later. Stone could do nothing but accept.

Rather than pass the time waiting in public he looked about for the sign 'Toilets' and headed for them. There was an anonymous row of twenty cubicles. He chose one in the middle, went in, locked the door and sat down. It was the one place he was unlikely to run into his friends or enemies. Once, during the thirty minutes he spent silently enclosed, the Algerian who cleaned up behind people knocked on the door and asked if he were all right. Stone, the steel box on his knees, upright in Spartan comfort, replied yes loudly.

At the last moment he left his cubicle, gave the attendant a franc, walked quickly to the passport desk and on into the departure lounge. He had been there five minutes when a Customs official approached and spoke to him. 'I am sorry to interrupt you, sir, but there is a small problem with your papers.'

'What do you mean?'

'Simply a formality, sir. Would you please come with me?'

Stone followed him back to the Customs section where he was ushered into an office. As he entered his eyes were on the floor. They saw two feet, one of them in a correctional shoe. He looked up. The man was dressed in brown and wore a beard. 'Monsieur Stone, we have been looking for you,' he said with a large smile.

Stone glanced behind him. The way was blocked by the Customs officer. He swung the steel box into the man's gut and pushed the gasping body back out of the entrance. A second later he was running. He heard the police at passport control calling out. They were too surprised to follow. That surprise would not last long. He only prayed that the Renault was still illegally parked before the building. He could hear the pursuit beginning behind him.

There was no time to look back. He stumbled once on the stairs but managed to catch himself by clinging to a man climbing up. Their eyes met and Stone pushed himself away down the last few steps. He could see the car through the glass across the entrance hall. There was a policeman not far from it, probably considering whether it should be towed off. Stone did not stop to explain. Nor did he look back as he pulled away. If he had, he might have recognized a square solid silhouette running among the police who chased without knowing why.

Chapter Twenty-two

An unpleasant surprise. That was what Pierre Dehal thought when Courman's card was placed on his desk. An extremely unpleasant surprise. Life was delicate enough without people breaking the rules. And one of the rules was that Courman would not come to his office. Never.

It was not Courman's past life which made the General nervous for his own reputation. Not at all. No one else knew about that. It was his present life. Courman was officially a Gaullist organizer and therefore a political hack – both basic faults in the eyes of the rue St Dominique, Army Headquarters.

The sooner he saw him the fewer people would notice.

Courman chose the most uncomfortable chair in the large office, which smelt of sumptuous sterility. He brought the chair with his slow limp up to Dehal's desk and sat down. Silent as always and perfectly still.

'Why have you come? Couldn't you have telephoned?'

Courman bowed his head slightly and recounted what had happened since their last conversation. Dehal appeared indifferent. He adopted a sarcastic air and said: 'You mean you found him and lost him twice today?'

'Correct,' Courman replied coldly. 'Partially through error and partially through lack of co-operation. So long as I am limited to dealing with this man by small measures he will always escape. Now we have passed that stage. Limited measures are no longer possible. If I am to be sure of finding him I need the whole works.'

'What do you mean?'

'The works, Dehal. The whole weight of legal force. Your

contacts and my contacts are not enough.'

'The others will never go along with it. Every time we twist the police into action, it costs something. It's a debt which we have to repay. It is also a weakness on our part. Does it really matter? From what you say he has nothing but verbal evidence. That can be squashed and it will never see the light of day in France.'

'No, Dehal. It's worse than that. Do you remember the letter you wrote to me about the Ailleret affair?'

'Of course.'

'I never received it.'

'You. . . .'

'You remember it was to be passed on by Bertiaud. Well, it wasn't. He kept it. He has had it all the time.'

'You never told me that.'

Courman seemed to lose his patience and leant forward across the desk.

'Of course I never told you, you fool. Why should I tell you? You were the last person to know.'

Dehal sat back and waited. A jade songbird flitted through his mind.

'Bertiaud's dead. Stone's got it.'

Neither moved. It was Courman's turn to wait. Dehal's reply came quicker than he expected.

'What do you want?'

'Everything. I want the police and the immigration officials alerted. If they find him they are to hold him. No interrogations, no charge. Simply hold him. That is essential. Above all, we need the gendarmerie. If they can pick him up before he gets near a border or a port, all the better. What I really want are their eyes. If they can tell me where he is, my men can do their work without any official interference. I suggest you tell them he's some sort of spy. That will explain why they should go carefully.'

'Once the gendarmerie are involved it will only be a few

hours before Interior bring the DST into play, and they won't be happy just to hold the man.'

'If we don't work quickly we shall have to call in the DST anyway. Otherwise they won't know until it's all over. One other thing. I need manœuvrability. My people are deployed. Theoretically there is someone, or soon will be, on most exit-points. But I want to be on the spot myself to be sure there is no foul-up. You will put a helicopter at my disposal until we have finished.'

'If you bugger it, Courman. . . .'

'We are both finished. That in any case.'

It was four o'clock before Stone arrived at Boulogne. He had decided to avoid the borders and the other airports and even the ferries. The hovercraft port was well isolated outside the town and it was freer from red tape. It would get him to England quicker than most things. He left his car on the main road and began to walk toward the hangar. It was the last day of June and there were large groups of tourists milling about outside in the sun.

Stone mixed in among them as quickly as he could and looked carefully about. There was nothing suspicious. Nothing. He moved toward the ticket counter inside and joined the queue.

Then he looked sideways and noticed two men. They were waiting beside the passport control. Simply waiting and watching. Stone slipped out of the queue and around behind them. He knew the type. They weren't going anywhere and they weren't employees. The one on the right had a slight bulge half-way up his jacket.

Behind Stone was a public toilet. He slipped into it. It was filthy and smelt. His mind went back to the airport. It was definitely an unpleasant day. High on the wall there was a window just large enough for him to slip through except that it swung out on a hinge at the bottom and stopped half-way.

Stone pulled a small knife from his pocket and unscrewed the sides until the window dropped right down. He then eased his way out and cut back to the car by a long round-about route.

He drove twenty kilometres out of Boulogne before pulling off on to a dirt road over the sea and switching off the motor. There he remained for some time, thinking.

He needed time, but time was not to his advantage. Every hour they would be tightening the knot. He thought of going into hiding, perhaps in Maupans' house on Noirmoutier — that was a good ten hours away — or even at St Benoit again. But they would find him sooner or later wherever he hid; of that he was now convinced. There had to be a solution. It was the unexpected which he needed. That and enough time to warn London. The unexpected.

He pulled from a pocket the address Mélanie had written on a scrap of paper. The house was in western Normandy — for a Frenchman, the end of the world. They would never expect him to try that. He knew there were ferries from Cherbourg to Southampton, and Mélanie wasn't far from Cherbourg.

He drew out an atlas. It was another three hours at least. They wouldn't think of it. Why would he drive so far only to be faced with a long boat-trip?

It was six o'clock when Stone turned on the ignition and pulled out of the dirt track. He stuck to the small country roads which cut across northern Normandy. He was obliged to go slowly and stop every thirty minutes to ensure the direction was more or less correct. The roads were deserted except for the odd local car. Only once did he see a police patrol. It was from the gendarmerie. Stone had been forced to cross a main highway and the gendarme was waiting there, controlling the Friday traffic coming from Paris.

He stared at Stone as the Renault went by, then waved for him to stop. Stone put his foot on the accelerator and disappeared into the small road on the other side, but not before he saw the gendarme jump into his car and begin to follow. He pushed the Renault faster until there was no sign of car lights behind, then pulled off on to a forest track and waited.

He remained there for an hour. The gendarme had apparently given up or gone the wrong way.

After that he was more careful. It was clear that he was no longer running from a small gang, but from the entire police force. In that case the later into the night he drove the more alone he would be. He knew the French police. Most of them went to bed early, and even in the most stirring times they stuck to main roads.

He changed his route, cutting well south before going west again. By doing so most towns were avoided, especially on the last part of the voyage across the Suisse Normande. That was hilly country which had always been poor and was therefore deserted. Only at the last minute did he turn north and drive up through the centre of the Manche on the twisting lanes lined by hedges which appeared to be no more than a continuation of south-west England.

Shortly before eleven he drew up outside the gates of a dark house. He was a few miles from the town of St Lo on a small lane in a valley. He could make out behind the gates a large stone building covered in vines.

He rang and waited. No one appeared. He rang again. It was a cloudy night, but he managed to find a low part of the wall and climb over. Inside was a paved courtyard. He crossed it and banged at the closed shutters on the ground floor, then called loudly, 'Mélanie. It's Charles Stone.'

He called twice before a light appeared in an upper window, followed by a head which withdrew immediately. Minutes later he heard the door being unlocked. A small figure appeared and embraced him.

'I thought it was them.' She held on to him and repeated

herself.

'Where is Maupans?' Stone asked.

'They couldn't come tonight. They're arriving tomorrow morning.' She drew back and stared at him in the dark. 'Why are you here?'

'I was stopped. They've blocked the exits.'

She didn't answer but went to unlock the gate, then opened a garage. He put his car away and followed her inside.

She lit a long hall which served as a dining-room and drawing-room. She explained that they seldom came to Normandy; it was hardly worth opening the rest of the house.

There was a large sixteenth-century fireplace in which a fire was dying. Stone added some wood and asked for something to eat. He had had nothing since breakfast.

She had recovered from her fright and was suddenly quite gay. He told her about the airport and Boulogne and his long drive across northern France.

She couldn't help laughing at the description of him sitting in a cubicle for thirty minutes and squeezing out through the lavatory window. Her laugh cheered him up. He told her to come and sit beside him. She brought a filthy bottle with her and two small glasses. 'It's Calvados produced here by my grandfather.' He looked doubtfully at the bottle. 'The filth is age, nothing more. Taste it.'

The liquor had a slow fine burn which seeped down through his system. They drank three glasses of it each, sitting before the fire, and then crawled up a winding stuccoed staircase to the second floor.

They slept in a room which Mélanie said had been her grandmother's. It was as it had always been − the bed was set into the wall in elaborate panelling, a large crucifix hung above it in the alcove. The sheets were hand-embroidered with an elaborate filigree of leaves and flowers. They were slightly damp, but that was not a problem; no, it drew them together. Religious statues and books watched over them and linen cloths protected all the furniture.

Even in the darkness Stone could see the Virgin Mary, insistent in carved wood painted over, basking in a brief ray of moonlight, holding out her arms, smiling in eternal peace and despair or thwarted surprise.

They were both alone, profoundly alone, perhaps more that evening than ever before. Feeling themselves together beneath heavy linen sheets in a dead world created the illusion of being together. Their illusion came from their bodies — urgent and agitated as if the very candour of each gesture might crash through the barriers of solitude and make the union real.

Stone pulled the sheets up over their heads, shut out the world and the saints staring down from the walls; almost like children wrestling with phantoms in a fabricated cavern, they wrestled, with anticipation and fear and nervousness.

Beneath the sheets he could smell her opening up with invitation, throwing out sweet liquid scent. His belly was taut, almost trembling against her. He ran his tongue repeatedly down over her eyes, around her nostrils into her mouth. Her breath was coloured by the dry scent of the Calvados. He freed himself slightly, bent down to kiss her breasts, ran his tongue on down over the slight cascade of her ribs, into a slight valley, then the rise of her stomach and the open warmth. She shivered, pulled him back up against her, pushed her thighs open. He slipped between them and brought himself home. It was a night to come home, a night to stay home.

She went to sleep in Stone's arms and woke again later in the night to his caresses. They forgot as best they could that they were alone.

The next morning Stone made her telephone Cherbourg. There was a car ferry at one o'clock, an English boat. That was all he needed to know.

He placed a call to Williams in London. It was Saturday, but he knew he would be in his office. The editor took the call immediately and did not wait for an explanation:

'Where are you?'

'I couldn't get out. Their goons were at the airport and, I might add, at Boulogne. I imagine they are waiting at all the exits. And the police are on to it as well.'

'The police?'

'The whole fucking country.'

'I've got Sherbrooke here with me. We thought you were caught. We were about to print a call for an enquiry.'

'Not yet. Not quite. I'm near Cherbourg. I want to catch the ferry at one o'clock. It's an English boat and I want you to arrange everything from your end. I can't risk coming into contact with the French office. Just make sure they know I'm coming. I may have to get on illegally.'

'What do you mean?'

'I don't know yet. I'll have to see the set-up.'

He put the receiver down and turned to Mélanie.

'I shall leave here at eleven-thirty. There is no point in hanging about on the road. The last moment is the best moment to arrive. Do you have any weapons in this place?'

She took him to a room where there were a series of shotguns and rifles in wall racks. He opened the drawer beneath them. In one there was a black pistol with wooden plates on either side of the handle. He turned it over in his hand.

'What's this?'

'My father had it in the Resistance. I think he took it from a German.'

The make was STAR, Spanish. It took a clip of eight bullets in the handle and was charged by pulling back the sliding hood on the barrel. He found a box of shells. They appeared to be all right.

He closed the door of the small room and installed himself at the large table by the fire where he set about taking the pistol to pieces and cleaning it. Mélanie said that her father had used it from time to time until a few years before when his health collapsed.

When the pistol was cleaned and back together he asked: 'Is there somewhere I can fire this thing?'

She led him out into a large garden. It was overgrown in a gentle way and thick green like the country side around. The garden itself gave out on to an apple orchard which stretched to the top of the valley. He collected eight small stones and set them on a low wall. From twenty yards he began to fire. He missed the first three and she began to laugh behind him. He looked back at her and began to laugh himself. It seemed ridiculous, target practice in the peace of Normandy, surrounded by nature in its most unaggressive form. He kissed her and went back to his targets. Two of the last three shots struck home.

'Where are the tools kept in this house?'

She led him into one of the garages and opened a cupboard. He searched about, picked up a file and put it back; searched again until he found a much smaller one.

When they were again installed before the fire he placed eight more shells on the table and one after the other began filing fine Xs into their heads.

She looked at him questioningly.

'Like the Ritz, this is a very old trick, illegal since the Boer War. It was invented by the British at a place called Dum-Dum in India. The X causes a curious reaction when the ball strikes something. Instead of going straight through, the lead comes to pieces, explodes. The result is either very nasty, or efficient, depending on your point of view. Above all, it is a compensation for my being out of practice and outnumbered.'

Chapter Twenty-three

As Stone shoved the clip into the handle, the telephone began to ring.

'Only François knows you are here?'

She nodded.

'Answer it. Go on. You can always pretend you're a maid.'

They climbed to the landing of the first floor where the telephone sat in an alcove. He picked it up and gave her the receiver, then took the ear-piece for himself.

'Hello. Hello.' They listened in the silence of the house. 'Hello. Is Madame Barre there?' It was Maupans' voice.

'François, what is it?'

'Thank goodness. Look, something has happened. Are you alone?'

'What?'

'I mean is Charles there?'

Stone took the receiver and answered curtly, 'What's the matter?'

'I don't know. But, look, we were just about to leave to join Mélanie when I had a call. It was her father. He wanted to know if she was in Normandy. Afterwards I thought it was a bit funny. I mean it wasn't his voice, not a sick man's voice. So I rang him up and he didn't know anything about it.'

'You told them she was here?'

'I thought maybe Mélanie had mentioned the weekend to him. Yes, I told him. He seemed to know and only wanted confirmation. I can't understand it.'

'How long ago?'

'A quarter of an hour. They have a long way to go to get there. Charles, are you all right?'

'That depends on where they start from.'

Stone hung up as he finished the phrase.

'Let's get out of here. I'm afraid you've got to come with me. They are on their way.'

What Maupans couldn't understand was, in fact, deceptively simple.

The police had traced the number of Stone's rented Renault to the airport hotel. A visit to the manager by an inspector had confirmed that the client was Stone. They added that he had left his own car in their garage.

Was it still there?

No. A woman had paid and taken it away that afternoon. Her name?

They didn't know. She had paid cash.

The inspector, by experience, continued to apply pressure. Sometimes even innocent people forget something. The manager began to fret and called in different members of the staff. He was a young, ambitious man and did not want trouble. But, then, who did?

A desk clerk remembered that the woman had made a telephone call.

Did they have the number?

Of course. They always kept the numbers. Normal book-keeping.

The list was produced and the number noted. When traced it turned out to be that of a small company. The police turned this information over to General Dehal in a sealed envelope and he, without deigning to look inside, communicated it to Courman. He had no intention of becoming involved in unpleasant details. It was mid-evening.

Courman looked up the company in a reference book and found the owner: François de Maupans. He checked the list of people Stone had seen since they began to follow him. Maupans' name appeared twice.

Courman also guessed that the woman was Mélanie Barre. That was not difficult. After all, Stone had left his flat with her and arrived at the airport alone.

Finally, Courman received the gendarme's sighting late that evening. On the strength of the report he immediately transferred his headquarters to central Normandy; an air force station near Caen.

In the helicopter, Colbert beside him, hidden in the darkness, he reviewed the situation.

Stone was west of Boulogne. Had he been scared off? Where was he going? Courman had a second thought. Where was Mélanie Barre going with his car? He leant forward and asked the pilot to switch on an interior light. He pulled out a summary Peduc had prepared on her. His eyes stopped on the tenth line. A house in Normandy.

According to Stone's calculation, Cherbourg was one hour and a quarter away. That was why he had wanted to leave at 11.30. He wanted to arrive on the boat at the last moment.

Instead they left the house at eleven. It was better to go slowly on the road than to risk being caught like a rat. He found a detailed map in the house, studied it and chose a small road which wound up to the north without passing through any towns.

Before leaving the courtyard he charged the pistol, showed Mélanie how to release the safety-catch if he needed it quickly and put it in her lap. She was nervous with the solid black metal sliding between her legs. He kissed her and told her to hold it firmly to avoid the safety-catch being knocked off.

The sky had clouded over and a thin Normandy rain had begun to fall by the time the doors and gate were locked and they had turned out into the lane.

Five minutes later a car appeared from the other direction and drew up before the gate. The men inside had come from St Lo. One was a former Milice. The other practised the dying trade of smuggling. They climbed over the wall and forced the door to the house. They carried out a hurried search before reporting via the telephone on the first floor to Courman who was still at Caen. There was little they could say. The house was empty. The Alpine was gone. The Renault was there. There was a fire still burning. If Stone had been there, he had just left. Probably in his own car.

Courman told them to head north to the next large town, Carenton, as quickly as possible and to telephone him from there. He had his eyes on a map of the peninsula, specifically on Cherbourg, as he alerted the police then headed for the helicopter, Colbert beside him.

Stone said nothing. He drove slowly and carefully, watching for any signs of trouble. From time to time he turned and smiled at Mélanie, who had recovered her calm. She had on a sweater and jeans, country clothes, and her hair was simply tied back. She seemed to be happy in a resigned way. Rather like Stone himself. He could still feel a layer of satisfaction in his chest. She held the pistol in her right hand, firmly on her knees. Her left hand was on Stone's thigh.

She did not expect anything from him. Now or the next day. There was little point in wasting the present.

Near the village of St Jores, Stone saw a gendarme. He was coming out of the village café. It was one of those things. He did not see the man until the last moment and could not change direction. The only other possibility was to continue as if there were nothing.

He was not sure if the gendarme had noticed them. Perhaps the man was not even part of Courman's team. In any case they were gone, around a corner, before they could see whether there had been a reaction.

But Stone did not want to take chances. He changed his route, cutting east for ten miles, speeding up slightly in order not to lose too much time. Then he turned north again toward Cherbourg and slowed slightly.

It was eleven-thirty and they had covered a third of the distance.

The gendarme had noticed. He went to his car and radioed that he had seen a blue Alpine heading north-east through his village. There were a man and a woman in it; probably the suspects. It was ten minutes before the message was relayed to the two men who had telephoned Courman from Carenton, where they were waiting for instructions.

They decided to head north-west in the hope of overtaking Stone. In fact, they were soon travelling on the same road in the opposite direction.

Stone was not surprised when he saw a car pass him, then brake abruptly and swing about. He had not expected to be left alone. That was one of the reasons he was content to have retrieved his own car.

On those small roads more than speed was needed to lose their tail. They were narrow and winding. They hid more than they revealed. For the next seven minutes he had glimpses of their pursuers appearing behind them on straight stretches or below them on long hills. Yet each time the distance was greater and eventually they had disappeared.

He kept up his speed and again changed routes. They were thirty miles from Cherbourg and the choices were becoming limited.

A nervous desire was growing in his gut to accelerate and get to the boat; but he fought it back. He knew the last moment was still the right moment to arrive. And yet with the roads apparently covered by Courman's men it was dangerous to go slowly. He decided to pull off into a wood near Briquebec and then make a dash for it in the last few minutes. While they sat in the wood he took the pistol from Mélanie's hand and released the safety-catch, checked that it was charged, put the catch back into place. This he did

several times until Mélanie stopped him, took the pistol back
and held his hand. He smiled at her, then looked down at his
lap and waited. It was a pine wood. He wound down his
window and watched the light rain breaking slowly on the
dead needles which covered the ground.

Petit Colbert had taken a calculated risk. What he called a
calculated choice. On arriving in Cherbourg with Courman he
had been given the gendarme's sighting at St Jores. He had
examined the map of the peninsula and shrugged in despair at
the rabbit warren of roads between that village and Cherbourg.

Shortly afterwards he had been given the last sighting
made by the two men from St Lo when they gave up their
chase and began to search for a telephone to report in.

He looked at the map again. There was still a multiple
choice. He looked closely, trying to make sense out of the
white and yellow lines. He was sure that Stone would avoid
the main highways. In any case, they were already blocked
by the police.

He ran his fingers over and over the map until suddenly
they stopped inadvertently. There. At fifteen miles from the
city. There he fell on a short stretch where the choice of
roads was reduced to two. He looked carefully and chose the
one he would take if he were in Stone's position. Then, in a
mute tribute to Stone's superior intelligence or twisted
nature, he decided to head for the other.

The piece of road was four miles long without any
intersections. He drove slowly along it until he found a part
which was reasonably straight. There he parked on a dirt path
the car he had been given and began to look for a clear
observation-point in the trees. In his right hand he carried a
rifle.

He did not have a new rifle, or anything elaborate. It was a
.303 which he had used for years. It was a friend. He knew its

quirks and weaknesses. There was an elaborate sighting device which Colbert had adapted not long before; in the interests of science.

He chose a spot which gave him a long view of the road. If he acted quickly there would be time for three shots. Colbert settled his feet into the wet earth to be sure they would not slip and left them in place. Then lowered his arms and waited, limp, a shadow lost and resigned under the fine drizzle.

It was ten minutes before he heard the faint roar of a motor. He raised his rifle, sighted the farthest section of the road and released the safety-catch.

When the Alpine came into view it was travelling quickly, at perhaps ninety. There were two figures inside. Colbert caught the driver in the sights, then the driver's head. Then he squeezed.

A short explosion made Mélanie look to her left. She saw Stone, arched back, then slumped over the wheel. His foot came off the accelerator as he arched and slipped down on to the brake. She was thrown against the disintegrating windscreen as the car began to skid. It twisted on the road but the weight of his body held them in line.

The car halted half on the gravel shoulder. She pushed herself back into the seat. Stone was still hunched motionless forward. She looked around. A figure had emerged from the woods a hundred yards away. She looked back at Stone. Raised her left hand and nudged him. He did not move.

She felt a desire to scream rising in her throat; fought to control it. Looked up again. The figure was at fifty yards. Square. Dark and wet under the rain. She looked at his hands held calmly before him and recognized a rifle.

Her fingers began to twitch. She began to call out to him. Stopped herself. Tried to open the door to run. Found her hand was full. She looked down surprised. The pistol was still clutched in the fingers of her right hand. She stared hard at it. Tried to bring it into focus. Into memory. She turned it over, looked up again. She could make out the man's eyes staring at her. They held an expression of curiosity.

She looked down again. Put a finger on the catch. Pushed. Pushed again. It moved back. She raised the pistol in the direction of the wet square twenty yards away. Pulled.

She saw him stop. Surprised. Look down. There was a round red hole in his abdomen. Several inches across. She pulled the trigger head back and fired again. His throat opened up before her eyes like an over-ripe fig and then disappeared. She fired a third time but missed. The body had already fallen out of her aim to the ground.

She checked the pistol was still loaded, pushed the safety-catch into place and set it carefully on the dashboard. Her fingers nudged Stone again without success.

She climbed out of the car and tried to pull him from the driver's seat. He was heavy and limp. She pushed him back from the wheel; then took his legs, one after the other, and pulled them over to the passenger's side. The rest followed more easily and was eventually propped up in her place. She climbed behind the wheel.

She retained no memory of the last fifteen miles to Cherbourg. They were driven quickly. There was a vague impression at one point of a police car but that was quickly forgotten.

The city itself was crossed effortlessly and she stopped only once; at the entrance to the ferry loading-zone. There was a large expanse of concrete between her and the boat. Almost empty. She perceived, more clearly this time, three men approaching and a man in uniform whose head turned and whose mouth opened to call out to her to stop. She did not notice a bearded man in a brown suit waiting patiently at the side.

A car had just disappeared up the ramp into the boat. There was another car following it yards behind. She placed her foot on the accelerator and one hand on the horn. Two of the men had to jump out of the way as she skidded across the pavement. The second car came to a sudden halt as she passed before it, hitting the ramp at fifty miles an hour, crossing it more in the air than on her wheels and screeching into a barrier half-way in the hold.

She leapt out of the car, clutching the steel box, and locked the door behind her. Then turned looking for something.

She could see the policeman running across the loading-zone towards the ship. One of the three men was already on the loading-ramp, pushing aside a ship's officer. She turned. The floor was painted with arrows.

She tried to follow their directions. Finally her eyes fell on an arrowed sign: DECK.

A sailor approached. She pushed him out of the way and ran for the hatch.

On the other side of it she found a stairway and ran up until it stopped. She shoved open another door. It gave on to the upper deck. There were feet echoing on the metal steps below. She ran out on to the deck and forward.

At the end there was a barrier and beyond it an open door. She slipped under the barrier and into the wheelhouse. There was a man in uniform. Middle-aged. Solid.

In halting English she gasped: 'Are you the Captain?'

He looked at her surprised and nodded.

'I come from Charles Stone.'

'Stone. Yes. Where is he?'

'Below in his car, dead. I have brought you his papers.'

She held out the steel box.

He looked at her, still surprised. Then recovered. Locked the doors at either end of the wheelhouse. Placed the box on the floor and picked up his internal phone.

Within moments he had blocked the ramp and ordered all officials ashore. There were three cars left to load. 'Too fucking bad,' he told a complaining First Officer.

When he turned back to the young woman she was seated on the floor, face hidden in her hands. At first he thought she was crying. But no. She lifted her eyes and returned his gaze. They did not ask any questions. Nor did they offer any reply.

Epilogue

Both Williams and Sherbrooke met the boat in Southampton. They were accompanied by a delegation of police who detained two passengers for questioning.

After a short conference between Williams, the Captain and a Chief Inspector, Mélanie was released into the editor's care and arrangements were made to transport Stone's body to London.

Williams' plan was to begin publishing on Monday. He had in fact put a preliminary article in on Saturday morning in the hope that Courman would believe the necessary information was already delivered.

That Saturday evening he received a telephone call threatening violence if he published any more. Within an hour of his negative reply there were shots fired through the windows of his London house, followed by a second threatening call. For the next ten days he was given police protection.

On Sunday his offices were burgled. Nothing was taken. Apparently the thieves were looking for something which they had not found.

On Monday, as intended, he began to publish a quickly written account of both the Ailleret assassination and the crusade that Charles Stone had undertaken to expose it. Whether Stone would have recognized himself in this knight-crusader is perhaps irrelevant.

As for his body, it was buried a week later in Chelsea Cemetery; a large, old-fashioned, overgrown place, inhabited by forgotten poets and Victorian do-gooders. There were few people at the service – Williams, Sherbrooke and his wife, Mélanie, Maupans who had insisted on coming over, and odd friends that Stone apparently had in London. They had seen the articles in the newspapers.

Mélanie remained in England for six months, until all was published and the danger passed. On returning to Paris she was told that her job had been phased out. They no longer needed her services. Privately she was told that there had been too much publicity and her superiors felt they could do without the unwelcome light her presence brought.

And General Pierre Dehal did not become Chief of the Army Staff. A certain amount of pressure from the Government encouraged him to offer his resignation a year later. The friendly conspiracy whom he had served served him in their turn, and he was found a directorship on the board of a large nationalized company.

The Minister of Defence of the day, Michel Debré, did, however, take advantage of the scandal. He was well aware of a drive for power by the main body of the officer corps. He seized the opportunity to reduce the Chief of Staff's powers; taking away what Charles Ailleret had won for his successors and naming a last lot of loyal Gaullist generals.

However, he was succeeded by ministers who had little experience in dealing with the military morass (Robert Galley, Jacques Soufflet, Yvon Bourges). They did and still do have difficulty not doing what the generals ask. On top of which the new President of the Republic, Valéry Giscard d'Estaing, and his prime minister proved to be equally inexperienced and vulnerable in the military field.

They went so far as to name a junior minister of defence who was a serving general and who, although tough and effective, had always taken the side of the 'Army'.

Almost the first of his acts on taking office was to encourage the politicians to give back to the Chief of Staff the powers which Ailleret had won at the expense of his life in 1968, and which Debré had taken away four years later. But in 1974 it was neither the opportunists nor the Gaullists who benefited. Their time was over and the old main line of the officer corps received the full heritage which had been denied them since the day when they had opted for Pétain and collaboration with the Germans thirty years before.

Finally Philippe Courman. He had watched powerless on the dockside as the boat sailed away with the documents. His efforts to have it confined to port succeeded five minutes too late. And so in disgrace he was obliged to abandon his office and his role in the UDR and return to his turnips.

He declared that it was not the first time and spent the period between 1972 and 1974 tightening up his organization. On the death of President Georges Pompidou he was one of the first to offer his services to the aspiring but not yet victorious Giscardiens.

Those who lacked all the essential infrastructure or grass roots – or what Courman calls the screwdrivers and bottle-openers – necessary to holding the country welcomed him with joy. He became, or rather has returned to his position as a bastion of those in power and of the forces of order.